The Brotherhood of the Seven Kings

by

L. T. Meade and Robert Eustace

Ulwencreutz Media

ISBN 978-1-365-20523-1

INTRODUCTION

THAT a secret society, based upon the lines of similar institutions so notorious on the Continent during the last century, could ever have existed in the London of our day may seem impossible. Such a society, however, not only did exist, but through the instrumentality of a woman of unparalleled capacity and genius, obtained a firm footing. A century ago the Brotherhood of the Seven Kings was a name hardly whispered without horror and fear in Italy, and now, by the fascinations and influence of one woman, it began to accomplish fresh deeds of unparalleled daring and subtlety in London. By the wide extent of its scientific resources, and the impregnable secrecy of its organisations, it threatened to become, a formidable menace to society, as well as a source of serious anxiety to the authorities of the law. It is to the courtesy of Mr. Norman Head that we are indebted for the subject-matter of the following hitherto unpublished revelations.

Chapter I

AT THE EDGE OF THE CRATER

TOLD BY NORMAN HEAD

IT was in the year 1894 that the first of the remarkable events which I am about to give to the world occurred. They found me something of a philosopher and a recluse, having, as I thought, lived my life and done with the active part of existence. It is true that I was young, not more than thirty-five years of age, but in the ghastly past I had committed a supreme error, and because of that paralyzing experience I had left the bustling world and found my solace in the scientist's laboratory and the philosopher's study.

Ten years before these stories begin, when in Naples studying biology, I fell a victim to the wiles and fascinations of a beautiful Italian. A scientist of no mean attainments herself, with beauty beyond that of ordinary mortals, she had appealed not only to my head, but also to my heart. Dazzled by her beauty and intellect, she led me where she would. Her aims and ambitions, which in the false glamour she threw over them I thought the loftiest in the world, became also mine. She introduced me to the men of her set—I was quickly in the toils, and on a night never to be forgotten, I took part in a grotesque and horrible ceremony, and became a member of her Brotherhood.

It was called the Brotherhood of the Seven Kings, and dated its origin from one of the secret societies of the Middle Ages. In my first enthusiasm it seemed to me to embrace all the principles of true liberty. Katherine was its chief and queen. Almost immediately after my initiation, however, I made an appalling discovery. Suspicion pointed to the beautiful Italian as the instigator, if not the author, of a most terrible crime. None of the details could be brought home to her, but there was little, doubt that she was its moving spring. Loving her passionately as I then did, I tried to close my intellect against the all too conclusive evidence of her guilt. For a time I succeeded, but when I was ordered myself to take part in a transaction both dishonourable and treacherous, my eyes were opened. Horror seized me, and I fled to England to place myself under the protection of its laws.

Ten years went by, and the past was beginning to fade. It was destined to be recalled to me with startling vividness.

When a young man at Cambridge I had studied physiology, but never qualified myself as a doctor, having independent means; but in my laboratory in the vicinity of Regent's Park I worked at biology and physiology for the pure love of these absorbing sciences.

I was busily engaged on the afternoon of the 3rd of August, 1894, when Mrs. Kenyon, an old friend, called to see me. She was shown into my study, and I went to her there. Mrs. Kenyon was a widow, but her son, a lad of about twelve years of age, had, owing to the unexpected death of a relative, just come in for a large fortune and a title. She took the seat I offered her.

"It is too bad of you, Norman," she said; "it is months since you have been near me. Do you intend to forget your old friends?"

"I hope you will forgive me," I answered; "you know how busy I always am."

"You work too hard," she replied. "Why a man with your brains and opportunities for enjoying life wishes to shut himself up in the way you do, I cannot imagine."

"I am quite happy as I am, Mrs. Kenyon," I replied; "why, therefore, should I change? By the way, how is Cecil?"

"I have come here to speak about him. You know, of course, the wonderful change in his fortunes?"

"Yes," I answered.

"He has succeeded to the Kairn property, and is now Lord Kairn. There is a large rent-roll and considerable estates. You know, Norman, that Cecil has always been a most delicate boy."

6

"I hoped you were about to tell me that he was stronger," I replied.

"He is, and I will explain how in a moment. His life is a most important one. As Lord Kairn much is expected of him. He has not only, under the providence of God, to live, but by that one little life he has to keep a man of exceedingly bad character out of a great property. I allude to Hugh Doncaster. Were Cecil to die, Hugh would be Lord Kairn. You have already doubtless heard of his character?"

"I know the man well by repute," I said.

I thought you did. His disappointment and rage at Cecil succeeding to the title are almost beyond bounds. Rumours of his malevolent feelings towards the child have already reached me. I am told that he is now in London, but his life, like yours, is more or less mysterious. I thought it just possible, Norman, that you, as an old friend, might be able to get me some particulars with regard to his whereabouts."

"Why do you want to know?" I asked.

"I feel a strange uneasiness about him; something which I cannot account for. Of course, in these enlightened days he would not attempt the child's life, but I should be more comfortable if I were assured that he were nowhere in Cecil's vicinity."

"But the man can do nothing to your boy!" I said. "Of course, I will find out what I can, but—-"

Mrs. Kenyon interrupted me.

"Thank You. It is a relief to know that you will help me. Of course, there is no real danger; but I am a widow, and Cecil is only a child. Now, I must tell you about his health. He is almost quite well. The most marvellous resurrection has taken place. For the last two months he has been under the care of that extraordinary woman, Mme. Koluchy. She has worked miracles in his case, and now to complete the cure she is sending, him to the Mediterranean. He sails to-morrow night under the care of Dr.

7

Fietta. I cannot bear parting with him, but it is for his good, and Mme. Koluchy insists that a sea voyage is indispensable."

"But won't you accompany him?" I asked.

"I am sorry to say that is impossible. My eldest girl, Ethel, is about to be married, and I cannot leave her on the eve of her wedding; but Cecil will be in good hands. Dr. Fietta is a capital fellow—I have every faith in him."

"Where are they going?"

"To Cairo. They sail to-morrow night in the Hydaspes."

"Cairo is a fearfully hot place at this time of year. Are you quite sure that it is wise to send a delicate lad like Cecil there in August?"

"Oh, he will not stay. He sails for the sake of the voyage, and will come back by the return boat. The voyage is, according to Mme. Koluchy, to complete the cure. That marvellous woman has succeeded where the medical profession gave little hope. You have heard of her, of course?"

"I am sick of her very name," I replied; "one hears it everywhere. She has bewitched London with her impostures and quackery."

"There is no quackery about her, Norman. I believe her to be the cleverest woman in England. There are authentic accounts of her wonderful cures which cannot be contradicted. There are even rumours that she is able to restore youth and beauty by her arts. The whole of society is at her feet, and it is whispered that even Royalty are among her patients. Of course, her fees are enormous, but look at the results! Have you ever met her?"

"Never. Where does she come from? Who is she?"

"She is an Italian, but she speaks English perfectly. She has taken a house which is a perfect palace in Welbeck Street."

"And who is Dr. Fietta?"

"A medical man who assists Madame in her treatments. I have just seen him. He is charming, and devoted to Cecil. Five o'clock! I had no idea it was so late. I must be going. You will let me know when you hear any news of Mr. Doncaster? Come and see me soon."

I accompanied my visitor to the door, and then, returning to my study, sat down to resume the work I had been engaged in when I was interrupted.

But Mrs. Kenyon's visit had made me restless. I knew Hugh Doncaster's character well. Reports of his evil ways now and then agitated society, but the man had hitherto escaped the stern arm of justice. Of course, there could be no real foundation for Mrs. Kenyon's fears, but I felt that I could sympathize with her. The child was young and delicate; if Doncaster could injure him without discovery, he would not scruple to do so. As I thought over these things, a vague sensation of coming trouble possessed me. I hastily got into my evening dress, and having dined at my club, found myself at half-past ten in a drawing-room in Grosvenor Square. As I passed on into the reception-rooms, having exchanged a few words with my hostess, I came across Dufrayer, a lawyer, and a special friend of mine. We got into conversation. As we talked, and my eyes glanced idly round the groups of smartly dressed people, I noticed where a crowd of men were clustering round and paying homage to a stately woman at the farther end of the room. A diamond star flashed in her dusky hair. On her neck and arms diamonds also glittered. She had an upright bearing and a regal appearance. Her rosy lips were smiling. The marked intelligence and power of her face could not fail to arrest attention, even in the most casual observer. At the first glance I felt that I had seen her before, but could not tell when or where.

"Who is that woman?" I asked of my companion.

"My dear fellow," he replied, with an amused smile, "don't you know? That is the great Mme. Koluchy, the rage of the season, the great specialist, the great consultant. London is mad about her. She has only been here ten minutes, and look, she is going already. They say she has a dozen engagements every night."

Mme. Koluchy began to move towards the door, and, anxious to get a nearer view, I also passed rapidly through the throng. I reached the head of the stairs before she did, and as she went by looked her full in the face. Her eyes met mine. Their dark depths seemed to read me through. She half smiled, half paused as if to speak, changed her mind, made a stately inclination of her queenly head, and went slowly downstairs. For a moment I stood still, there was a ringing in my ears, and my heart was beating to suffocation. Then I hastily followed her. When I reached the pavement Mme. Koluchy's carriage stopped the way. She did not notice me, but I was able to observe her. She was bending out and talking eagerly to some one. The following words fell on my ear:

"It is all right. They sail to-morrow evening."

The man to whom she spoke made a reply which I could not catch, but I had seen his face. He was Hugh Doncaster.

Mme. Koluchy's carriage rolled away, and I hailed a hansom. In supreme moments we think rapidly. I thought quickly then.

"Where to?" asked the driver.

"No. 140, Earl's Terrace, Kensington," I called out. I sat back as I spoke. The horror of past memories was almost paralyzing me, but I quickly pulled myself together. I knew that I must act, and act quickly. I had just seen the Head of the Brotherhood of the seven Kings. Mme. Koluchy, changed in much since I last saw her, was the woman who had wrecked my heart and life ten years ago in Naples.

With my knowledge of thepast, I was well aware that where this woman appeared victims fell. Her present victim was a child. I must save that child, even if my own life were the penalty. She had ordered the boy abroad. He was to sail to-morrow with an emissary of hers. She was in league with Doncaster. If she could get rid of the boy, Doncaster would doubtless pay her a fabulous sum. For the working of her she above all things wanted money. Yes, without doubt the lad's life was in the gravest danger, and I had not a moment to lose. The first thing was to communicate with the mother, and if possible put a stop to the intended voyage.

I arrived at the house, flung open the doors of the hansom, and ran up the steps. Here unexpected news awaited me. The servant who answered my summons said that Mrs. Kenyon had started for Scotland by the night mail—she had received a telegram announcing the serious illness of her eldest girl. On getting it she had started for the north, but would not reach her destination until the following evening.

"Is Lord Kairn in?" I asked.

"No, sir," was the reply. "My mistress did not like to leave him here alone, and be has been sent over to Mme. Koluchy's, 100, Welbeck Street. Perhaps you are not aware, sir, that his lordship sails to-morrow evening for Cairo?"

"Yes, I know all about that," I replied "and now, if you will give me your mistress's address, I shall be much obliged to you."

The man supplied it. I entered my hansom again. For a moment it occurred to me that I would send a telegram to intercept Mrs. Kenyon on her rapid journey north, but I finally made up my mind not to do so. The boy was already in the enemy's hands, and I felt sure that I could now only rescue him by guile. I returned home, having already made up my mind how to act. I would accompany Cecil and Dr. Fietta to Cairo.

At eleven o'clock on the following morning I had taken my berth in the Hydaspes, and at nine that evening was on board. I caught a momentary glimpse of young Lord Kairn and his attendant, but in order to avoid explanations kept out of their way. It was not until the following morning, when the steamer was well down Channel, that I made my appearance on deck, where I at once saw the boy sitting at the stern in a chair. Beside him was a lean, middle-aged man wearing a pair of pince-nez. He looked every inch a foreigner, with his pointed beard, waxed moustache, and deep-set, beady eyes. As I sauntered across the deck to where they were sitting, Lord Kairn looked up and instantly recognised me.

"Mr. Head!" he exclaimed, jumping from his chair, "you here? I am very glad to see you."

"I am on my way to Cairo, on business," I said, shaking the boy warmly by the hand.

"To Cairo? Why, that is where we are going; but you never told mother you were coming, and she saw you the day before yesterday. It was such a pity that mother had to rush off to Scotland so suddenly; but last night, just before we sailed, there came a telegram telling us that Ethel was better. As mother had to go away, I went to Mme. Koluchy's for the night. I love going there. She has a lovely house, and she is so delightful herself. And this is Dr. Fietta, who has come with me." As the boy added these words Dr. Fietta came forward and peered at me through his pince-nez. I bowed, and he returned my salutation.

"This is an extraordinary coincidence, Dr. Fietta!" I exclaimed. "Cecil Kenyon happens to be the son of one of my greatest friends. I am glad to see him looking so well. Whatever Mme. Koluchy's treatment has been, it has had a marvellous effect. I am told that you are fortunate enough to be the participator in her wonderful secrets and cures."

"I have the honour of assisting Mme. Koluchy," he replied, with a strong foreign accent; "but may I take the liberty of inquiring who gave you the information about myself?"

"It was Mrs. Kenyon," I answered. "She told me all about you the other day."

"She knew, then, that you were going to be a fellow-passenger of her son's?"

"No, for I did not know myself. An urgent telegram calling me to Egypt arrived that evening, and I only booked my passage yesterday. I am fortunate in having the honour of meeting so distinguished a savant as yourself. I have heard much about Mme. Koluchy's marvellous occult powers, but I suppose the secrets of her success are very jealously guarded. The profession, of course, pooh-pooh her, I know, but if one may credit all one hears, she possesses remedies undreamt-of in their philosophy."

"It is quite true, Mr. Head. As a medical man myself, I can vouch for her capacity, and, unfettered by English professional scrupulousness, I appreciate it. Mme. Koluchy and I are proud of our young friend here, and hope that the voyage will complete his cure, and fit him for the high position he is destined to occupy."

The voyage flew by. Fietta was an intelligent man, and his scientific attainments were considerable. But for my knowledge of the terrible past my fears might have slumbered, but as it was they were always present with me, and the moment all too quickly arrived when suspicion was to be plunged into certainty.

On the day before we were due at Malta, the wind sprang up and we got into a choppy sea. When I had finished breakfast I went to Cecil's cabin to see how he was. He was just getting up, and looked pale and unwell.

"There is a nasty sea on," I said, "but the captain says we shall be out of it in an hour or so."

"I hope we shall," he answered, "for it makes me feel squeamish, but I daresay I shall be all right when I get on deck. Dr. Fietta has given me something to stop the sickness, but it has not me had much effect."

"I do not know anything that really stops sea-sickness," I answered; "but what has he done?"

"Oh: a curious thing, Mr. Head. He pricked my arm with a needle on a syringe, and squirted something in. He says it is a certain cure for sea-sickness. Look," said the child, baring his arm, "that is where he did it."

I examined the mark closely. It had evidently been made with a hypodermic injection needle.

"Did Dr. Fietta tell you what he put into your arm?" I asked.

"Yes, he said it was morphia."

"Where does he keep his needle?"

"In his trunk there under his bunk. I shall be dressed directly, and will come on deck."

I left the cabin and went up the companion. The doctor was pacing to and fro on the hurricane-deck. I approached him.

"Your charge has not been well," I said, "I have just seen him. He tells me you have give him a hypodermic of morphia."

He turned round and gave me a quick glance of uneasy fear.

"Did Lord Kairn tell you so?"

"Yes."

"Well, Mr. Head, it is the very best cure for sea-sickness. I have found it most efficacious."

"Do you think it wise to give a child morphia?" I asked.

"I do not discuss my treatment with an unqualified man," he replied brusquely, turning away as he spoke. I looked after him, and as he disappeared down the deck my fears became certainties. I determined, come what would, to find out what he had given the boy. I knew only too well the infinite possibilities of that dangerous little instrument, a hypodermic syringe.

As the day wore on the sea moderated, and at five o'clock it was quite calm again, a welcome change to the passengers, who, with the permission of the captain, had arranged to give a dance that evening on deck. The occasion was one when ordinary scruples must fade out of sight. Honour in such a mission, as I had set myself must give place to the watchful zeal of the detective. I was determined to take advantage of the dance to explore Dr. Fietta's cabin. The doctor was fond of dancing, and as soon as I saw that he and Lord Kairn were well engaged, I descended the

14

companion, and went to their cabin. I switched on the electric light, and, dragging the trunk from beneath the bunk, hastily opened it. It was unlocked and only secured by straps. I ran my hand rapidly through the contents, which were chiefly clothes, but tucked in one corner I found a case, and, pulling it out, opened it. Inside lay the delicate little hypodermic syringe which I had come in search of.

I hurried up to the light and examined it. Smeared round the inside of the glass, and adhering to the bottom of the little plunger, was a whitish, gelatinous-looking substance. This was no ordinary hypodermic solution. It was half-liquefied gelatine such as I knew so well as the medium for the cultivation of *biological* micro-organisms. For a moment I felt half-stunned. What infernal *science* culture might it not contain?

Time was flying, and at any moment I might be discovered. I hastily slipped the syringe into my pocket, and closing the trunk, replaced it, and, switching off the electric light, returned to the deck. My temples were throbbing, and it was with difficulty I could keep my self-control. I made up my mind quickly. Fietta would of course miss the syringe, but the chances were that he would not do so that night. As yet there was nothing apparently the matter with the boy, but might there not be flowing through his veins some poisonous germs of disease, which only required a *germ theory* period of incubation for their development?

At daybreak the boat would arrive at Malta. I would go on shore at once, call upon some medical man, and lay the case before him in confidence, in the hope of his having the things I should need in order to examine the contents of the syringe. If I found any organisms, I would take the law into my own hands, and carry the boy back to England by the next boat.

No sleep visited me that night, and I lay tossing to and fro in my bunk longing for daylight. At 6 a.m. I heard the engine-bell ring, and the screw suddenly slow down to half-speed. I leapt up and went on deck. I could see the outline of the rock-bound fortress and the lighthouse of St. Elmo looming more vividly every moment. As soon as we were at anchor and the gangway down, I hailed one of the little green boats and told the men to row me to the shore. I drove at once to the Grand Hotel in the Strada Reale, and asked the Italian guide the address of a medical man. He gave me the address of an English doctor who lived close by, and I went there at once to see him. It was now seven o'clock, and I found him up. I made my apologies for the early hour of my visit, put the whole matter before him, and produced the syringe. For a moment he was inclined to take my story with incredulity, but by degrees he became interested, and ended by inviting me to breakfast with him. After the meal we repaired to his consulting-room to make our investigations. He brought out his microscope, which I saw, to my delight, was of the latest design, and I set to work at once, while he watched me with evident interest. At last the crucial moment came, and I bent over the instrument and adjusted the focus on my preparation. My suspicions were only too well confirmed by which I had extracted what I saw. The substance from the syringe was a mass of micro-organisms, but of what nature I did not know. I had never seen any quite like them before. I drew back.

"I wish you would look at this," I said. "You tell me you have devoted considerable attention to bacteriology. Please tell me what you see."

Dr. Benson applied his eye to the instrument, regulating the focus for a few moments in silence, then he raised his head, and looked at me with a curious expression.

"Where did this culture come from?" he asked.

"From London, I presume," I answered.

"It is extraordinary," he said, with emphasis, "but there is no doubt whatever that these organisms are the specific germs of the very disease I have studied here so assiduously; they are the micrococci of Mediterranean fever, the minute round or oval bacteria. They are absolutely characteristic."

I jumped to my feet.

"Is that so?" I cried. The diabolical nature of the plot was only too plain. These germs injected into a patient would produce a fever which only occurs in the Mediterranean. The fact that the boy had been in the Mediterranean even for a short time would be a complete blind as to the way in which they obtained access to the body, as every one would think the disease occurred from natural causes.

"How long is the period of incubation?" I asked.

"About ten days," replied Dr. Benson.

I extended my hand.

"You have done me an invaluable service," I said.

"I may possibly be able to do you a still further service," was his reply. "I have made Mediterranean fever the study of my life, and have, I believe, discovered an antitoxin for it. I have tried my discovery on the patients of the naval hospital with excellent results. The local disturbance is slight, and I have never found bad symptoms follow the treatment. If you will bring the boy to me I will administer the antidote without delay."

I considered for a moment, then I said: "My position is a terrible one, and I am inclined to accept your proposition. Under the circumstances it is the only chance."

"It is," repeated Dr. Benson. "I shall be at your service whenever you need me."

I bade him good-bye and quickly left the house.

It was now ten o'clock. My first object was to find Dr. Fietta, to speak to him boldly, and take the boy away by main force if necessary. I rushed back to the Grand Hotel, where I learned that a boy and a man, answering to the description of Dr. Fietta and Cecil, had breakfasted there, but had gone out again immediately afterwards. The Hydaspes I knew was to coal, and would not leave Malta before one o'clock. My only chance, therefore, was to catch them as they came on board. Until then I could do nothing. At twelve o'clock I went down to the quay and took a boat to the Hydaspes. Seeing no sign of Fietta and the boy on deck, I made my way at once to Lord Kairn's cabin. The door was open and the place in confusion—every vestige of baggage had disappeared. Absolutely at a loss to divine the cause of this unexpected discovery, I pressed the electric bell. In a moment a steward appeared.

"Has Lord Kairn left the ship?" I asked, my heart beating fast.

"I believe so, sir," replied the man. "I had orders to pack the luggage and send it on shore. It went about an hour ago."

I waited to hear no more. Rushing to my cabin, I began flinging my things pell-mell into my portmanteau. I was full of apprehension at this sudden move of Dr. Fietta's. Calling a steward who was passing to help me, I got my things on deck, and in a few moments had them in a boat and was making rapidly for the shore. I drove back at once to the Grand Hotel in the Strada Reale.

"Did the gentleman who came here to-day from, the Hydaspes, accompanied by a little boy, engage rooms for the night?" I asked of the proprietor in the bureau at the top of the stairs.

"No, sir," answered the man; "they breakfasted here, but did not return. I think they said they were going to the gardens of San Antonio."

For a minute or two I paced the hall in uncontrollable excitement. I was completely at a loss what step to take next. Then suddenly an idea struck me. I hurried down the steps and made my way to Cook's office.

"A gentleman of that description took two tickets for Naples by the Spartivento, a Rupertino boat, two hours ago," said the clerk, in answer to my inquiries. "She has started by now," he continued, glancing up at the clock.

"To Naples?" I cried. A sickening fear seized me. The very name of the hated place struck me like a poisoned weapon.

"Is it too late to catch her?" I cried.

"Yes, sir, she has gone."

"Then what is the quickest route by which I can reach Naples?"

"You can go by the Gingra, a P. & O. boat, to-night to Brindisi, and then overland. That is the quickest way now."

I at once took my passage and left the office. There was not the least doubt what had occurred. Dr. Fietta had missed his syringe, and in consequence had immediately altered his plans. He was now taking the lad to the very fountain-head of the Brotherhood, where other means if necessary would be employed to put an end to his life.

It was nine o'clock in the evening, three days later, when, from the window of the railway carriage, I caught my first glimpse of the glow on the summit of Vesuvius. During the journey I had decided on my line of action. Leaving my luggage in the cloak-room I entered a carriage and began to visit hotel after hotel. For a long time I had no success. It was past eleven o'clock that night when, weary and heart-sick, I drew up at the Hotel Londres. I went to the concierge with my usual question, expecting the invariable reply, but a glow of relief swept over me when the man said:

"Dr. Fietta is out, sir, but the young man is in. He is in bed—will you call to-morrow? What name shall I say?"

"I shall stay here," I answered; "let me have a room at once, and have my bag taken to it. What is the number of Lord Kairn's room?"

"Number forty-six. But he will be asleep, sir; you cannot see him now."

I made no answer, but going quickly upstairs, I found the boy's room. I knocked; there was no reply, I turned the handle and entered. All was dark. Striking a match I looked round. In a white bed at the farther end lay the child. I went up and bent softly over him. He was lying with one hand beneath his cheek. He looked worn and tired, and now and then moaned as if in trouble. When I touched him lightly on the shoulder he started up and opened his eyes. A dazed expression of surprise swept over his face; then with an eager cry he stretched out both his hands and clasped one of mine.

"I am so glad to see you," he said. "Dr. Fietta told me you were angry—that I had offended you. I very nearly cried when I missed you that morning at Malta, and Dr. Fietta said I should never see you any more. I don't like him—I am afraid of him. Have you come to take me home?" As he spoke he glanced eagerly round in the direction of the door, clutching my hand still tighter as he did so.

"Yes, I shall take you home, Cecil. I have come for the purpose," I answered; "but are you quite well?"

"That's just it; I am not. I have awful dreams at night. Oh, I am so glad you have come back and you are not angry. Did you say you were really going to take me home?"

"To-morrow, if you like."

"Please do. I am—stoop down, I want to whisper to you—I am dreadfully afraid of Dr. Fietta."

"What is your reason?" I asked.

"There is no reason," answered the child, "but somehow I dread him. I have done so ever since you left us at Malta. Once I woke in the middle of the night and he was bending over me—he had such a queer look on his face, and he used that syringe again. He was putting something into my arm—he told me it was morphia. I did not want him to do it, for I thought you would rather he didn't. I wish mother had sent me away with you. I am afraid of him; yes, I am afraid of him."

"Now that I have come, everything will be right," I said.

"And you will take me home to-morrow?"

"Certainly."

"But I should like to see Vesuvius first. Now that we are here it seems a pity that I should not see it. Can you take me to Vesuvius to-morrow morning, and home in the evening, and will you explain to Dr. Fietta?"

"I will explain everything. Now go to sleep. I am in the house, and you have nothing whatever to fear."

"I am very glad you have come," he said wearily. He flung himself back on his pillow; the exhausted look was very manifest on his small, childish face. I left the room, shutting the door softly.

To say that my blood boiled can express but little the emotions which ran through my frame—the child was in the hands of a monster. He was in the very clutch of the Brotherhood, whose intention was to destroy his life. I thought for a moment. There was nothing now for it but to see Fietta, tell him that I had discovered his machinations, claim the boy, and take him away by force. I knew that I was treading on dangerous ground. At any moment my own life might be the forfeit for my supposed treachery to the cause whose vows I had so madly taken. Still, if I saved the boy nothing else really mattered.

I went downstairs into the great central hall, interviewed the concierge, who told me that Fietta had returned, asked for the number of his private sitting-room, and, going there, opened the door without knocking. At a writing-table at the farther end sat the doctor. He turned as I entered, and, recognising me, started up with a sudden exclamation. I noticed that his face changed colour, and that his beady eyes flashed all ugly fire. Then, recovering himself, he advanced quietly towards me.

"This is another of your unexpected surprises, Mr. Head," he said with politeness. "You have not, then, gone on to Cairo? You change your plans rapidly."

"Not more so than you do, Dr. Fietta," I replied, watching him as I spoke.

"I was obliged to change my mind," he answered. "I heard in Malta that cholera had broken out in Cairo. I could not therefore take my patient there. May I inquire why I have the honour of this visit? You will excuse my saying so, but this action of yours forces me to suspect that you are following me. Have you a reason?"

He stood with his hands behind him, and a look of furtive vigilance crept into his small eyes.

"This is my reason," I replied. I boldly drew the hypodermic syringe from my pocket as I spoke.

With an inconceivably rapid movement he hurried past me, locked the door, and placed the key in his pocket. As he turned towards me again I saw the glint of a long, bright stiletto which he had drawn and was holding in his right hand, which he kept behind him.

"I see you are armed," I said quietly, "but do not be too hasty. I have a few words to say to you." As I spoke I looked him full in the face, then I dropped my voice.

"I am one of the Brotherhood of the Seven King's!"

When I uttered these magical words he started back and looked at me with dilated eyes.

"Your proofs instantly, or you are a dead man," he cried hoarsely. Beads of sweat gleamed upon his forehead.

"Put that weapon on the table, give me your right hand, and you shall have the proofs you need," I answered.

He hesitated, then changed the stiletto to his left hand, and gave me his right. I grasped it in the peculiar manner which I had never forgotten, and bent my head close to his. The next moment I had uttered the pass-word of the Brotherhood.

"La Regina," I whispered.

"E la regina," he replied, flinging the stiletto on the carpet.

22

"Ah!" he continued, with an expression of the strongest relief, while he wiped the moisture from his forehead. "This is too wonderful. And now tell me, my friend, what your mission is? I knew you had stolen my syringe, but why did you do it? Why did you not reveal yourself to me before? You are, of course, under the Queen's orders?"

"I am," answered, "and her orders to me now are to take Lord Kairn home to England overland to-morrow morning."

"Very well. Everything is finished—he will die in one month."

"From Mediterranean fever? But it is not necessarily fatal," I continued.

"That is true. It is not always fatal acquired in the ordinary way, but by our methods it is so."

"Then you have administered more of the micro-organisms since Malta?"

"Yes; I had another syringe in my case, and now nothing can save him. The fever will commence in six days from now."

He paused for a moment or two.

"It is very odd," he went on, "that I should have had no communication. I cannot understand it." A sudden flash of suspicion shot across his dark face. My heart sank as I saw it. It passed, however, the next instant; the man's words were courteous and quiet.

"I of course accede to your proposition," he said: "everything is quite safe. This that I have done can never by any possibility be discovered. Madame is invincible. Have you yet seen Lord Kairn?"

"Yes, and I have told him to be prepared to accompany me home to-morrow."

"Very well."

Dr. Fietta walked across the room, unlocked the door and threw it open.

"Your plans will suit me admirably," he continued. "I shall stay on here for a few days more, as I have some private business to transact. To-night I shall sleep in peace. Your shadow has been haunting me for the last three days."

I went from Fietta's room to the boy's. He was wide awake and started up when he saw me.

"I have arranged everything, Cecil," I said, "and you are my charge now. I mean to take you to my room to sleep."

"Oh," he answered, "I am glad. Perhaps I shall sleep better in your room. I am not afraid of you—I love you." His eyes, bright with affection, looked into mine. I lifted him into my arms, wrapped his dressing-gown over his shoulders, and conveyed him through the folding-doors, down the corridor, into the room I had secured for myself. There were two beds in the room, and I placed him in one.

"I am so happy," he said, "I love you so much. Will you take me to Vesuvius in the morning, and then home in the evening?"

"I will see about that. Now go to sleep," I answered.

He closed his eyes with a sigh of pleasure. In ten minutes he was sound asleep. I was standing by him when there came a knock at the door. I went to open it. A waiter stood without. He held a salver in his hand. It contained a letter, also a sheet of paper and an envelope stamped with the name of the hotel.

"From the doctor, to be delivered to the signor immediately," was the laconic remark.

Still standing in the doorway, I took the letter from the tray, opened it, and read the following words:

"You have removed the boy and that action arouses my mistrust. I doubt your having received any Communication from Madame.

If you wish me to believe that you are a bonâ-fide member of the Brotherhood, return the boy to his own sleeping-room, immediately."

I took a pencil out of my pocket and hastily wrote a few words on the sheet of paper, which had been sent for this purpose.

"I retain the boy. You are welcome to draw your own conclusions."

Folding up the paper I slipped it into the envelope, and wetting the gum with my tongue, fastened it together, and handed it to the waiter who withdrew. I re-entered my room and locked the door. To keep the boy was imperative, but there was little doubt that Fietta would now telegraph to Mme. Koluchy (the telegraphic office being open day and night) and find out the trick I was playing upon him. I considered whether I might not remove the boy there and then to another hotel, but decided that such a step would be useless. Once the emissaries of the Brotherhood were put upon my track the case for the child and myself would be all but hopeless.

There was likely to be little sleep for me that night. I paced up and down my lofty room. My thoughts were keen and busy. After a time, however, a strange confusion seized me. One moment I thought of the child, the next of Mme. Koluchy, and then again I found myself pondering some abstruse and comparatively unimportant point in science, which I was perfecting at home. I shook myself free of these thoughts, to walk about again, to pause by the bedside of the child, to listen to his quiet breathing.

Perfect peace reigned over his little face. He had resigned himself to me, his terrors were things of the past, and he was absolutely happy. Then once again that queer confusion of brain returned. I wondered what I was doing, and why I was anxious about the boy. Finally I sank upon the bed at the farther end of the room, for my limbs were tired and weighted with a heavy oppression. I would rest for a moment, but nothing would induce me to close my eyes. So I thought, and flung myself back on my pillow. But the next instant all present things were forgotten in dreamless and heavy slumber.

I awoke long hours afterwards, to find the sunshine flooding the room, the window which led on to the balcony wide open, and Cecil's bed empty. I sprang up with a cry; memory returned with a flash. What had happened? Had Fietta managed to get in by means of the window? I had noticed the balcony outside the window on the previous night. The balcony of the next room was but a few feet distant from mine. It would be easy for any one to enter there, spring from one balcony to the other, and so obtain access to my room. Doubtless this had been done. Why had I slept? I had firmly resolved to stay awake all night. In an instant I had found the solution. Fietta's letter bad been a trap. The envelope which he sent me contained poison on the gum. I had licked it, and so received the fatal soporific. My heart beat wildly. I knew I had not an instant to lose. With hasty strides I went into Fietta's sitting-room: there was no one there; into his bedroom, the door of which was open: it was also empty. I rushed into the hall.

"The gentleman and the little boy went out about half an hour ago," said the concierge, in answer to my inquiries. "They have gone to Vesuvius—a fine day for the trip." The man smiled as he spoke.

My heart almost stopped.

"How did they go?" I asked.

"A carriage, two horses—best way to go."

In a second I was out in the Piazza del Municipio. Hastily selecting a pair-horse carriage out of the group of importunate drivers, I jumped in.

"Vesuvius," I shouted, "as hard as you can go."

The man began to bargain. I thrust a roll of paper-money into his hand. On receiving it he waited no longer, and we were soon dashing at a furious speed along the crowded, ill-paved streets, scattering the pedestrians as we went. Down the Via Roma, and out on to the Santa Lucia Quay, away and away through endless labyrinths of noisome, narrow streets, till at length we got out into the more open country at the base of the burning mountain. Should I be in time to prevent the catastrophe which I dreaded? For I had been up that mountain before, and knew well the horrible danger at the crater's mouth—a slip, a push, and one would never be seen again.

The ascent began, and the exhausted horses were beginning to fail. I leapt out, and giving the driver a sum which I did not wait to count, ran up the winding road of cinders and pumice that curves round beneath the observatory. My breath had failed me, and my heart was beating so hard that I could scarcely speak when I reached the station where one takes ponies to go over the new, rough lava. In answer to my inquiries, Cook's agent told me that Fietta and Cecil had gone on not a quarter of an hour ago.

I shouted my orders, and flinging money right and left, I soon obtained a fleet pony, and was galloping recklessly over the broken lava. Throwing the reins over the pony's head I presently jumped off, and ran up the little, narrow path to the funicular wire-laid railway that takes passengers up the steep cone to the crater.

"Just gone on, sir," said a Cook's official, in answer to my question.

"But I must follow at once," I said excitedly, hurrying towards the little shed.

The man stopped me.

"We don't take single passengers," he answered.

"I will, and must, go alone," I said. "I'll buy the car, and the railway, and you, and the mountain, if necessary, but go I will. How much do you want to take me alone?"

"One hundred francs," he answered impertinently, little thinking that I would agree to the bargain.

"Done!" I replied.

In astonishment he counted out the notes which I handed to him, and hurried at once into the shed. Here he rang an electric bell to have the car at the top started back, and getting into the empty car, I began to ascend—up, and up, and up. Soon I passed the empty car returning. How slowly we moved! My mouth was parched and dry, and I was in a fever of excitement. The smoke from the crater was close above me in great wreaths. At last we reached the top. I leapt out, and without waiting for a guide, made my way past, and rushed up the active cone, slipping in the shifting, loose, gritty soil. When I reached the top a gale was blowing, and the scenery below, with the Bay and Naples and Sorrento, lay before me, the most magnificent panorama in the world. I had no time to glance at it, but hurried forward past crags of hot rock, from which steam and sulphur were escaping. The wind was taking the huge volumes of smoke over to the farther side of the crater, and I could just catch sight of two figures as the smoke cleared for a moment. The figures were those of Fietta and the boy. They were evidently making a détour of the crater, and had just entered the smoke. I heard a guide behind shout something to me in Italian, but I took no notice, and plunged at once into the blinding, suffocating smoke that came belching forth from the crater.

I was now close behind Fietta and the boy. They held their handkerchiefs up to their faces to keep off the choking sulphurous fumes, and had evidently not seen me. Their guide was ahead of them. Fietta was walking slowly; he was farthest away from the crater's mouth. The boy's hand was within his; the boy was nearest to the yawning gulf. A hot and choking blast of smoke blinded me for a moment, and hid the pair from view; the next instant it passed. I saw Fietta suddenly turn, seize the boy, and push him towards the edge. Through the rumbling thunder that came from below I heard a sharp cry of terror, and bounding forward I just caught the lad as he reeled, and hurled him away into safety.

With a yell of baffled rage Fietta dashed through the smoke and flung himself upon me. I moved nimbly aside, and the doctor, carried on by the impetus of his rush, missed his footing in the crumbling ashes and fell headlong down through the reeking smoke and steam into the fathomless, seething caldron below.

Fietta falls into the crater.

"The Doctor ... missed his footing."

What followed may be told in a few words. That evening I sailed for Malta with the boy. Dr. Benson administered the antitoxin in time, and the child's life was saved. Within a fortnight I brought him back to his mother.

It was reported that Dr. Fietta had gone mad at the edge of the crater, and in an excess of maniacal fury had first tried to destroy the boy and then flung himself in. I kept my secret.

Chapter II

THE WINGED ASSASSIN

MY scientific pursuits no longer interested me. I returned to my house in Regent's Park, but only to ponder recent events. With the sanction of conscience I fully intended to be a traitor to the infamous Brotherhood which, in a moment of mad folly, I had joined. From henceforth my object would be to expose Mme. Koluchy. By so doing, my own life would be in danger; nevertheless, my firm determination was not to leave a stone unturned to place this woman and her confederates in the felon's dock of an English criminal court. To effect this end one thing was obvious: single-handed I could not work. I knew little of the law, and to expose a secret society like Mme. Koluchy's, I must invoke the aid of the keenest and most able legal advisers.

Colin Dufrayer, the man I had just met before my hurried visit to Naples, was assuredly the person of all others for my purpose. He was one of the smartest lawyers in London. I went therefore one day to his office. I was fortunate in finding him in, and he listened to the story, which I told him in confidence, with the keenest attention.

"If this is true, Head," he said, "you yourself are in considerable danger."

"Yes," I answered; "nevertheless, my mind is made up. I will enter the lists against Mme. Koluchy."

His face grew grave, furrows lined his high and bald forehead, and knitted themselves together over his watchful, grey eyes.

"If any one but yourself had brought me such an incredible story, Head, I should have thought him mad," he said, at last. "Of course, one knows that from time to time a great master in crime arises and sets justice at defiance; but that this woman should be the leader of a deliberately organized crusade against the laws of England is almost past my belief. Granted it is so, however, what do you wish me to do?"

"Give me your help," I answered; "use your ingenuity, employ your keenest agents, the most trusted and experienced officers of the law, to watch this woman day and night, and bring her and her accomplices to justice. I am a rich man, and I am prepared to devote both my life and my money to this great cause. When we have obtained sufficient evidence," I continued, "let us lay our information before the authorities."

He looked at me thoughtfully; after a moment he spoke.

"What occurred in Naples has doubtless given the Brotherhood a considerable shock," he said, "and if Mme. Koluchy is as clever as you suppose her to be, she will remain quiet for the present. Your best plan, therefore, is to do nothing, and allow me to watch. She suspects you, she does not suspect me."

"That is certainly the case," I answered.

"Take a sea voyage, or do something to restore your equilibrium, Head; you look overexcited."

"So would you be if you knew the woman, and if you had just gone through my terrible experiences."

"Granted, but do not let this get on your nerves. Rest assured that I won't leave a stone unturned to convict the woman, and that when the right moment comes I will apply to you."

I had to be satisfied with this reply, and soon afterwards I left Dufrayer. I spent a winter of anxiety, during which time I heard nothing of Mme. Koluchy. Once again my suspicions were slumbering, and my attention was turned to that science which was at once the delight and solace of my life, when, in the May of the following year, I received a note from Dufrayer. It ran as follows:—-

"MY DEAR HEAD,—I have received an invitation both for you and myself to dine and sleep next Friday at Sir John Winton's place at Epsom. You are, of course, aware that his horse, Ajax, is the favourite for the Derby. Don't on any account refuse this invitation—throw over all other engagements for the sake of it. There is more in this than meets the eye.

"Yours sincerely.

"COLIN DUFRAYER."

I wired back to Dufrayer to accept the invitation, and on the following Friday went down to Epsom in time for dinner. Dufrayer had arrived earlier in the day, and I had not yet had an opportunity of seeing him alone. When I entered the drawing-room before dinner I found myself one of a large party. My host came forward to receive me. I happened to have met Sir John several times at his club in town, and he now signified his pleasure at seeing me in his house. A moment afterwards he introduced me to a bright-eyed girl of about nineteen years of age. Her name was Alison Carr. She had very dark eyes and hair, a transparent complexion and a manner full of vivacity and intelligence. I noticed, however, an anxious expression about her lips, and also that now and then, when engaged in the most animated conversation, she lost herself in a reverie of a somewhat painful nature. She would wake from these fits of inattention with an obvious start and a heightened colour. I found she was to be my companion at dinner, and soon discovered that hers was an interesting, indeed, delightful, personality. She knew the world and could talk well. Our conversation presently drifted to the great subject of the hour, Sir John Winton's colt, Ajax.

"He is a beauty," cried the girl. "I love him for himself, as who would not who had ever seen him?—but if he wins the Derby, why, then, my gratitude—-" She paused and clasped her hands, then drew herself up, colouring.

"Are you very much interested in the result of the race?" I could not help asking.

"All my future turns on it," she said, dropping her voice to a low whisper. "I think," she continued, "Mr. Dufrayer intends to confide in you. I know something about you, Mr. Head, for Mr.

Dufrayer has told me. I am so glad to meet you. I cannot say any more now, but my position is one of great anxiety."

Her words somewhat surprised me, but I could not question her further at that moment. Later on, however, when we returned to the drawing-room, I approached her side. She looked up eagerly when she saw me.

"I have been all over Europe this summer," she said gaily; "don't you want to see some of my photographs?"

She motioned me to a seat near her side, and taking up a book opened it. We bent over the photographs; she turned the pages, talking eagerly. Suddenly, she put her hand to her brow, and her face turned deadly pale.

"What is the matter?" I asked.

She did not speak for a moment, but I noticed that the moisture stood on her forehead. Presently she gave a sigh of relief.

"It has passed," she said. "Yes, I suffer in my head an indescribable agony, but it does not last now more than a moment or two. At one time the pain used to stay for nearly an hour, and I was almost crazy at the end. I have had these sharp sort of neuralgic pains from a child, but since I have consulted Mme. Koluchy——"

I started. She looked up at me and nodded.

"Of course you have heard of her," she said; "who has not? She is quite the most wonderful, delightful woman in existence. She, indeed, is a doctor to have confidence in. I understand that the men of the profession are mad with jealousy, and small wonder, her cures are so marvellous. Yes, Mr. Head, I went to quite half a dozen of our greatest doctors, and they could do nothing for me; but since I have been to Mme. Koluchy the pain comes but seldom, and when it does arise from any cause it quickly subsides. I have much to thank her for. Have you ever seen her?"

"Yes," I replied.

"And don't you like her?" continued the girl eagerly. "Is she not beautiful, the most beautiful woman in the world? Perhaps you have consulted her for your health; she has a great many men patients."

I made no reply; Miss Carr continued to speak with great animation.

"It is not only her beauty which impresses one," she said, "it is also her power—she draws you out of yourself completely. When I am away from her I must confess I am restless—it is as though she hypnotized me, and yet she has never done so. I long to go back to her even when——" She hesitated and trembled. Some one came up, and commonplace subjects of conversation resumed their sway.

That evening late I joined Dufrayer in the smoking-room. We found ourselves alone, and I began to speak at once.

"You asked me to come here for a purpose," I said. "Miss Carr, the girl whom I took in to dinner, further told me that you had something to communicate. What is the matter?"

"Sit down, Head; I have much to tell you."

"By the way," I continued, as I sank into the nearest chair, "do you know that Miss Carr is under the influence of Mme. Koluchy?"

"I know it, and before I go any further, tell me what you think of her."

"She is a handsome girl," I replied, "and I should say a good one, but she seems to have trouble. She hinted at such, and in any case I observed it in her face and manner."

"You are right, she is suffering from a very considerable anxiety. I will explain all that to you presently. Now, please, give your best attention to the following details. It is about a month ago that I first received a visit from Frank Calthorpe, Sir John Winton's nephew, and the junior partner of Bruce, Nicholson, & Calthorpe, the great stockjobbers in Garrick Gardens. I did some legal business for his firm some years ago, but the matter on which Calthorpe came to see me was not one connected with his business, but of a purely private character."

"Am I to hear what it is?"

"You are, and the first piece of information I mean to impart to you is the following. Frank Calthorpe is engaged to Miss Carr."

"Indeed!"

"The engagement is of three months' date."

"When are they to be married?"

"That altogether depends on whether Sir John Winton's favourite, Ajax, wins the Derby or not."

"What do you mean?"

"To explain, I must tell you something of Miss Carr's early history." I sat back in my chair and prepared to listen. Dufrayer spoke slowly.

"About a year ago," he began, "Alison Carr lost her father, She was then eighteen years of age, and still at school. Her mother died when she was five years old. The father was a West Indian merchant, and had made his money slowly and with care. When he died he left a hundred thousand pounds behind him and an extraordinary will. The girl whom you met to-night was his only child. Henry Carr, Alison's father, had a brother, Felix Carr, a clergyman. In his will Henry made his brother Alison's sole guardian, and also his own residuary legatee. The interest of the hundred thousand pounds was to be devoted altogether to the girl's benefit, but the capital was only to come into her possession on certain conditions. She was to live with her uncle, and receive the interest of the money as long as she remained single. After the death of the uncle she was still, provided she was unmarried, to receive the interest during her lifetime. At her death the property was to go to Felix Carr's eldest son, or, in case he was dead, to his children. Provided, however, Alison married according to the conditions of the will, the whole of the hundred thousand pounds was to be settled on her and her children. The conditions were as follows:

conditions of the will

"The man who married Alison was to settle a similar sum of one hundred thousand upon her and her children, and he was also to add the name of Carr to his own. Failing the fulfilment of these two conditions, Alison, if she married, was to lose the interest and capital of her father's fortune, the whole going to Felix Carr for his life, and after him to his eldest son. On this point the girl's father seems to have had a crank—he was often heard to say that he did not intend to amass gold in order to provide luxuries for a stranger.

"'Let the man who marries Alison put pound to pound,' he would cry; 'that's fair enough, otherwise the money goes to my brother.'

"Since her father's death, Alison has had one or two proposals from elderly men of great wealth, but she naturally would not consider them. When she became engaged, however, to Calthorpe, he had every hope that he would be able to fulfil the strange conditions of the will and meet her fortune with an equal sum on his own account. The engagement is now of three months' date, and here comes the extraordinary part of the story. Calthorpe, like most of his kind, is a speculator, and has large dealings both in stocks and shares and on the turf. He is a keen sportsman.

"Now, pray, listen. Hitherto he has always been remarkable for his luck, which has been, of course, as much due to his own common sense as anything else; but since his engagement to Miss Carr his financial ventures have been so persistently disastrous, and his losses so heavy, that he is practically now on the verge of ruin. Several most remarkable and unaccountable things have happened recently, and it is now almost certain that some one with great resources has been using his influence against him. You will naturally say that the person whose object it would be to do so is Alison's uncle, but beyond the vaguest suspicion, there is not the slightest evidence against him. He has been interested in the engagement from the first, and preparations have even been made for the wedding. It is true that Alison does not like him, and resents very much the clause in the will which compels her to live with him; but as far as we can tell, he has always been systematically kind to her, and takes the deepest interest in Calthorpe's affairs. Day by day, however, these affairs grow worse and worse.

"About a fortnight ago, Calthorpe actually discovered that shares were being held against him on which he was paying enormous differences, and had finally to buy them back at tremendous loss. The business was done through a broker, but the identity of his client is a mystery. We now come to his present position, which is a most crucial one. Next Wednesday is the Derby Day, and Calthorpe hopes to retrieve his losses by a big coup, as he has backed Ajax at an average price of five to two in order to win one hundred thousand on the horse alone. He has been quietly getting his money on during the last two months through a lot of different commission agents. If he secures this big haul he will be in a position to marry Alison, and his difficulties will be at an end. If, on the other hand, the horse is beaten, Calthorpe is ruined."

"What are the chances for the horse?" I asked.

"As far as I can tell, they are splendid. He is a magnificent creature, a bay colt with black points, and comes of a splendid stock. His grandsire was Colonel Gillingham's Trumpeter, who was the champion of his year, winning the Derby, the Two Thousand Guineas, and St. Leger. There is not a three-year-old with such a fashionable ancestry as Ajax, and Sir John Winton is confident that he will follow their glorious record."

"Have you any reason to suspect Mme. Koluchy in this matter?" I asked.

"None. Without doubt Calthorpe possesses an enemy, but who that enemy is remains to be discovered. His natural enemy would be Felix Carr, but to all appearance the man has not moved a finger against him. Felix is well off, too, on his own account, and it is scarcely fair to suspect him of the wish to deliberately ruin his niece's prospects and her happiness. On the other hand, such a series of disasters would not happen to Calthorpe without a cause, and we have got to face that fact. Mme. Koluchy would, of course, be capable of doing the business, but we cannot find that Felix Carr even knows her."

"His niece does," I cried. "She consults her—she is under her care."

"I know that, and have followed up the clue very carefully," said Dufrayer. "Of course, the fact that Alison visits her two or three times a week, and in all probability confides in her fully, makes it all-important to watch her carefully. That fact, with the history which you have unfolded of Mme. Koluchy, makes it essential that we should take her into our calculations, but up to the present there is not a breath of suspicion against her. All turns on the Derby. If Ajax wins, whoever the person is who is Calthorpe's secret enemy, will have his foul purpose defeated."

Early the following morning, Sir John Winton took Dufrayer and myself to the training stables. Miss Carr accompanied us. The colt was brought out for inspection, and I had seldom seen a more magnificent animal. He was, as Dufrayer had described him, a bright bay, with black points. His broad forehead, brilliant eyes, black muzzle, and expanded nostrils proclaimed the Arab in his blood, while the long, light body, with the elongated limbs, were essentially adapted for the maximum development of speed. As the spirited creature curveted and pranced before us, our admiration could scarcely be kept in bounds. Miss Carr in particular was almost feverishly excited. She went up to the horse and patted him on his forehead. I heard her murmur something low into his ear. The creature turned his large and beautiful eye upon her as if he understood; he further responded to the girl's caress by pushing his nose forward for her to stroke.

"I have no doubt whatever of the result," said Sir John Winton, as he walked round and round the animal, examining his points and emphasizing his perfections. "If Ajax does not win the Derby, I shall never believe in a horse again." He then spoke in a low tone to the trainer, who nodded; the horse was led back to his stables, and we returned to the house.

As we crossed the Downs I found myself by Miss Carr's side.

"Yes," she exclaimed, looking up at me, her eyes sparkling, "Ajax is safe to win. Has Mr. Dufrayer confided in you, Mr. Head?"

"He has," I answered.

"Do you understand my great anxiety?"

"I do, but I think you may rest assured. If I am any judge of a horse, the favourite is sure to win the race."

"I wish Frank could hear you," she cried; "he is terribly nervous. He has had such a queer succession of misfortunes. Of course, I would marry him gladly, and will, without any fortune, if the worst comes to the worst; but there will be no worst," she continued brightly, "for Ajax will save us both." Here she paused, and pulled out her watch.

"I did not know it was so late," she exclaimed. "I have an appointment with Mme. Koluchy this morning. I must ask Sir John to send me to the station at once."

She hurried forward to speak to the old gentleman, and Dufrayer and I fell behind.

Soon afterwards we all returned to London, and on the following Monday I received a telegram from Dufrayer.

"Come to dinner—seven o'clock, important," was his brief message.

I responded in the affirmative, and at the right hour drove off to Dufrayer's flat in Shaftesbury Avenue, arriving punctual to the moment.

"I have asked Calthorpe to meet you," exclaimed Dufrayer, coming forward when I appeared; "his ill-luck dogs him closely.

If the horse loses he is absolutely ruined. His concealed enemy becomes more active as the crucial hour approaches. Ah, here he comes to speak for himself."

The door was thrown open, and Calthorpe was announced. Dufrayer introduced him to me, and the next moment we went into the dining-room. I watched him with interest. He was a fair man, somewhat slight in build, with a long, thin face and a heavy moustache. He wore a worried and anxious look painful to witness; his age must have been about twenty-eight years. During dinner he looked across at me several times with an expression of the most intense curiosity, and as soon as the meal had come to an end, turned the conversation to the topic that was uppermost in all our minds.

"Dufrayer has told me all about you, Mr. Head; you are in his confidence, and therefore in mine."

"Be assured of my keen interest," I answered. "I know how much you have staked on the favourite. I saw the colt on Saturday. He is a magnificent creature, and I should say is safe to win, that is—-" I paused, and looked full into the young man's face. "Would it not be possible for you to hedge on the most advantageous terms?" I suggested. "I see the price to-night is five to four."

"Yes, and I could win thirty thousand either way if I could negotiate the transaction, but that would not effect my purpose. You have heard, I know, from Dufrayer, all about my engagement and the strange conditions of old Carr's will. There is no doubt that I possess a concealed enemy, whose object is to ruin me; but if Ajax wins I could obtain sufficient credit to right myself, and also to fulfil the conditions of Carr's will. Yes, I will stand to it now, every penny. The horse can win, and by God he shall!"

As he spoke Calthorpe brought down his fist with a blow on the table that set the glasses dancing. A glance was sufficient to show that his nerves were strung up to the highest pitch, and that a little more excitement would make him scarcely answerable for his actions.

"I have already given you my advice on this matter," said Dufrayer, in a grave tone. He turned and faced the young man as he spoke. "I would say emphatically, choose the thirty thousand now, and get out of it. You have plunged far too heavily in this matter. As to your present run of ill-luck, it will turn, depend upon it, and is only a question of time. If you hedge now you will have to put off your marriage, that is all. In the long run you will be able to fulfil the strange conditions which Carr has enjoined on his daughter's future husband, and if I know Alison aright, she will be willing to wait for you. If, on the other hand, you lose, all is lost. It is the ancient adage, 'A bird in the hand.'"

"It would be a dead crow," he interrupted excitedly, "and I want a golden eagle." Two hectic spots burned his pale cheeks, and the glitter in his eye showed how keen was the excitement which consumed him.

"I saw my uncle this morning," he went on. "Of course, Sir John knows my position well, and there is no expense spared to guard and watch the horse. He is never left day or night by old and trusted grooms in the training stables. Whoever my enemy may be, I defy him to tamper with the horse. By the way, you must come down to see the race, Dufrayer; I insist upon it, and you too, Mr. Head. Yes, I should like you both to be there in the hour of my great success. I saw Rushton, the trainer, to-day, and he says the race is all over, bar shouting."

This was Monday night, and the following Wednesday was Derby Day. On the next evening, impelled by an uncontrollable desire to see Calthorpe, I called a hansom and gave the driver the name of his club. I felt certain that I should find him there. When I arrived the porter told me that he was in the house, and sending up my card, I went across to the tape machine, which was ticking away under its glass case in the hall. Two or three men were standing beside it, chatting. The Derby prices had just come through, and a page-boy was tearing the tape into lengths and pinning them on a green baize board in the hall. I glanced hurriedly through them. Evens Ajax, four to one Bright Star, eleven to two Midge, eight to one Day Dawn. I felt a hand on my shoulder, and Calthorpe stood beside me. I was startled at his appearance. There was a haggard, wild look in his eyes.

"It seems to be all right," I said cheerfully. "I see Ajax has gone off a point since this morning, but I suppose that means nothing?"

"Oh, nothing," he replied; "there has been a pot of money going on Bright Star all day, but the favourite can hold the field from start to finish. I saw him this morning, and he is as fit as possible. Rushton, the trainer, says he absolutely can't lose."

A small, dark, man in evening dress approached us and overheard Calthorpe's last remark.

"I'll have a level monkey about that, if you like, Mr. Calthorpe," he said, in a low, nasal voice.

"It's a wager," retorted Calthorpe, drawing out his pocket-book with silver-bound edges, and entering the bet. "I'll make it a thousand, if you like?" he added, looking up.

"With pleasure," cried the little man. "Does your friend fancy anything?"

"No, thank you," I replied.

The man turned away, and went back to his companions.

"Who is that fellow?" I asked of Calthorpe.

"Oh, a very decent little chap. He's on the Stock Exchange, and makes a pretty big book on his own account."

"So I should think," I replied. "Why do you suppose he wants to lay against Ajax?"

"Hedging, I should imagine," answered Calthorpe carelessly. "One thousand one way or the other cannot make any difference now."

He had scarcely said the words before Dufrayer entered the hall.

"I have been looking for you, Head," he said, just nodding to Calthorpe as he spoke, and coming up to my side. "I went to your house and heard you were here, and hoped I should run you to earth. I want to speak to you. Can you come with me?"

"Anything wrong?" asked Calthorpe uneasily.

"I hope not," replied Dufrayer, "but I want to have a word with Head. I will see you presently, Calthorpe."

He linked his hand through my arm, and we left the club.

"What is it?" I asked, the moment we got into the street.

"I want you to come to my flat. Miss Carr is there, and she wishes to see you."

"Miss Carr at your flat, and she wishes to see me?"

"She does. You will soon know all about it, Head. Here, let us get into this hansom."

He hailed one which was passing; we got into it and drove quickly to Shaftesbury Avenue. Dufrayer let himself in to his rooms with a latchkey, and the next moment I found myself in Alison's presence. She started up when she saw the lawyer and myself.

"Now, Miss Carr," said Dufrayer, shutting the door hastily, "we have not a moment to lose, Will you kindly repeat the story to Head which you have just told me?"

"But is there anything to be really frightened about?" she asked.

"I do not know of any one who can judge of that better than Mr. Head. Tell him everything, please, and at once."

Thus adjured, the girl began to speak.

"I went as usual to Mme. Koluchy this afternoon," she began; "her treatment does me a great deal of good. She was even kinder than usual. I believe her to be possessed of a sort of second sight.

When she assured me that Ajax would win the Derby, I felt so happy that I laughed in my glee. She knows, no one better, how much this means to me. I was just about to leave her when the door of the consulting-room was opened, and who should appear standing on the threshold but my uncle, the Rev. Felix Carr! There is no love lost between my uncle and myself, and I could not help uttering a cry, half of fear and half of astonishment. I could see that he was equally startled at seeing me.

"'What in the name of fortune has brought you to Mme. Koluchy?' he cried.

"Madame rose in her usual stately way and went forward to meet him.

"'Your niece, Alison, is quite an old patient of mine,' she said; 'but did you not receive my telegram?'

"'No; I left home before it arrived,' he answered. 'The pains grew worse, and I felt I must see you. I have taken a horrible cold on the journey.' As he spoke he took his handkerchief out of his pocket, and sneezed several times. He continued to stand on the threshold of the room.

"'Well, good-bye, Alison, keep up your courage,' cried Mme. Koluchy. She kissed me on my forehead and I left. Uncle Felix did not take any further notice of me. The moment I went out the door of the consulting-room was closed, and the first thing I saw in the corridor was a torn piece of letter. It lay on the floor, and must have dropped out of Uncle Felix's pocket. I recognized the handwriting to be that of Mme. Koluchy, I picked it up, and these words met my eyes: 'Innocuous to man, but fatal to the horse.' I could not read any further, as the letter was torn across and the other half not in my possession, but the words frightened me, although I did not understand them. I became possessed with a dreadful sense of depression. I hurried out of the house. I was so much at home with Mme. Koluchy now that I could go in and out as much as I pleased. I drove straight to see you, Mr. Dufrayer. I hoped you would set my terrors at rest, for surely Ajax cannot be the horse alluded to. The words haunt me, but there is nothing in

45

them, is there? Please tell me so, Mr. Head—please allay my fears."

"May I see the torn piece of paper?" I asked gravely.

The girl took it out of her pocket and handed it to me.

"You don't mind if I keep this?" I said.

"No, certainly; but is there any cause for alarm?"

"I hope none, but you did well to consult Dufrayer. Now, I have something to ask you."

"What is that?"

"Do not repeat what you were good enough to tell Dufrayer and me to Calthorpe."

"Why so?"

"Because it would give him needless anxiety. I am going to take the matter up, and I trust all will be well. Keep your own counsel; do not tell what you have just told us to another living soul; and now I must ask you to leave us."

Her face grew whiter than ever; her anxious eyes travelled from my face to Dufrayer's.

"I will see you to a hansom," I said. I took her downstairs, put her into one, and returned to the lawyer's presence.

"I am glad you sent for me, Dufrayer," I answered. "Don't you see how grave all this is? If Ajax wins the Derby, the Rev. Felix Carr—I know nothing about his character, remember—will lose the interest on one hundred thousand pounds and the further chance of the capital being secured to his son. You see that it would be very much to the interest of the Rev. Felix if Ajax loses the Derby. Then why does he consult Mme. Koluchy? The question of health is surely a mere blind. I confess I do not like the aspect of affairs at all. That woman has science at her fingers' ends. I shall go down immediately to Epsom and insist on Sir

46

John Winton allowing me to spend the night in the training stables."

"I believe you are doing the right thing," answered Dufrayer. "You, who know Mme. Koluchy well, are armed at a thousand points."

"I shall start at once," I said.

I bade Dufrayer good-bye, hailed a hansom, desired the man to drive me to Victoria Station, and took the next train to Epsom.

I arrived at Sir John Winton's house about ten o'clock. He was astonished to see me, and when I begged his permission to share the company of the groom in the training stables that night, he seemed inclined to resent my intrusion. I did not wish to betray Alison, but I repeated my request with great firmness.

"I have a grave reason for making it," I said, "but one which at the present moment it is best for me not to disclose. Much depends on this race. From the events which have recently transpired, there is little doubt that Calthorpe has a secret enemy. Forewarned is forearmed. Will you share my watch to-night in the training stables, Sir John?"

"Certainly," he answered. "I do not see that you have any cause for alarm, but under the circumstances, and in the face of the mad way that nephew of mine has plunged, I cannot but accede to your request. We will go together."

We started to walk across the Downs. As we did so, Sir John became somewhat garrulous.

"I thought Alison would have come by your train," he said, "but have just had a telegram asking me not to expect her. She is probably spending to-night with Mme. Koluchy. By the way, Head, what a charming woman that is."

"Do you know her?" I asked.

"She was down here on Sunday. Alison begged me to invite her. We all enjoyed her company immensely. She has a wonderful knowledge of horses; in fact, she seems to know all about everything."

"Has she seen Ajax?" I asked. My heart sank, I could not tell why.

"Yes, I took her to the stables. She was interested in all the horses, and above all in Ajax. She is certain he will win the Derby."

I said nothing further. We arrived at the stables. Sir John and I spent a wakeful night. Early in the morning I asked to be allowed to examine the colt. He appeared in excellent condition, and the groom stood by him, admiring him, praising his points, and speaking about the certain result of the day's race.

"Here's the Derby winner," he said, clapping Ajax on his glossy side. "He'll win the race by a good three lengths. By the way, I hope he won't be off his feed this morning."

"Off his feed exclaimed Sir John. What do you mean?"

"What I say, sir. We couldn't get the colt to touch his food last night, although we tempted him with all kinds of things. There ain't nothing in it, I know, and he seems all right now, don't he?"

"Try him with a carrot," said Sir John.

The man brought a carrot and offered it to the creature. He turned away from it, and fixed his large, bright eyes on Sir John's face. I fancied there was suffering in them. Sir John seemed to share my fears. He went up to the horse and examined it critically, feeling its nose and ears.

"Tell Saunders to step across," he said, turning to the groom. He mentioned a veterinary surgeon who lived close by. "And look you here, Dan, keep your own counsel. If so much as a word of this gets out, you may do untold mischief."

"No fear of me, sir," said the man. He rushed off to fetch Saunders, who soon appeared.

The veterinary surgeon was a thickly built man, with an intelligent face. He examined the horse carefully, taking his temperature, feeling him all over, and finally stepping back with a satisfied smile.

"There's nothing to be alarmed about, Sir John," he said. "The colt is in perfect health. Let him have a mash presently with some crushed corn in it. I'll look in in a couple of hours, but there's nothing wrong. He is as fit as possible."

As the man left the stables, Sir John uttered a profound yawn.

"I confess I had a moment's fright," he said; "but I believe it was more from your manner than anything else, Mr. Head. Well, I am sleepy. Won't you come back to the house and let me offer you a shake-down?"

"No," I replied, "I want to return to town. I can catch an early train if I start at once."

He shook hands with me, and I went to the railway station. The oppression and apprehension at my heart got worse moment by moment. For what object had Mme. Koluchy visited the stables? What was the meaning of that mysterious writing which I had in my pocket—"Innocuous to man, but fatal to the horse"? What did the woman, with her devilish ingenuity, mean to do? Something bad, I had not the slightest doubt.

I called at Dufrayer's flat and gave him an account of the night's proceedings.

"I don't like the aspect of affairs, but God grant my fears are groundless," I cried. "The horse is off his feed, but Sir John and the vet. are both assured there is nothing whatever the matter with him. Mme. Koluchy was in the stables on Sunday; but, after all, what could she do? We must keep the thing dark from Calthorpe and trust for the best."

At a quarter to twelve that day I found myself at Victoria. When I arrived on the platform I saw Calthorpe and Miss Carr coming to meet me. Dufrayer also a moment afterwards made his appearance. Miss Carr's eyes were full of question, and I avoided her as much as possible. Calthorpe, on the contrary, seemed to have recovered a good bit of nerve, and to be in a sanguine mood. We took our seats, and the train started for Epsom. As we alighted at the Downs station, a man in livery hurried up to Calthorpe.

"Sir John Winton is in the paddock, sir," he said, touching his hat. "He sent me to you, and says he wishes to see you at once, sir, and also Mr. Head."

The man spoke breathlessly, and seemed very much excited.

"Very well; tell him we'll both come," replied Calthorpe. He turned to Dufrayer. "Will you take charge of Alison?" he said.

Calthorpe and I moved off at once.

"What can be the matter?" cried the young man. "Nothing wrong, I hope. What is that?" he cried the next instant.

The enormous crowd was increasing moment by moment, and the din that rose from Tattersall's ring seemed to me unusually loud so early in the day's proceedings. As Calthorpe uttered the last words he started and his face turned white.

"Good God! Did you hear that?" he cried, dashing forward. I followed him quickly; the ring was buzzing like an infuriated beehive, and the men in it were hurrying to and fro as if possessed by the very madness of excitement. It was an absolute pandemonium. The stentorian tones of a brass-voiced bookmaker close beside us fell on my ears:

"Here, I'll bet five to one Ajax—five to one Ajax!"

The voice was suddenly drowned in the deafening clamour of the crowd, the air seemed to swell with the uproar. Were my worst fears confirmed? I felt stunned and sick. I turned round; Calthorpe had vanished.

Several smart drags were drawn up beside the railings. I glanced up at the occupants of the one beside me. From the box-seat looking down at me with the amused smile of a spectator sat Mme. Koluchy. As I caught her eyes I thought I detected a flash of triumph, but the next moment she smiled and bowed gracefully.

"You are a true Englishman, Mr. Head," she said. "Even your infatuated devotion to your scientific pursuits cannot restrain you from attending your characteristic national fête. Can you tell me what has happened? Those men seem to have suddenly gone mad—is that a part of the programme?"

"'Innocuous to man, but fatal to the horse," was my strange reply. I looked her full in the face. The long lashes covered her brilliant eyes for one flashing moment, then she smiled at me more serenely than ever.

"I will guess your enigma when the Derby is won," she said.

I raised my hat and hurried away. I had seen enough: suspicion was changed into certainty. The next moment I reached the paddock. I saw Calthorpe engaged in earnest conversation with his uncle.

"It's all up, Head," he said, when he saw me.

"Don't be an idiot, Frank," cried Sir John Winton angrily. "I tell you the thing is impossible. I don't believe there is anything the matter with the horse. Let the ring play their own game, it is nothing to us. Damn the market! I tell you what it is, Frank. When you plunged as you did, you would deserve it if the horse fell dead on the course; but he won't—he'll win by three lengths. There's not another horse in the race."

Calthorpe muttered some inaudible reply and turned away. I accompanied him.

"What is the matter?" I asked, as we left the paddock.

"Saunders is not satisfied with the state of the horse. His temperature has gone up; but, there! my uncle will see nothing wrong. Well, it will be all over soon. For God's sake, don't let us say anything to Alison."

"Not a word," I replied.

We reached the grand stand. Alison's earnest and apprehensive eyes travelled from her lover's face to mine. Calthorpe went up to her and endeavoured to speak cheerfully.

"I believe it's all right," he said. "Sir John says so, and he ought to know. It will be all decided one way or another soon. Look, the first race is starting."

We watched it, and the one that followed, hardly caring to know the name of the winner. The Derby was timed for three o'clock— it only wanted three minutes to the hour. The ring below was seething with excitement, Calthorpe was silent, now gazing over the course with the vacant expression of a man in a day-dream.

Bright Star was a hot favourite at even money.

"Against Ajax, five to one," rang out with a monotonous insistence.

There was a sudden lull, the flag had fallen. The moments that followed seemed like years of pain—there was much senseless cheering and shouting, a flash of bright colours, and the race was over. Bright Star had won. Ajax had been pulled up at Tattenham Corner, and was being led by his jockey.

Twenty minutes later Dufrayer and I were in the horse's stable.

"Will you allow me to examine the horse for a moment?" I said to the veterinary surgeon.

"It will want some experience to make out what is the matter," replied Saunders; "it's beyond me."

I entered the box and examined the colt carefully. As I did so the meaning of Mme. Koluchy's words became plain. Too late now to do anything—the race was lost and the horse was doomed. I looked around me.

"Has any one been bitten in this stable?" I asked.

"Bitten!" cried one of the grooms. "Why, I said to Sam last night"—he apostrophized the stable-boy—"that there must be gnats about. See my arm, it's all inflamed."

"Hold!" I cried, "what is that on your sleeve?"

"A house-fly, I suppose, sir," he answered.

"Stand still," I cried. I put out my hand and captured the fly. "Give me a glass," I said. "I must examine this."

One was brought and the fly put under it. I looked at it carefully. It resembled the ordinary house-fly, except that the wings were longer. Its colour was like an ordinary humming-bee.

"I killed a fly like that this morning," said Sam, the stable-boy, pushing his head forward.

"When did you say you were first bitten?" I asked, turning to the groom.

"A day or two ago," he replied. "I was bitten by a gnat, I don't rightly know the time. Sam, you was bitten too. We couldn't catch it, and we wondered that gnats should be about so early in the year. It has nothing to do with the horse, has it, sir?"

I motioned to the veterinary surgeon to come forward, and once more we examined Ajax. He now showed serious and unmistakable signs of malaise.

"Can you make anything out?" asked Saunders.

"With this fly before me, there is little doubt," I replied; "the horse will be dead in ten days—nothing can save him. He has been bitten by the tse-tse fly of South Africa—I know it only too well."

My news fell on the bystanders like a thunderbolt.

"Innocuous to man, but fatal to the horse," I found myself repeating. The knowledge of this fact had been taken advantage of—the devilish ingenuity of the plot was revealed. In all probability Mme. Koluchy had herself let the winged assassin loose when she had entered the stables on Sunday. The plot was worthy of her brain, and hers alone.

"You had better look after the other horses," I said, turning to the grooms. "If they have not been bitten already they had better be removed from the stables immediately. As for Ajax, he is doomed."

Late that evening Dufrayer dined with me alone. Pity for Calthorpe was only exceeded by our indignation and almost fear of Mme. Koluchy.

"What is to happen?" asked Dufrayer.

"Calthorpe is a brave man and will recover," I said. "He will win Miss Carr yet. I am rich, and I mean to help him, if for no other reason than in order to defeat that woman."

"By the way," said Dufrayer, "that scrap of paper which you hold in your possession, coupled with the fact that Mr. Carr called upon Mme. Koluchy, might induce a magistrate to commit them both for conspiracy."

"I doubt it," I replied; "the risk is not worth running. If we failed, the woman would leave the country, to return again in more dangerous guise. No, Dufrayer, we must bide our time until we get such a case against her as will secure conviction without the least doubt."

"At least," cried Dufrayer, "what happened to-day has shown me the truth of your words—it has also brought me to a decision. For the future I shall work with you, not as your employed legal adviser, but hand in hand against the horrible power and machinations of that woman. We will meet wit with wit, until we bring her to the justice she deserves."

Chapter III

THE SWING OF THE PENDULUM

THERE was now little doubt that Mme. Koluchy knew herself to be in personal danger. On the Derby Day I had thrown down the gauntlet with a vengeance—her object henceforth would be to put me out of the way. I lived in an atmosphere of intangible mystery, which was all the darker and more horrible because it was felt, not seen.

By Dufrayer's advice, I left the bringing of this dangerous woman to justice in his hands. He employed the cleverest and most up-to-date detectives to have her secretly watched, and from time to time they brought us their reports. Clue after clue arose: each clue was carefully followed, but it invariably led to disappointing results. Madame eluded every effort to bring a definite charge against her. The money we were spending, however, was not entirely in vain. We learned that her influence and the wide range of her acquaintances were far beyond what we had originally surmised. Her fame as a healer, her marvellous and occult cures, the reputation of her great wealth and dazzling beauty, increased daily, and I was certain that before long I should meet her in the lists. The encounter was destined to come sooner even than I had anticipated, and in a manner most unexpected.

It was the beginning of the following November that I received an invitation to dine with an old friend, Harry de Brett. He was several years my senior, and had recently succeeded to his father's business in the City—an old-established firm of bankers, whose house was in St. Mark's Court, Gracechurch Street. Only a few days previously I had seen it announced in the society papers that a marriage had been arranged between De Brett's only daughter, Geraldine, and the Duke of Friedeck, a foreign nobleman, whose name I had seen figuring prominently at many a function the previous season. I had known Geraldine since she was a child, and was glad to have an opportunity of offering my congratulations.

At the appointed hour, I found myself at De Brett's beautiful house in Bayswater, and Geraldine, who was standing near her father, came eagerly forward to welcome me. She was a pretty and very young girl, with a clear, olive complexion and soft, dark eyes. She had the innocent and naïve manner of a schoolgirl. She was delighted to see me, and began to talk eagerly.

"Come and stand by this window, Mr. Head. I am so glad you were able to come—I want to introduce you to Karl—the Duke of Friedeck, I mean; he will be here in a minute or two." As she spoke she dropped her voice to a semi-whisper.

"You know, of course, that we are to be married soon?" she continued.

"I have heard of the engagement," I answered, "and I congratulate you heartily. I should like much to meet the Duke. His name is, of course, familiar to any one who reads the society papers."

"He is anxious to make your acquaintance also," she replied. "I told him you were coming, and he said——" She paused.

"But surely the Duke of Friedeck has never heard of me before?" I answered, in some surprise.

"I think he has," she answered. "He was quite excited when I spoke of you. I asked him if he had met you; he said 'No,' but that you were very well known in scientific circles as a clever man. The Duke is a great scientist himself, Mr. Head, and I know he would like to have a chat with you. I am certain you will be friends."

Just at that moment the Duke was announced. He was a tall and handsome man of about five and thirty, with the somewhat florid complexion, blue eyes, and fair, curling hair of the Teuton. He was well dressed, and had the indescribable air of good breeding which proclaims the gentleman. I looked at him with much curiosity, being puzzled by an intangible memory of having seen his face before—where and how I could not tell.

Geraldine tripped up to him and brought him to my side.

"Karl," she cried, "this is my friend Mr Head. Don't you remember we talked about him this morning?"

Friedeck bowed.

"I am glad to make your acquaintance," he said to me. "Yours is a name of distinction in the world of science."

"That can scarcely be the case," I answered. "It is true I am fond of original research, but up to the present I have worked for my own pleasure alone."

"Nevertheless, the world has whispered of you," he replied. "I, too, am fond of science, and have lost myself more than once in its tortuous mazes. I have lately started a laboratory of my own, but just now other matters—-" He broke off abruptly, and glanced at Geraldine, who smiled and blushed.

Dinner was announced. I happened to sit not far from the guest of the evening, and noticed that he was a good conversationalist. There was scarcely a subject mentioned on which he had not something to say; and on more than one occasion his repartee was brilliant, and his remarks, touched with humour. Geraldine, in her white dress, with her soft, rather sad, eyes, her manner at once bright, sweet, and timid, made a contrast to this astute-looking man of the world.

I glanced from one to the other, and an uneasiness which I could scarcely account for sprang up within me. Notwithstanding his handsome appearance and his easy and courteous manner, I wondered if this man, nearly double her age, was likely to make the pretty English girl happy.

As dinner progressed I observed that the Duke often took the trouble to look at me. I also noticed that whenever our eyes met he turned away. How was it possible for him to have heard of me before? Although I was a scientist, my researches were unknown to the world. I determined to take the first opportunity of solving this mystery.

Soon after eleven o'clock the guests took their leave, and I was just about to follow their example when De Brett asked me to have a pipe with him in his smoking-room. As we seated ourselves by the fire, he began to talk at once of his future son-in-law.

"He is a capital fellow, is he not, Head?" exclaimed my host. "I hope you have formed a favourable opinion of him?"

"I never form an opinion quickly," I answered, with caution. "The Duke of Friedeck is certainly distinguished in appearance, and—-"

"Oh, you are too cautious," cried De Brett, in some irritation; "you may take my word for it that he is all right. This is a great catch for my little girl. Of course, she will have plenty of money on her own account; but the Duke is not only of high family, he is also rich. He comes from Bavaria, and his title is absolutely genuine. Soon after the great Duke of Marlborough's wars, and almost immediately after the Battle of Blenheim, the Austrian Government took possession of the Dukedom of Friedeck, and until lately the family have remained in exile. It was only a year ago that the present Duke regained his rights and all the great estates. He was introduced to us by no less a person than Madame Koluchy. Ah! I see you start. You have heard of her, of course?"

"Who has not?" I replied.

"Do you know her?"

"I have met her," I said. It was only with an effort I could control the ungovernable excitement which seized me at the mere mention of this woman's name.

"She dines with us next week," continued De Brett; "a wonderful woman, wonderful! Her cures are marvellous; but that is after all the least part of her interesting personality. She is so fascinating, so wise and good-natured, that men and women alike fall at her feet. As to Geraldine, she has taken an immense fancy to her."

"Where did you first meet her?" I asked.

"In Scotland last summer. She was staying with my old friends, the Campbells, for a couple of nights, and Friedeck was also one of the guests. If she is a friend of yours, Head—and I rather expect so from your manner—will you dine with us again next Thursday in order to meet her? We are going down to my place, Forest Manor, in Essex, and Madame is to stay with us for a couple of nights. We expect quite a large party, and can give you a bed—will you come?"

"I wish I could, but I fear it will be impossible," I replied. "It is true that I know Madame Koluchy, but——" I broke off. "Don't ask me any more at the moment, De Brett. The fact is, your news has excited me, you will say unreasonably."

De Brett gazed at me with earnestness.

"You have fallen under the spell of the most beautiful woman in London," he said, after a pause; "is that so, Head?"

"You may put it that way if you like," I said, "but I cannot explain myself to-night. Be assured, however, of my deep interest in this matter. Pray tell me anything more you may happen to know with regard to the Duke of Friedeck."

"You certainly are a strange fellow," said my host. "You are wearing at the present moment an air of quite painful mystery. However, here goes. You wish to hear about the Duke—I have nothing but good to tell of him. He is a rich man, and dabbles now and then on the Stock Exchange, but not to any serious extent. A week ago be arranged for a loan from my bank, depositing as security some of the most splendid diamonds I have ever seen. They are worth a king's ransom and each stone is historical. He brought the diamonds away from the estates in Bavaria, and they are to be reset and presented to Geraldine just before the wedding."

"How large was the amount of the loan?" I asked.

De Brett raised his eyebrows. He evidently thought that I was infringing on the privileges even of an old friend.

"Compared with the security, the loan was a trifling one," he said, after a pause; "not more than £10,000. Friedeck will pay me back next week, as he wishes to release the diamonds in order to have them ready to give to Geraldine on her wedding-day."

"And when do you propose that the wedding shall take place?" I continued.

"Ah, you have me there, Head; that is the painful part. You know what my motherless girl is to me—well, the Duke insists upon taking her away between now and Christmas. They are to spend Christmas in the old feudal style in the old castle in Bavaria. It is a great wrench parting from the little one, but she will be happy. I never met a man I took more warmly to than Karl Duke of Friedeck. You can see for yourself that the child is devoted to him."

"I can," I said. "I will wish you good-night now, De Brett. Be assured once again of my warm interest in all that concerns you and Geraldine."

I shook hands with my host, and a moment later found myself in the street. I called a hansom, and desired the man to drive straight to Dufrayer's flat in Shaftesbury Avenue. He had just come in, and welcomed me eagerly.

"By all that's fortunate, Head!" he exclaimed. "I was just on my way to see you."

"Then we have well met," I answered.

"Dufrayer, I have come here on a most important matter. But first of all tell me, have you ever heard of the Duke of Friedeck?"

"The Duke of Friedeck!" cried Dufrayer. "Why, it was on that very subject I wished to see you. You have, of course, observed the announcement of his approaching marriage in the society papers?"

"I have," I replied. "He is engaged to Geraldine de Brett. I have been dining at De Brett's house to-night, and met the Duke at dinner. De Brett has been telling me all about him. Dufrayer, I have learned to my consternation that the man was introduced to the De Bretts by Mme. Koluchy. That fact is quite enough to rouse my suspicions, but I see you have something to communicate on your own account. What is it?"

"Sit down, Head. You know, of course, that I am having Madame watched. The Duke of Friedeck is beyond doubt one of her satellites, and I am strongly inclined to think that this is a new plot brewing."

"Just my own opinion," I replied; "but tell me what you know."

"I was coming to see you, for I hoped that you might remember the Duke's name from your old association with the Brotherhood."

"I do not recall it, but names mean nothing. The man is handsome, and has the manners of a gentleman. When he entered De Brett's drawing-room I thought for a moment that I must have met him before, but that idea quickly vanished. Nevertheless, he contrived to arouse my suspicions by more than one stealthy glance which he favoured me with, even before his connection with Mme. Koluchy was mentioned. I regard him now as a highly suspicious individual, and I fully believe he is playing some game a little deeper than appears."

"Beyond doubt, the man has plenty of money, and moves in good circles," said Dufrayer. "He is known, however, to live a pretty fast life. He shoots at Hurlingham, drives his own drag, rents a moor in Scotland, and has a suite at the Hotel Cecil; but nothing can be discovered against him except that he is constantly seen in Madame's company."

"And that is quite enough," I replied. "Friedeck is one of Madame's satellites. Without doubt, there is mischief ahead."

"I agree with you," said Dufrayer; "I think it more than possible that this plausible Duke is simply another serpent springing from the head of this modern Medusa. In that case, De Brett ought to be warned."

I rose uneasily.

"I would have warned him to-night," I answered, "but I want more evidence. How are we to get it?"

"Tyler's agents are doing their best, and Madame is closely watched."

"Yes, but that woman could deceive the devil himself," I said bitterly.

"That is true," answered Dufrayer, "and to show our hand too soon might be fatal. We cannot move in this matter until we have got more circumstantial evidence. How we are to set to work is the puzzle!"

"Well," I said, "I shall move Heaven and earth in this matter. I have known Geraldine since she was a child. She is a sweet, innocent, motherless girl. The great risk to her happiness that may now be impending is too serious to contemplate quietly. If I had time I should go to Bavaria in order to find out if the Duke's story is true; but in any case, it might be well to send one of Tyler's agents to look up the supposed estates."

"I will do so," said Dufrayer.

"And in the meantime I shall watch," I said, "and if an opportunity occurs, believe me, De Brett shall have his warning."

As I spoke I bade my friend good-night and returned to my own house.

The next few days were spent in anxious thought, but no immediate action seemed possible. Clue after clue still arose, but only to vanish into nothing. I seldom now went into society without hearing Mme. Koluchy's name, and all the accounts of her were favourable. She was the sort of Woman to charm the eye and fire the imagination. Her personal attractions were some of her strongest potentialities.

On the following Tuesday, as I was walking down Oxford Street, a brougham drew up suddenly at the pavement, the window was lowered, and a girlish face looked eagerly out.

"Mr. Head," cried Geraldine de Brett eagerly, "you are the very man I want. Come here, I have something to say." I approached her at once. "We are dreadfully disappointed at your refusing to come to us on Thursday," she continued. "We are making up a delightful party. My father and I are going down to Forest Manor for a fortnight, in order to have plenty of room to entertain our friends. This is a personal matter with me. I ask you to come to us as a personal favour. Will you refuse?"

I looked full into the sparkling and lovely eyes of the young girl. The colour came and went in her cheeks; she laid one of her small hands for a moment on mine.

"I must tell you everything," she continued eagerly. "Of course I want you, but I am not the only one. Mme. Koluchy—ah, you have heard of her?"

"Who has not?" was my cautious reply.

"Yes, but, Mr. Head, you are concealing something. Madame is one of your very greatest friends: she has told me so. It is only an hour since I left her. She is most anxious to meet you on Thursday at our house. I promised you should be there—wasn't it rash of me? But I made up my mind that I would insist on your coming. Now, you won't allow me to break my word, will you?"

"Did Mme. Koluchy really say that she wished to see me?" I asked. As I put the question I felt my face turning pale. I looked again full at Miss de Brett. It was evident that she misinterpreted my emotion. Well, that mattered nothing. I quickly made up my mind.

"I had an engagement for Thursday," I said, "but your word is law—I cannot refuse you."

Geraldine laughed.

"Madame doubted my power to bring you, but I knew you would come, if I could really see you."

"Suppose we had not met in this chance sort of way?"

"I was going to your house. I had no intention of leaving a stone unturned. Without you my party will not be complete. Yes, you will come, and it is all right. You will hear from father to-morrow. He very often drives out to Forest Manor from the bank, and perhaps you can arrange to come with him, but you will get all particulars straight from him. Thank you a thousand times— you have made me a happy girl."

She waved her hand to me in farewell, and the brougham rolled out of sight.

My blood was coursing quickly through my veins and my mind was made up. Madame would not wish me to meet her at De Brett's house without a strong reason. With her usual astuteness she was using Geraldine de Brett as her tool in more senses than one. I must not delay another moment in warning the banker.

Calling a hansom, I desired the man to drive me straight to De Brett's bank in the City, and soon after twelve o'clock I found myself in Gracechurch Street. In a few moments the hansom turned down a narrow lane leading into St. Mark's Court. Here I paid my driver, and a moment later found myself in the open space in front of the bank. This was a cul-de-sac, but there was another lane leading into it also from Gracechurch Street running parallel to the one I had come down, and separated from it by a narrow row of buildings, which came to an abrupt termination about fifty feet from the houses forming the farther side of the court.

Well as I knew De Brett, I had not been at the old bank for some years, and looked around me now eagerly, until my eye fell upon the large brass plate bearing the well-known name. I entered the office, and going up to the counter asked if Mr. De Brett were in. The clerk replied in the affirmative, and giving him my card he passed through a door into an inner room. The next moment he reappeared and requested me to step inside: I found De Brett seated at a writing-table, upon which a circle of light fell from a shaded incandescent.

"Welcome, Head," he exclaimed, rising and coming forward with his usual heartiness of manner. "To what am I indebted for this visit? Sit down. I am delighted to see you. By the way, Geraldine tells me—-"

"I have just met your daughter," I interrupted, "and it is principally on account of that meeting that I have come here to trouble you during business hours."

"Oh, I can spare you ten minutes," he answered, looking around him as he spoke. "The fact is this, Head, Geraldine is anxious that you should join our party at Forest Manor, and I wish you would reconsider your determination. The Duke has taken a fancy to you, and as you happen to know Mme. Koluchy, it would be a pleasure to us all if you would give us the benefit of your society for a night or two."

"I have promised Geraldine to come," I answered gravely: "but, De Brett, you must pardon me. I have intruded on you in your business hours to speak on a most delicate private matter. However you may receive what I have to say, I must ask you to hear it in confidence, and with that good feeling that has prompted me to come to you."

"My dear Head, what do you mean? Pray explain yourself."

"I am uneasy," I continued, "very uneasy. I am also in a peculiar position, and cannot disclose the reason of my fears. You are pleased with the match which Geraldine is about to make. Now, I have reasons for doubting the Duke of Friedeck, reasons which I cannot at the present moment disclose, but I am bound—yes, bound, De Brett, in your girl's interests—to warn you as to your dealings with him."

De Brett looked at me through his gold-rimmed spectacles with a blank expression of amazement.

"If it were any other man who spoke to me in this strain," he said at last, "I believe I should show him the door. Are you aware, Head, that this is a most serious allegation? You are bound in all honour to explain yourself."

"I cannot do so at the present moment. I can only repeat that my fears are grave. All I ask of you is to use double caution, to find out all you can about the man's antecedents——"

De Brett interrupted me, rising hastily from his seat.

"In our dealings one with the other," he said, "this is the first time in which you have shown bad taste. I shall see the Duke this afternoon, and shall be bound to acquaint him, in his and my own interests, with your communication."

"I hope you won't do so. Remember, my warning is given in confidence."

"It is not fair to give a man such a warning, and then to give him no reason for it," retorted the banker.

"I will give you my reasons."

"When?"

"On Thursday night. Will you regard my confidence as sacred until then?"

"You have disturbed me considerably, but I will do so. I should be sorry to alarm Geraldine unnecessarily. I am quite certain you are mistaken. You never saw the Duke until you met him at my house?"

"That I believe to be true, but I cannot say anything further now. I will explain my reasons fully on Thursday night."

De Brett rose from his seat. He bade me good-bye, but not with his customary friendliness. I went away, to pass the time until Thursday in much anxiety.

After grave thought I resolved, if I discovered nothing fresh with regard to Friedeck, to acquaint De Brett with what I knew of Mme. Koluchy. If Geraldine married the Duke, she should at least do so with her father's eyes opened. I little guessed, however, when I made these plans, what circumstances were about to bring forth.

On the following Thursday morning I awoke from a disturbed sleep to find London enveloped in one of the thickest fogs that had been known for some years. The limit of my vision scarcely extended beyond the area railings round which the soot-laden mist clung in a breathless calm.

In the course of the morning I received a telegram from De Brett.

"Meet me at the bank not later than a quarter-past four," were the few words which it contained.

Soon after three o'clock I started for my destination, avoiding omnibuses and preferring to walk the greater part of the way. I arrived at St. Mark's Court at the time named, and was just approaching the bank when two men knocked violently against me in the thick fog. One of them apologized, but before I could make any reply vanished into the surrounding gloom. I had caught a glimpse of his features, however. He was the Duke of Friedeck. Across the narrow court, at the opposite side from the bank, I saw a stream of light from an open door making a blurred gleam in the surrounding darkness. I crossed the court to see what this indicated. I then discovered that the light came from an old-fashioned eating-house, something in the style of the celebrated "Cock" in Fleet Street. As I stood in the shadow, the two men who had knocked against me entered the eating-house.

I returned now to the bank. As soon as I arrived the manager came up to me.

"Mr. De Brett was called out about half an hour ago," he said, "but he has asked you to wait for him here, Mr. Head. He expects to be back not later than half-past four."

I seated myself accordingly, a clerk brought me the Times and I drew up my chair in front of a bright fire. Now and then some one made a desultory remark about the fog, which was thickening in intensity each moment.

The time flew by: the bank had, of course, closed at four o'clock, but the clerks were busy finishing accounts and putting the place in order for the night. The different tills were emptied of their contents, and the money was taken down to the great vaults where the different safes were kept. The hands of the clock over the mantel-piece pointed to a quarter to five, when the sound of wheels was heard distinctly outside, and the next moment I saw a splendidly equipped brougham and pair draw up outside the bank. A footman dismounted and handed the commissionaire a note. This was brought into the office. It was for me; a clerk gave it to me. I glanced at the writing, and saw that the letter was from De Brett. I tore open the envelope, and read as follows:—-

"DEAR HEAD,—I have been unexpectedly detained at Lynn's bank, in Broad Street, so have sent the brougham for you. Will you come on at once and pick me up at Lynn's? Please ask Derbyshire, the manager, for the keys of the small safe. He will give them to you after he has locked up the strong-room.

"Yours,

"HARRY DE BRETT."

I turned to the manager. He was an elderly man, with grizzled hair and an anxious expression of face.

"Mr. de Brett wants me to bring him the keys of the small safe," I said. I saw the man raise his brows in surprise.

"That is an unusual request," he answered "but, of course, it must be as Mr. de Brett wishes. As a rule, either Mr. Frome or I keep the keys, as Mr. de Brett never cares to be troubled with them."

"Here is his letter," I replied, handing it to the manager. He read it, retaining it in his hand.

"Do you object to my keeping this, Mr. Head? The request is so unusual, that I should like to have this note as my authority."

"You can certainly keep the note," I said.

"Very well, sir: I shall have to detain you for a few moments, as we have not quite cleared the tills. The keys of all the other safes are kept in the small one. I will bring you the keys of the small safe in a moment or two."

The clerks bustled about, the work of the night was quickly accomplished, and shortly after five o'clock I was seated in De Brett's luxurious brougham, with the keys of the small safe in my pocket.

We went along very slowly, as the fog seemed to grow thicker each moment. Suddenly as the coachman piloted his way in the direction of Broad Street I began to feel a peculiar sensation. My head was giddy, an unusual weakness trembled through my nerves, and for the first time I noticed that the brougham was full of a faint, sweet odour. Doubtless the smell of the fog had prevented my observing this at first. The sensation of faintness grew worse, and I now made an effort to attract the coachman's attention. This I altogether failed to do, and becoming seriously alarmed I tried to open the door; but it resisted all my efforts, as also did the windows, which were securely fixed. The horrible feeling that I was the victim of some dastardly plot came over me with force. I shouted and struggled to attract attention, and finally tried to break the windows. All in vain—the sense of giddiness grew worse, everything seemed to whirl before my mental vision—the bank, De Brett, the keys of the safe which I had in my pocket, the thought of Geraldine and her danger, were mixed up in a hideous phantasmagoria. The next moment I had lost consciousness.

When I came to myself I found that I was lying on a piece of waste ground which I afterwards found to be in the neighbourhood of Putney. For one or two moments I could not in the least recall what had happened. Then my memory came back with a quick flash.

"The Duke of Friedeck! The bank! Geraldine!" I said to myself. I sprang to my feet and began a hasty examination of my pockets. Yes, my worst conjectures were confirmed, for the keys of the small safe were gone!

My watch and money were intact; the keys alone were stolen. I stood still for a moment half-dazed from the anæsthetic fumes which by some means had been liberated in the brougham. Then the need of immediate action came over me, and I made my way at once to the nearest railway station. I found to my relief that it was only a little past eleven o'clock. Beyond doubt, I had recovered consciousness much sooner than the villains who had planned this terrible plot intended.

I took the next train to town, and on my way up resolved on my line of action. To warn De Brett was impracticable, for the simple reason that he was out of town—to waste time visiting Dufrayer was also not to be thought of. Without the least doubt, the bank was in imminent danger, and I must not lose an unnecessary moment in getting to St. Mark's Court.

As I thought over matters I felt more and more certain that the eating-house facing the bank was a rendezvous for Madame's agents. I hastily resolved, therefore, to disguise myself and go there. Once I had belonged to the infamous Brotherhood. I knew their password. By this means, if my suspicions were true, I could doubtless gain admission—as for the rest, I must leave it to chance.

As soon as I reached town I drove off at once to a theatrical agent, whose acquaintance I had already made. He remembered me, and I explained enough of the situation to induce him to render me assistance. In a very short time I was metamorphozed. By a few judicious touches twenty years were added to my age, a wig of dark hair completely covered my own, my complexion was dyed to a dark olive, and in a thick travelling cloak, with a high fur collar, I scarcely knew myself. My final act was to slip a loaded revolver into my pocket, and then, feeling that I was prepared for the worst, I hurried forth.

It was now between twelve and one in the morning, and the fog was denser than ever. Few men know London better than I do, but once or twice in that perilous journey I lost my way. At last, however, I found myself in St. Mark's Court. I was now breathing with difficulty: the fog was piercing my lungs and hurting my throat, my eyes watered. When I got into the court I heard the steady tramp of the policeman whose duty it was to guard the place at night. Taking no notice of him, I went across the court in the direction of the eating-house. The light within still burned, but dimly. There was a blur visible, nothing more. This came through one of the windows, for the door was shut. I tapped at the door. A man came immediately and opened it. He asked me what my business was. I repeated the password of the society. A change came over his face. My conjectures were verified—I was instantly admitted.

"Are you expecting to see a friend here to-night?" said the man. "It is rather late, and we are just closing."

As he uttered the words, like a flash of lightning, an old memory returned to me. I have said that when I first saw the Duke at De Brett's house I was puzzled by an intangible likeness. Now I knew who the man really was. In the old days in Naples, an English boy of the name of Drake was often seen in Madame's salons. Drake and the Duke of Friedeck were one and the same.

"I have come here to see Mr. Drake," I said stoutly.

The man nodded. My chance shot had found its billet.

"Mr. Drake is upstairs," he said. "Will you find your own way up, or shall I announce you?"

"I will find my own way," I said. "He is in the——"

"Room to the front—third floor," answered the man.

He returned to the dining-saloon, and I heard the swing-door close behind him. Without a moment's hesitation I ascended the stairs. The stairs and passage were in complete darkness. I went up, passed the first and second stories, and on to the third. As I approached the landing of the third story I saw an open door and a gleam of light in a small room which faced the court. The light was caused by a lamp which stood on a deal table, the wick of which was turned down very low. Except the lamp and table there was no other furniture in the room. I went in and looked around me. The Duke was not present. I was just considering what my next step should be, when I heard voices and several steps ascending the stairs. I saw an empty cupboard, the door of which stood ajar. I made for it, and closed the door softly behind me. As the men approached, I slipped the revolver from my pocket and held it in my hand. It was probable that Friedeck had been told of my arrival. If so, he would search for me, and in all probability look in the cupboard. Three or four men at least were coming up the stairs, and I knew that my life was scarcely worth a moment's purchase. I had a wild feeling of regret that I had not summoned the policeman in the court to my aid, and then the men entered the room. When they did so, I breathed a sigh of relief. They talked to one another as if I did not exist. Evidently the waiter downstairs had thought that my knowledge of the password was all-sufficient, and had not troubled himself to mention my appearance on the scene.

One of the men went up to the lamp, turned it on to a full blaze, and then placed it in the window.

"This will be sufficient for our purpose," he said, with a laugh: "otherwise, with the fog as thick as it is now, the bolt might miss its mark."

"The thicker the fog the safer," said another voice, which I recognized as that of the Duke. "I am quite ready, gentlemen, if you are."

"All right," said the man who had first spoken, "I will go across to Bell's house and fix the rope from the bar outside the window. As the bob of the pendulum you will swing true, Drake, no fear of that. You will swing straight to the balcony, as sure as mathematics. Have you anything else to ask?"

"No," answered Friedeck. "I am ready. Get your part of the work through as quickly as you can: you cannot fail to see this window with the bright light in it. I will have the lower sash open, and be ready to receive the bolt from the crossbow with the light string attached."

"That will do the business," answered his confederate; "when the bolt reaches you, pull in as hard as you can, for the rope will be attached to the light string. The crossbar is here. You have only to attach it to the rope and swing across. Well, all right, I'm off."

The man whose mission it was to send the bolt into the open window now left the room, and I heard his footsteps going softly downstairs. I opened the cupboard door about half an inch, and was able to watch the proceedings of the other three men who remained on the scene. The window was softly opened. They spoke in whispers. I could judge by their attitudes that all three were in the highest state of nervous excitement.

Presently a low cry of satisfaction from Friedeck reached my ears; something shot into the room and struck against the opposite wall. The next moment the men were pulling in a silken string, to which a wire rope was attached. I then saw the Duke remove his coat. A wooden crossbar was securely fastened to the end of the stout rope, the rope was held outside the window by the two confederates, and the Duke got upon the window-sill, slipped his legs over the crossbar, and the next instant had disappeared into space.

Where he had gone, what he was doing, were mysteries yet to be solved. The men remained for a moment longer beside the window, then they softly closed the sash, and putting out the lamp left the room. I heard their steps descending the stairs, the sounds died away into utter stillness. I listened intently, and then, softly leaving the cupboard, approached the window. In the intense darkness caused by the fog I could not see a yard in front of me. De Brett's bank was in danger—the Duke of Friedeck and his accomplices were burglars; but what the crossbow, the rope, the bolt, the crossbar of wood, and the sudden disappearance of the Duke himself through the open window portended I could not fathom. My duty, however, was clear. I must immediately give the alarm to the policeman in the court, whose tramp I even now heard coming up to me through the fog.

I waited for a few moments longer, and then determined to make my exit. I ran downstairs, treading as softly as I could. I had just reached the little hall and put my hand on the latch of the door, when I was accosted.

"Who is there?" said a voice.

I replied glibly, "I am going in search of Drake."

"You cannot see him, he is engaged," said the same voice, and now a man came forward. He held a dark lantern in his hand and suddenly threw its bull's-eye full on my face. Perhaps he saw through my disguise; anyhow, he must have observed that my face was unfamiliar to him. The expression on his own changed to one of alarm. He suddenly made a low and peculiar whistle, and two or three other men entered the hall. The first man said something, the words of which I could not catch, and all four made a rush for me. But the door was on the latch. I burst it open, and escaped into the court. The thick fog favoured me, and I hoped that I had escaped the gang, when a heavy blow on the back of my head rendered me, for the second time within that ominous twenty-four hours, unconscious.

When I awoke I found myself in the ward of a London hospital, and the kind face of a house surgeon was bending over me.

"Ah! you'll do," I heard him say: "you are coming to nicely. You had a nasty blow on your head, though. Don't talk just at present; you'll be all right in a couple of hours."

I lay still, feeling bewildered. Figures were moving about the room, and the daylight was streaming in at the windows. I saw a nurse come up and look at me. She bent down.

"You feel better? You are not suffering?" she said.

"I am not," I replied; "but how did I get here? What has happened?"

"A policeman heard you cry and picked you up unconscious in a place called St. Mark's Court. Some one gave you a bad blow on your head—it is a wonder your skull was not cracked, but you are better. Have you a message to give to any one?"

"I must get up immediately," I said; "I have not a moment to lose. Something dreadful has happened, and I must see to it. I must leave the hospital at once."

"Not without the surgeon's permission," said the nurse. "Have you any friend you would like to be sent to you?"

I mentioned Dufrayer's name. The nurse said she would dispatch a messenger immediately to his house and ask him to come to me.

I waited with what patience I could. The severe blow had fortunately only stunned me. I was not seriously hurt, and all the events of the preceding night, previous to the blow, presented themselves clearly before my memory.

In a little over an hour Dufrayer arrived. His eyes were blazing with excitement. He came up to me full of consternation.

"What has happened, Head?" he asked.

"Oh! I am all right; don't bother about me," I said. "But listen, Dufrayer, I must go to St. Mark's Court immediately—there is mischief."

"St. Mark's Court Are you mad? Have you heard anything?"

"Heard what?" I asked.

"They have done it, that's all," cried Dufrayer.

"What?" I exclaimed.

"Well, there's the very devil to pay in the City this morning. De Brett's bank was broken into last night, the night watchman seriously injured, and securities and cash to the tune of one hundred thousand pounds taken from the strong-room, and the man has got clean away. Your messenger from here followed me to the bank. Tyler is there and De Brett. The daring of the robbery is unparalleled."

"I can throw light on this matter," I said. "Get the surgeon to give me leave to go, Dufrayer. There is not a moment to lose if we are to catch the scoundrel. I must accompany you to the bank."

"Well, you seem all right, old chap, and if you have anything to say—-"

"I have," I cried impatiently. "See the surgeon. I must get off immediately."

Dufrayer did as I requested him. The surgeon shook his head over what he called my imprudence, but said he could not detain me against my will. Dufrayer and I stepped into a hansom, and on my way to the bank I repeated my strange adventures of the previous night.

"Did ever any one hear of another man doing such a foolhardy thing?" cried Dufrayer. "What possessed you to enter that hell alone beats my comprehension."

"Never mind that now," I replied. "Remember, I knew the Brotherhood; my one chance consisted in going alone. Thank goodness the fog has risen."

A light breeze was blowing over the city, and as we entered St. Mark's Court a ray of sunshine cast a watery gleam over the old smoke-begrimed buildings. We entered the bank and found De Brett, his manager, two police inspectors, and Tyler's agent awaiting us.

De Brett exclaimed, when he caught sight of me:

"Ah, Head, here's a pretty business! I'm a ruined man. The bank cannot stand a blow of this kind."

"Courage," I replied; "we may be able to put things right yet. I have a story to tell. Mr. Derbyshire, you have doubtless kept the note which Mr. de Brett wrote to me last night?"

"The note I wrote to you!" cried De Brett. "What do you mean?"

"Will you produce the note?" I said to the manager.

The man brought it and put it into his chief's hand. De Brett read it with increasing amazement.

"But I never put pen to paper on such a fool's errand," he cried. "Why, I never take the keys of the small safe. Derbyshire and Frome have charge of them. Head, this note is a forgery. What in the name of Heaven does it mean?"

"It meant for me a brougham which was a death-trap," I replied: "and it also meant the most dastardly scheme to rob you, and perhaps murder me, which has ever been conceived. But listen, let me tell my story."

I did so, amidst the breathless silence of the spectators.

"And now," I continued, "the best thing we can do, gentlemen, is to go across to the house from which the bolt was shot. It is possible that we may see something in that upper room which will explain the manner in which the burglar entered the bank."

"I am at your service, Mr. Head," said Inspector Brown, in a cheerful tone; "a mystery of this sort is quite to my mind. All the same, sir," he continued, as he and I took the lead of the little procession which crossed St. Mark's Court, "I cannot imagine how any man got into that window of the bank on the second floor without wings. There is a constable on patrol in the court all night, so ladders are out of the question. The annihilation of gravity is a new departure in the burglar's art."

We had now reached the building which faced the court, and which was between the bank and eating-house. It was composed entirely of offices—we went up at once to the top floor. The door of the room which faced the court was locked. The inspector took a step back, and, flinging his shoulders against it, it flew open. The room was bare and unoccupied, but, as we entered, Inspector Brown uttered a cry.

"Here is confirmation of your story, Mr. Head." As he spoke he lifted up a coil of strong rope which lay in a corner of the room. Attached to it was a crossbar of wood. A strong iron bar with a hook at one end and a crossbow also lay in the neighbourhood of the rope.

"The thing is as clear as daylight," I exclaimed. "I could not put two and two together last night, for the fog fairly bewildered me, but now I see the whole scheme. Let me explain. This rope was sent by means of the crossbow across to the window in the eating-house. To the bolt of the crossbow was attached a silken cord, to which again the rope was fastened. The man who swung himself out of the window by the rope last night acted as the bob of the pendulum, and so reached the window of the bank. Swinging through the eating-house window and rising to the balcony outside the bank window, he then doubtless seized the handle of the outside frame and, settling on the balcony, cut out the glass with a diamond."

"We will go at once and see the room in the eating-house," said the inspector.

We did so, and found to our amazement that the door of the eating-house was locked and the place empty. After some slight difficulty we got the door burst open and went upstairs. Here we found the final confirmation of my words—the silken string which had been attached to the rope and cut from it before the Duke made his aerial flight.

"But who did it?" cried De Brett. "We must secure the scoundrel without a moment's delay, for amongst other things he has stolen the Duke of Friedeck's priceless securities, the diamonds. By the way," continued the banker, "where is the Duke? I sent him a telegram and expected him here before now."

An ominous silence fell upon every one. De Brett's face grew white; he looked at me.

"For God's sake, speak," he cried. "Have you anything else to confide?"

"You must be prepared for bad news, De Brett," I said. I went up and laid my hand on my old friend's shoulder. "Thank God, I was in time. Your little girl is saved from the most awful fate which could overtake any woman. The man who committed the burglary was known to you as the Duke of Friedeck."

De Brett stepped back: his face changed from white to purple.

"Then that accounts for the telegrams," he said. "I received two yesterday, one from you telling me to expect you by a late train at Forest Manor, the other from that scoundrel. In it he said that be was unexpectedly detained in town. Doubtless both telegrams were sent by the same man."

"Without doubt," I replied. "The whole thing was carefully planned, and not a stone left unturned to secure the success of this most dastardly scheme. But, De Brett, I have one thing more to say. There is no Duke of Friedeck: it was an assumed name. I am prepared to swear to the man's real identity when the police have secured him."

The remainder of this story can be told in a few words. The ruffian who had posed as the Duke of Friedeck was captured a few days later, but the greater part of the securities and money which he had stolen were never recovered. Doubtless Mme. Koluchy had them in her possession. The man passed through his trial and received his sentence, but that has nothing to do with the story.

By the energetic aid of his many friends De Brett escaped ruin, and his bank still exists and prospers. He is a sadder and a wiser man.

Chapter IV

THE LUCK OF PITSEY HALL

AS the days and weeks went on Mme. Koluchy became more than ever the talk of London. The medical world agitated itself about her to an extraordinary degree. It was useless to gainsay the fact that she performed marvellous cures. Under her influence and treatment weak people became strong again. Those who stood at the door of the Shadow of Death returned to their intercourse with the busy world. Beneath her spell pain vanished. What she did and how she did it remained more than ever a secret. She dispensed her own prescriptions, but although some of her medicines were analyzed by experts, nothing in the least extraordinary could be discovered in their composition. The cure did not therefore lie in drugs. In what did it consist? Doctors asked this question one of another, and could find no satisfactory answer. The rage to consult Madame became stronger and stronger. Her patients adored her. The magnetic influence which she exercised was felt by each person with whom she came in contact.

Meanwhile Dufrayer and I watched and waited. The detective officers in Scotland Yard knew of some of our views with regard to this woman. Led by Dufrayer they were ceaselessly on the alert; but, try as the most able of their staff did, they could learn nothing of Mme. Koluchy which was not to her credit. She was spoken of as a universal benefactress, taking, it is true, large fees from those who could afford to pay; but, on the other hand, giving her services freely to the people to whom money was scarce. This woman could scarcely walk down the street without heads being turned to look after her, and this not only on account of her remarkable beauty, but still more because of her genius and her goodness. As she passed by, blessings were showered upon her, and if the person who called down these benedictions was rewarded by even one glance from those lovely and brilliant eyes, he counted himself happy.

About the middle of January the attention of London was diverted from Mme. Koluchy to a murder of a particularly mysterious character. A member of the Cabinet of the name of Delacour was found dead in St. James's Park. His body was discovered in the early morning, in the neighbourhood of Marlborough House, with a wound straight through the heart. Death must have been instantaneous. He was stabbed from behind, which showed the cowardly nature of the attack. I knew Delacour, and for many reasons was appalled when the tidings reached me. As far as any one could tell, he had no enemies. He was a man in the prime of life, of singular power of mind and strength of character, and the only possible motive for the murder seemed to be to wrest some important State secrets from his possession. He had been attending a Cabinet meeting in Downing Street, and was on his way home when the dastardly deed was committed. Certain memoranda respecting a loan to a foreign Government were abstracted from his person, but his watch, a valuable ring, and some money were left intact. The police immediately put measures in active train to secure the murderer, but no clue could be obtained. Delacour's wife and only daughter were broken-hearted. His position as a Cabinet Minister was so well known, that not only his family but the whole country rang with horror at the dastardly crime, and it was fervently hoped that before long the murderer would be arrested, and receive the punishment which he so justly merited.

On a certain evening, about a fortnight after this event, as I was walking slowly down Welbeck Street, and was just about to pass the door of Mme. Koluchy's splendid mansion, I saw a young girl come down the steps. She was dressed in deep mourning, and glanced around from right to left, evidently searching for a passing hansom. Her face arrested me; her eyes met mine, and, with a slight cry, she took a step forward.

"You are Mr. Head?" she exclaimed.

"And you are Vivien Delacour," I replied. "I am glad to meet you again. Don't you remember the Hotel Bellevue at Brussels?"

When I spoke her name she coloured perceptibly and began to tremble. Suddenly putting out one of her hands, she laid it on my arm.

"I am glad to see you again," she said, in a whisper. "You know of our—our most terrible tragedy?

"I do," I replied.

"Mother is completely prostrated from the shock. The murder was so sudden and mysterious. If it were not for Mme.——-"

"Mme. Koluchy?" I queried.

"Yes, Mr. Head; Mme. Koluchy, the best and dearest friend we have in the world. She was attending mother professionally at the time of the murder, and since then has been with her daily. On that first terrible day she scarcely left us. I don't know what we should have done were it not for her great tact and kindness. She is full of suggestions, too, for the capture of the wretch who took my dear father's life."

"You look shaken yourself," I said; "ought you to be out alone at this hour?"

"I have just seen Madame with a message from mother, and am waiting here for a hansom. If you would be so kind as to call one, I should be much indebted to you."

"Can I do anything to help you, Vivien?" I said; "you know you have only to command me."

A hansom drew up at the pavement as I spoke. Vivien's sad grey eyes were fixed on my face.

"Find the man who killed my father," she said; "we shall never rest until we know who took his life."

"May I call at your house to-morrow morning?" I asked suddenly.

"If you will be satisfied with seeing me. Mother will admit no one to her presence but Mme. Koluchy."

"I will come to see you then; expect me at eleven."

I helped Miss Delacour into her hansom, gave directions to the driver, and she was quickly bowled out of sight.

On my way home many thoughts coursed through my brain. A year ago the Delacours, a family of the name of Pitsey, and I had made friends when travelling through Belgium. The Pitseys, of old Italian origin, owned a magnificent place not far from Tunbridge Wells—the Pitseys and the Delacours were distant cousins. Vivien at that time was only sixteen, and she and I became special chums. She used to tell me all about her ambitions and hopes, and in particular descanted on the museum of rare curios which her cousins, the Pitseys, possessed at their splendid place, Pitsey Hall. I had a standing invitation to visit the Hall at any time when I happened to have leisure, but up to the present had not availed myself of it. Memories of that gay time thronged upon me as I hurried to my own house, but mixed with the old reminiscences was an inconceivable sensation of horror. Why was Mme. Koluchy a friend of the Delacours? My mind had got into such a disordered state that I, more or less, associated her with any crime which was committed. Hating myself for what I considered pure morbidness, I arrived at my own house. There I was told that Dufrayer was waiting to see me. I hurried into my study to greet him; he came eagerly forward.

"Have you any news?" I cried.

"If you allude to Delacour's murder, I have," he answered.

"Then, pray speak quickly," I said.

"Well," he continued, "a curious development, and one which may have the most profoundly important bearing on the murder, has just taken place—it is in connection with it that I have come to see you." Dufrayer stood up as he spoke. He never liked to be interrupted, and I listened attentively without uttering a syllable. "Yesterday," he continued, "a man was arrested on suspicion. He was examined this morning before the magistrate at Dow Street. His name is Walter Hunt—he is the keeper of a small marine store at Houndsditch. For several nights he has been found hovering in a suspicious manner round the Delacours' house. On being questioned he could give no straightforward account of himself, and the police thought it best to arrest him. On his person was discovered an envelope, addressed to himself, bearing the City post-mark and the date of the day the murder was committed. Inside the envelope was an absolutely blank sheet of paper. Thinking this might be a communication of importance it was submitted to George Lambert, the Government expert at Scotland Yard, for examination—he subjected it to every known test in order to see if it contained any writing on sympathetic ink, or some other secret cipher principles. The result is absolutely negative, and Lambert firmly declares that it is a blank sheet of paper and of no value. I heard all these particulars from Ford, the superintendent in charge of the case; and knowing of your knowledge of chemistry, and the quantity of odds and ends of curious information you possess on these matters, I obtained leave that you should come with me to Scotland Yard and submit the paper to any further tests you know of. I felt sure you would be willing to do this."

"Certainly," I replied; "shall I come with you now?"

"I wish you would. If the paper contains any hidden cipher, the sooner it is known the better."

"One moment first," I said. "I have just met Vivien Delacour. She was coming out of Mme. Koluchy's house. It is strange how that woman gets to know all one's friends and acquaintances."

"I forgot that you knew the Delacours," said Dufrayer.

"A year ago," I replied, "I seemed to know them well. When we were in Brussels we were great friends. Vivien looked ill and in great trouble—I would give the world to help her; but I earnestly wish she did not know Madame. It may be morbidness on my part, but lately I never hear of any crime being committed in London without instantly associating Mme. Koluchy with it. She has got that girl more or less under her spell, and Vivien herself informed me that she visits her mother daily. Be assured of this, Dufrayer, the woman is after no good."

As I spoke I saw the lawyer's face darken, and the cold, hard expression I knew so well came into it, but he did not speak a word.

"I am at your service now," I said. "Just let me go to my laboratory first. I have some valuable notes on these ciphers which I will take with me."

A moment later Dufrayer and I found ourselves in a hansom on our way to Scotland Yard. There we were met by Superintendent Ford, and also by George Lambert, a particularly intelligent-looking man who favoured me with a keen glance from under shaggy brows.

"I have heard of you, Mr. Head," he said courteously, "and shall be only too pleased if you can discover what I have failed to do. The sheet of paper in question is the sort on which ciphers are often written, but all my re-agents have failed to produce the slightest effect. My fear is that they may possibly have destroyed the cipher should such a thing exist."

"That is certainly possible," I said; "but if you will take me to your laboratory I will submit the paper to some rather delicate tests of my own."

The expert at once led the way, and Dufrayer, Superintendent Ford, and I followed him. When we reached the laboratory, Lambert put all possible tests at my disposal. A glance at the stain on the paper before me showed that cobalt, copper, etc., had been already applied. These tests had, in all probability, nullified any further chemical tests I might try, and had destroyed the result, even if there were some secret writing on the paper.

I spent some time trying the more delicate and less-known tests, with no success. Presently I rose to my feet.

"It is useless," I said; "I can do nothing with this paper. It is rather a presumption on my part to attempt it after you, Mr. Lambert, have given your ultimatum. I am inclined to agree with you that the paper is valueless."

Lambert bowed, and a look of satisfaction crept over his face. Dufrayer and I soon afterwards took our leave. As we did so, I heard my friend utter a quick sigh.

"We are only beating the air as yet," he said. "We must trust that justice and right will win the day at last."

He parted from me at the corner of the street, and I returned to my own house.

On the following day, at the appointed hour, I went to see Vivien Delacour. She received me in her mother's boudoir. Here the blinds were partly down, and the whole room had a desolate aspect. The young girl herself looked pale and sad, years older than she had done in the happy days at Brussels.

"Mother was pleased when I told her that I met you yesterday," she exclaimed. "Sit down, won't you, Mr. Head? You and my father were great friends during that happy time at the Bellevue. Yes, I feel certain of your sympathy."

"You may be assured of it," I said, "and I earnestly wish I could give you more than sympathy. Would it be too painful to give me some particulars in connection with the murder?"

She shuddered quite perceptibly.

"You must have read all there is to know in the newspapers," she said; "I can tell you nothing more. My father left us on that dreadful day to attend a Cabinet meeting at Downing Street. He never returned home. The police look in vain for the murderer. There seems no motive for the horrible crime—father had no enemies."

Here the poor girl sobbed without restraint. I allowed her grief to have its way for a few moments, then I spoke.

"Listen, Vivien," I said; "I promise you that I will not leave a stone unturned to discover the man or woman who killed your father, but you must help me by being calm and self-collected. Grief like this is quite natural, but it does no good to any one. Try, my dear girl, to compose yourself. You say there was no motive for the crime, but surely some important memoranda were stolen from your father?"

"His pocket-book in which he often made notes was removed, but nothing more, neither his watch nor his money. Surely no one would murder him for the sake of securing that pocket-book, Mr. Head?"

"It is possible," I answered gloomily. "The memoranda contained in the book may have held clues to Government secrets, remember."

Vivien looked as if she scarcely understood. Once more my thoughts travelled to Mme. Koluchy. She was a strange woman—she dealt in colossal crimes. Her influence permeated society through and through. With her a life more or less was not of the slightest consequence. And this terrible woman, whom, up to the present, the laws of England could not touch, was the intimate friend of the young girl by my side!

Vivien moved uneasily, and presently rose.

"I am glad you are going to help us," she said, looking at me earnestly. "Madame does all she can, but we cannot have too many friends on our side, and we are all aware of your wisdom, Mr. Head. Why do you not consult Madame?"

I shook my head.

"But you are friends, are you not? I told her only this morning how I had met you."

"We are acquaintances, but not friends," I replied.

"Indeed, you astonish me. You cannot imagine how useful she is, and how many suggestions she throws out. By the way, mother and I leave London to-day."

"Where are you going?" I asked.

"Away from here. It is quite too painful to remain any longer in this house. The shock has completely shattered mother's nerves, and she is now under Mme. Koluchy's care. Madame has just taken a house in the country called Frome Manor—it is not far from our cousins, the Pitseys—you remember them? You met them in Brussels."

I nodded.

"We are going there to-day," continued Vivien. "Of course we shall see no one, but mother will be under the same roof with Madame, and thus will have the benefit of her treatment day and night."

Soon afterwards I took my leave. All was suspicion and uncertainty, and no definite clue had been obtained.

About this time I began to be haunted by an air which had sprung like a mushroom into popularity. It was called the "Queen Waltz," and it was scarcely possible to pick up a dance programme without seeing it. There was something fascinating about its swinging measure, its almost dreamy refrain, and its graceful alternations of harmony and unison. No one knew who had really composed it, and still less did any one for a moment dream that its pleasant chords contained a dark or subtle meaning. As I listened to it on more than one occasion, at more than one concert—for I am a passionate lover of music, and seldom spend an afternoon without listening to it—I little guessed all that the "Queen Waltz" would bring forth. I was waiting for a clue. How could I tell that all too late and by such unlikely means it would be put into my hands?

A month and even six weeks went by, and although the police were unceasing in their endeavours to gain a trace of the murderer, they were absolutely unsuccessful. Once or twice during this interval I had letters from Vivien Delacour. She wrote with the passion and impetuosity of a very young girl. She was anxious about her mother, who was growing steadily weaker, and was losing her self-restraint more and more as the long weeks glided by. Mme. Koluchy was anxious about her. Madame's medicines, her treatment, her soothing powers, were on this occasion destitute of results.

"Nothing will rest her," said Vivien, in conclusion, "until the murderer is discovered. She dreams of him night after night. During the daytime she is absolutely silent, or she paces the room in violent agitation, crying out to God to help her to discover him. Oh, Mr. Head, what is to be done?"

The child's letters appealed to me strongly. I was obliged to answer her with extreme care, as I knew that Madame would see what I wrote; but none the less were all my faculties at work on her behalf. From time to time I thought of the mysterious blank sheet of paper. Was it possible that it contained a cipher? Was one of those old, incomparable, magnificent undiscovered ciphers which belonged to the ancient Brotherhood really concealed beneath its blank surface? That blank sheet of paper mingled with my dreams and worried me during my wakeful hours. I became nearly as restless as Vivien herself, and when a letter of a more despairing nature than usual arrived on a certain morning towards the end of February, I felt that I could no longer remain inactive. I would answer Vivien's letter in person. To do so I had but to accept my standing invitation to Pitsey Hall. I wrote, therefore, to my friend, Leonardo Pitsey, suggesting that if it were convenient to him and his wife I should like to go to Pitsey Hall on the following Saturday.

The next afternoon Pitsey himself called to see me.

"I received your letter this morning, and having to come to town to-day, thought I would look you up," he cried. "I have to catch a train at 5.30, so cannot stay a minute. We shall be delighted to welcome you at the Hall. My wife and I have never forgotten you, Head. You will be, I assure you, a most welcome guest. By the way, have you heard of our burglary?"

"No," I answered.   ~ waltz ?

"You do not read your paper, then. It is an extraordinary affair—
crime seems to be in the very air just now. The Hall was attacked
by burglars last week—a most daring and cunningly planned
affair. Some plate was stolen, but the plate-chest, built on the
newest principles, was untampered with. There was a desperate
attempt made, however, to get into the large drawing-room,
where all our valuable curios are kept. Druco, the mastiff, who is
loose about the house at night, was found poisoned outside the
drawing-room door. Luckily the butler awoke in time, gave the
alarm, and the rascals bolted. The country police have been after
them, and in despair I have come up to Scotland Yard and
engaged a couple of their best detectives. They come down with
me to-night, and I trust we shall soon get the necessary clue to the
capture of the burglars. My fear is that if they are not arrested
they will try again, for, I assure you, the old place is worth
robbing. But, there, I ought not to worry you about my domestic
concerns. We shall have a gay party on Saturday, for my eldest
boy Ottavio comes of age next week, and the event is to be
celebrated by a great ball in his honour."

"How are the Delacours?" I interrupted.

"Vivien keeps fairly well, but her mother is a source of great
anxiety. Mme. Koluchy and Vivien are constant guests at the
Hall. The Delacours return to town before the ball, but Madame
will attend it. It will be an honour and a great attraction to have
such a lioness for the occasion. Do you know her, Head? She is
quite charming."

"I have met her," I replied.

"Ah! that is capital; you and she are just the sort to hit it off. It's
all right, then, and we shall expect you. A good train leaves
Charing Cross at 4.30. I will send the trap to meet you."

"Thank you," I answered. "I shall be glad to come to Pitsey Hall,
but I do not know that I can stay as long as the night of the ball."

"Once we get you into our clutches, Head, we won't let you go; my young people are all anxious to renew their acquaintance with you. Don't you remember little Antonia—my pretty songstress, as I call her? Vivien, too, talks of you as one of her greatest friends. Poor child! I pity her from my heart. She is a sweet, gentle girl; but such a shock as she has sustained may leave its mark for life. Poor Delacour—the very best of men. The fact is this: I should like to postpone the ball on account of the Delacours, although they are very distant cousins; but Ottavio only comes of age once in his life, and, under the circumstances, we feel that we must go through with it. 'Pon my word, Head, when I think of that poor child and her mother, I have little heart for festivities. However, that is neither here nor there—we shall expect you on Saturday."

As Pitsey spoke, he took up his hat.

"I must be off now," he said, "for I have to meet the two detectives at Charing Cross by appointment."

On the following Saturday, the 27th, I arrived at Pitsey Hall, where a warm welcome awaited me. The ball was to be on the following Tuesday, the 2nd of March. There was a large house party, and the late burglary was still the topic of conversation.

After dinner, when the ladies had left the dining-room, Pitsey and I drew our chairs together, and presently the conversation drifted to Mrs. Delacour, the mysterious murder, and Mme. Koluchy.

"The police are completely nonplussed," said Pitsey. "I doubt if the man who committed that rascally crime will ever be brought to justice. I was speaking to Madame on the subject to-day, and although she was very hopeful when she first arrived at Frome Manor, she is now almost inclined to agree with me. By the way, Mrs. Delacour's state is most alarming—she loses strength hour by hour."

"I can quite understand that," I replied. "If the murderer were discovered it would be an immense relief to her."

"So Madame says. I know she is terribly anxious about her patient. By the way, knowing that she was an acquaintance of yours, I asked her here to-night, but unfortunately she had another engagement which she could not postpone. What a wonderfully well-informed woman she is! She spent hours at the Hall this morning examining my curios; she gave me information about some of them which was news to me, but she has been many times now round my collection. It is a positive treat to talk with any one so intelligent, and if she were not so keen about my Venetian goblet——"

"What!" I interrupted, "the goblet you spoke to me about in Brussels, the one which has been in your family since 1500?"

"The same," he answered, nodding his head, and lowering his voice a trifle. "It has been in the family, as you say, since 1500. Madame has shown bad taste in the matter, and I am surprised at her."

"Pray explain yourself," I said.

"She first saw it last November, when she came here with the Delacours. I shall never forget her stare of astonishment. She stood perfectly still for at least two minutes, gazing at it without speaking. When she turned round at last she was as white as a ghost, and asked me where I got it from. I told her, and she offered me £10,000 for it on the spot."

"A large figure," I remarked.

"I was much annoyed," continued Pitsey, "and told her I would not sell it at any price."

"Did she give any reason for wishing to obtain it?"

"Yes, she said she had a goblet very like it in her own collection, and wished to purchase this one in order to complete one of the most unique collections of old Venetian glass in England. The woman must be fabulously rich, or even her passion for curios would not induce her to offer so preposterous a sum. Since her residence at Frome Manor she has been constantly here, and still takes, I can see, the deepest interest in the goblet, often remarking about it. She says it has got a remarkably pure musical note, very clear and distinct. But come, Head, you would like to see it. We will go into the drawing-room, and I will show it to you."

As Pitsey spoke he rose and led me through the great central hall into the inner drawing-room, a colossal apartment supported by Corinthian pillars and magnificently decorated.

"As you know, the goblet has been in our family for many centuries," he went on, "and we call it, from Uhland's ballad of the old Cumberland tradition, 'The Luck of Pitsey Hall.' You know Longfellow's translation, of course? Here it is, Head. Is it not a wonderful piece of work? Have a close look at it, it is worth examining."

The goblet in question stood about 6ft. from the ground on a pedestal of solid malachite, which was placed in a niche in the wall. One glance was sufficient to show me that it was a gem of art. The cup, which was 8 in. in diameter, was made of thin glass of a pale ruby colour. Some mystical letters were etched on the outside of the glass, small portions of which could be seen; but screening them from any closer interpretation was some twisted fancy work, often to be observed on old Venetian goblets. If by any chance this fancy work were chipped off the letters would be plainly visible. The cup itself was supported on an open-work stem richly gilt and enamelled with coloured filigree work, the whole supported again on a base set with opal, agate, lapis lazuli, turquoise, and pearl. From the centre of the cup, and in reality supporting it, was a central column of pale green glass which bore what was apparently some heraldic design. Stepping up close I tapped the cup gently with my finger. It gave out, as Pitsey had described, a note of music singularly sweet and clear. I then proceeded to examine the stem, and saw at once that the design formed a row of separate crowns. Scarcely knowing why, I counted them. There were seven! A queer suspicion crept over me. The sequence of late events passed rapidly through my mind, and a strange relationship between circumstances apparently having no connection began to appear. I turned to Pitsey.

"Can you tell me how this goblet came into your possession?" I asked.

"Certainly," he replied; "the legend which is attached to the goblet is this. We are, as you know, descended from an old Italian family, the Pizzis, our present name being merely an Anglicized corruption of the Italian. My children and I still bear Italian Christian names, as you know, and our love for the old country amounts almost to a passion. The Pizzis were great people in Venice in the sixteenth century; at that time the city had an immense fame for its beautiful glass, the manufacturers forming a guild, and the secret being jealously kept. It was during this time that Catherine de Medici by her arbitrary and tyrannical administration roused the opposition of a Catholic party, at whose head was the Duke of Alençon, her own fourth son. Among the Duke's followers was my ancestor, Giovanni Pizzi. It was discovered that an order had been sent by Catherine de Medici to one of the manufacturers at Venice to construct that very goblet which you see there. After its construction it was for some secret purpose sent to the laboratory of an alchemist in Venice, where it was seized by Giovanni Pizzi, and has been handed down in our family ever since."

"But what is the meaning of the seven crowns on the stem?" I asked.

"That I cannot tell. They have probably no special significance."

I thought otherwise, but kept my ideas to myself.

We turned away. A beautiful young voice was filling the old drawing-room with sweetness. I went up to the piano to listen to Antonia Pitsey, while she sang an Italian song as only one who had Italian blood in her veins could.

Antonia was a beautiful girl, dark, with luminous eyes and an air of distinction about her.

"I wish you would tell me something about your friend Vivien," I said, as she rose from the piano.

"Oh, Mr. Head, I am so unhappy about her," was the low reply. "I see her very often—she is altogether changed; and as to Mrs. Delacour, the shock has been so sudden, so terrible, that I doubt if she will ever recover. Mr. Head, I am so glad you have come. Vivien constantly speaks of you. She wants to see you to-morrow."

"Is she coming here?"

"No, but you can meet her in the park. She has sent you a message. To-morrow is Sunday. Vivien is not going to church. May I take you to the rendezvous?"

I promised, and soon afterwards the evening came to an end.

That night I was haunted by three main thoughts: the old Italian legend of the goblet; the seven crowns, symbolic of the Brotherhood of the Seven Kings; and, finally, Madame's emotion when she first saw it, and her strong desire to obtain it. I wondered had the burglary been committed by her instigation? Sleep I could not, my brain was too active and busy. I was certain there was mischief ahead, but try as I would I could only lose myself in strange conjectures.

The following day I met Miss Delacour, as arranged, in the park. Antonia brought me to her, and then left us together. The young girl's worn face, the pathetic expression in her large grey eyes, her evident nervousness and want of self-control all appealed to me to a terrible degree. She asked me eagerly if any fresh clue had been obtained with regard to the murderer. I shook my head.

"If something is not done soon, mother will lose her senses," she remarked. "Even Mme. Koluchy is in despair about her. All her ordinary modes of treatment fail in mother's case, and the strangest thing is that mother has begun to take a most queer and unaccountable dislike to Madame herself. She says that Madame's presence in the room gives her an uncontrollable feeling of nervousness. This has become so bad that mother and I return to town to-morrow; my cousin's house is too gay for us at present, and mother refuses to stay any longer under Mme. Koluchy's roof."

"But why?" I asked.

"That I cannot explain to you. For my part, I think Madame one of the best women on earth. She has been kindness itself to us, and I do not know what we should have done without her."

I did not speak, and Vivien continued, after a pause:

"Mother's conduct makes Madame strangely unhappy. She told me so, and I pity her from my heart. We had a long talk on the subject yesterday. That was just before she began to speak of the goblet, and before Mr. Lewisham arrived."

"Mr. Lewisham—who is he?" I asked.

"A great friend of Madame's. He comes to see her almost daily. He is very handsome, and I like him, but I did not know she was expecting him yesterday. She and I were in the drawing-room. She spoke of mother, and then alluded to the goblet, the one at the Hall. You have seen it, of course, Mr. Head?"

I nodded—I was too much interested to interrupt the girl by words.

"My cousins call it 'The Luck of Pitsey Hall.' Well, Madame has set her heart on obtaining it, and she has gone to the length of offering Cousin Leonardo ten thousand pounds for it."

"Mr. Pitsey told me last night that Madame had offered an enormous sum for the vase," I said; "but it is useless, as he has no intention of selling."

"I told Madame so," replied Vivien. "I know well what value my cousins place upon the old glass. I believe they think that their luck would really go if anything happened to it."

"Heaven forbid!" I replied involuntarily; "it is a perfect gem of its kind."

"I know! I know! I never saw Madame so excited and unreasonable about anything. She begged of me to use my influence to try and get my cousin to let her have it. When I assured her that it was useless, she looked more annoyed than I had ever seen her. She took up a book, and pretended to read. I went and sat behind one of the curtains, near a window. The next moment Mr. Lewisham was announced. He came eagerly up to Madame—I don't think he saw me.

"'Well!' he cried; 'any success? Have you secured it yet? If you have, we are absolutely safe. Has that child helped you?'

"I guessed that they were talking about me, and started up and disclosed myself. Madame did not take the slightest notice, but she motioned to Mr. Lewisham to come into another room. What can it all mean, Mr. Head?"

"That I cannot tell you, Vivien; but may I ask you one thing?"

"Certainly you may."

"Will you promise me to keep what you have just told me a secret from anybody else? I allude to Madame's anxiety to obtain the old goblet. There may be nothing in what I ask, or there may be much. Will you do this?"

"Of course I will. How queer you look!"

I made no remark, and soon afterwards took my leave of her.

Late that same evening, Antonia Pitsey received a note from Vivien, in which she said that Mme. Koluchy, her mother, and herself were returning to town by an early train the following morning. The Delacours did not intend to come back to Frome Manor, but Madame would do so on Tuesday in order to be in time for the great ball. She was going to town now in order to be present at an early performance of "For the Crown" at the Lyceum, having secured a box on the grand tier for the occasion.

This note was commented on without any special interest being attached to it, but restless already, I now quickly made up my mind. I also would go up to town on the following day; I also would return to Pitsey Hall in time for the ball.

Accordingly, at an early hour on the following day, I found myself in Dufrayer's office.

"I tell you what it is," I said, "there is some plot deeper than we think brewing. Madame took Frome Manor after the murder of Delacour. She would not do so without a purpose. She is willing to spend ten thousand pounds in order to secure a goblet of old Venetian glass, which is one of the curios at Pitsey Hall. A man called Lewisham, who doubtless bears another alias, is in her confidence. Madame returns to town to-night with a definite motive, I have not the slightest doubt."

"This is all very well, Norman," replied Dufrayer, "but what we want are facts. You will lose your senses if you go on building up fantastic ideas. Madame comes up to town and is going to the Lyceum; at least, so you tell me?"

"Yes."

"And you mean to follow her to see if she has any designs on Forbes Robertson or Mrs. Patrick Campbell?"

"I mean to follow her," I replied gravely. "I mean to see what sort of man Lewisham is. It is possible that I may have seen him before."

Dufrayer shrugged his shoulders and turned away somewhat impatiently. As he did so a wild thought suddenly struck me.

"What would you say," I cried, "if I suggested an idea to force Madame to divulge some clue to us?"

"My dear Norman, I should say that your fancies are getting the better of your reason, that is all."

"Now listen to me," I said. I sat down beside Dufrayer. "I have an idea which may serve us well. It is, of course, a bare chance, and if you like you may call it the conception of a madman. Madame goes to the Lyceum to-night. She occupies a box on the grand tier. In all probability Lewisham will accompany her. Dufrayer, you and I will also be at the theatre, and, if possible, we will take a box on the second tier exactly opposite to hers. I will bring Robertson, the principal and the trainer of the new deaf and dumb college, with me. I happen to know him well."

Dufrayer stared at me with some alarm in his face.

"Don't you see?" I went on excitedly. "Robertson is a master of the art of lip language. We will keep him in the back of the box. About the middle of the play, and in one of the intervals when the electric light is full on, we will send a note to Madame's box saying that the cipher on the blank sheet of paper has been read. The note will pretend to be an anonymous warning to her. We shall watch her, and by means of Robertson hear—yes, hear—what she says. Robertson will watch her through opera-glasses, and he will be able to understand every word she speaks, just as you or I could if we were in her box beside her. The whole thing is a bare chance, I know, but we may learn something by taking her unsuspecting and unawares."

Dufrayer thought for a minute, then he sprang to his feet.

"Magnificent!" he cried. "Head, you are an extraordinary man! It is a unique idea. I will go off to the box-office at once and take a box if possible opposite Madame, or, failing that, the best seats we can get. I only hope you can secure Robertson. Go to his house at once and offer him any fee he wants. This is detection carried to a fine art with a vengeance. If successful, I shall class you as the smartest criminal agent of the day. We both meet at the Lyceum at a quarter to eight. Now, there is not a moment to lose."

I drove down to Robertson's house in Brompton, found him at home, and told him my wish. I strongly impressed upon him that if he would help he would be aiding in the cause of justice. He became keenly interested, entered fully into the situation, and refused to accept any fee.

At the appointed hour we met Dufrayer at the theatre door, and learned that he had secured a box on the second tier directly opposite Mme. Koluchy's box on the grand tier. I had arranged to have my letter sent by a messenger at ten o'clock.

We took our seats, and a few moments later Mme. Koluchy, in rose-coloured velvet and blazing with diamonds, accompanied by a tall, dark, clean-shaven man, entered her box. I drew back into the shadow of my own box and watched her. She bowed to one or two acquaintances in the stalls, then sat down, leaning her arm on the plush-covered edge of her box.

Robertson never took his eyes off her, and I felt reassured as he repeated to us the chance bits of conversation that he could catch between her and her companion.

The play began, and a few minutes past ten, in one of the intervals, I saw Madame turn and receive my note, with a slight gesture of surprise. She tore it open and her face paled perceptibly. Robertson, as I had instructed him, stood in front of me—his opera-glasses were fixed on the faces of Madame and her companion. I watched Madame as she read the note; she then handed it to Lewisham, who read it also. They looked at each other, and I saw Madame's lips moving. Simultaneously, Robertson began to make the following report verbatim:—-

"Impossible...some trick...quite safe goblet...key to cipher...to-morrow night."

Then followed a pause.

"Life and death to us... Signed ... My name."

There was another long pause, and I saw Madame twist the paper nervously in her fingers. I looked at Dufrayer, our eyes met. My heart was beating. His face had become drawn and grey. The ghastly truth and the explanation were slowly sealing their impress on our brains. The darkness of doubt had lifted, the stunning truth was clear. The paper which had defied us was a cipher written by Madame in her own name, and doubtless implicated her with Delacour's murder. Her anxiety to secure the goblet was very obvious. In some subtle way, handed down, doubtless, through generations, the goblet once in the possession of the ancient Brotherhood had held the key of the secret cipher.

But to-morrow night! To-morrow night was the night of the ball, and Madame was to be there. The reasoning was so obvious that the chain of evidence struck Dufrayer and me simultaneously.

We immediately left the theatre. There was one thing to be done, and that without delay. I must catch the first train in the morning to Pitsey Hall, examine the goblet afresh, and tell Pitsey everything, and thus secure and protect the goblet from harm. If possible, I would myself discover the key to the cipher, which, if our reasoning was true, would place Madame in a felon's dock and see the end of the Brotherhood.

At ten o'clock the following morning I reached Pitsey Hall. When I arrived I found, as I expected, the house in more or less confusion. Pitsey was busily engaged superintending arrangements and directing the servants in their work. It was some little time before I could see him alone.

"What is the matter, my dear fellow?" he said. "I am very busy now."

"Come into the library and I will tell you," I replied.

As soon as ever we were alone I unfolded my story. Hardened by years of contact with the world, it was difficult to startle or shake the composure of Leonardo Pitsey, and before I had finished my strange tale I could see from his expression the difficulty I should have in convincing him of the truth.

"I have had my suspicions for a long time," I said, in conclusion. "These are not the first dealings I have had with Mme. Koluchy. Hitherto she has eluded all my efforts to get her within the arm of the law, but I believe her time is near. Pitsey, your goblet is in danger. You will remove it to some place of safety?"

"Remove the luck of Pitsey Hall on the night when my boy comes of age!" replied Pitsey, frowning as he spoke. "It is good of you to be interested, Head; but really—well, I never knew you were such an imaginative man! As to any accident taking place to-night, that is quite outside the realms of probability. The band will be placed in front of the goblet, and it is impossible for anything to happen to it, as none of the dancers can come near it. Now, have you anything more to say?"

"I beg of you to be guided by me and to put the goblet into a place of safety," I repeated. "You don't suppose I would try to scare you with a cock-and-bull story. There is reason in what I say. I know that woman, my uneasiness is far more than due to mere imagination."

"To please you, Head, I will place two of my footmen beside the goblet during the ball, in order to prevent the slightest chance of any one approaching it. There, will that satisfy you?"

I was obliged to bow my acquiescence, and Pitsey soon left me in order to attend to his multifarious duties.

I spent nearly an hour that morning examining the goblet afresh. The mystical writing on the cup, concealed by the open-work design, engrossed my most careful attention, but so well were the principal letters concealed by the outside ornaments, that I could make nothing of them. Was I, after all, entirely mistaken, or did this beautiful work of art contain hidden within itself the power for which I longed, the strange key to the mysterious paper which would convict Mme. Koluchy of a capital charge?

The evening came at last, and about nine the guests began to arrive. The first dance had hardly come to an end before Mme. Koluchy appeared on the scene. She wore a dress of cloth of silver, and her appearance caused an almost imperceptible lull in the dancing and conversation. As she walked slowly up the great ballroom on the arm of a county magnate all eyes turned to look at her. She passed me with a hardening about the corners of her mouth as she acknowledged my bow, and I fancy I saw her eyes wander in the direction of the goblet at the other end of the room. Soon afterwards Antonia Pitsey came to my side.

"How beautiful everything is," she said. "Did you ever see any one look quite so lovely as Madame? Her dress to-night gives her a regal appearance. Have you seen our dance programme? The 'Queen Waltz' will be played just after supper."

"So you have fallen a victim to the popular taste?" I answered. "I hear that waltz everywhere."

"But you don't know who has composed it?" said the girl, with an arch look. "Now, I don't mind confiding in you—it is Mme. Koluchy."

I could not help starting.

"I was unaware that she was a musician," I remarked.

"She is, and a most accomplished one. We have included the waltz in our programme by her special request. I am so glad; it is the most lively and inspiriting air I ever danced to."

Antonia was called away, and I leant against the wall, too ill at ease to dance or take any active part in the revels of the hour. The moments flew by, and at last the festive and brilliant notes of the "Queen Waltz" sounded on my ears. Couples came thronging into the ballroom as soon as this most fascinating melody was heard. To listen to its seductive measures was enough to make your feet tingle and your heart beat. Once again I watched Mme. Koluchy as she moved through the throng. Ottavio Pitsey, the hero of the evening, was now her partner. There was a slight colour in her usually pale checks, and I had never seen her look more beautiful. I was standing not far from the band, and could not help noticing how the dominant note, repeated in two bars when all the instruments played together in harmony, rang out with a peculiar and almost passionate insistence. Suddenly, without a moment's warning, and with a clap that struck the dancers motionless, a loud crash rang through the room. The music instantly ceased, and the priceless heirloom of the Pitseys lay in a thousand silvered splinters on the polished floor. There was a moment's pause of absolute silence, followed by a sharp cry from our host, and then a hum of voices as the dancers hurried towards the scene of the disaster. The consternation and dismay were indescribable. Pitsey, with a face like death, was gazing horror-struck at the base and stem of the vase which still kept their place on the malachite stand, the cup alone being shivered to fragments. The two footmen, who had been standing under the pedestal, looked as if they had been struck by an unseen hand. Pushing my way almost roughly through the crowded throng I reached the spot. Nothing remained but the stem and jewelled base of the goblet.

The footmen looked struck.

"The two footmen ... looked as if they had been struck byan unseen hand."

Silent and gazing at the throng as one in a dream stood Mme. Koluchy. Antonia had crept up close to her father; her face was as white as her dress.

"The Luck of Pitsey Hall," she murmured, "and on this night of all nights!"

As for me, I felt my brain almost reeling with excitement. For the moment the thoughts which surged through it numbed my capacity for speech. I saw a servant gathering up the fragments. The evening was ended, and the party gradually broke up. To go on dancing would have been impossible.

It was not till some hours afterwards that the whole Satanic scheme burst upon me. The catastrophe admitted of but one explanation. The dominant note, repeated in two bars when all the instruments played together in harmony, must have been the note accordant with that of the cup of the goblet, and by the well-known laws of acoustics, when so played it shattered the goblet.

Next day there was an effort made to piece together the shattered fragments, but some were missing—how removed, by whom taken, no one could ever tell. Beyond doubt the characters cunningly concealed by the openwork pattern contained the key to the cipher. But once again Madame had escaped. The ingenuity, the genius, of the woman placed her beyond the ordinary consequences of crime.

Delacour's murder still remains unavenged. Will the truth ever come to light?

Chapter V

TWENTY DEGREES

A HOT and sultry day towards the end of June was drawing to a close. I had just finished dinner and returned to my laboratory to continue some spectroscopic work, when Dufrayer, whom I had not seen for more than a week, walked in. Noticing that I was busy, he took a cigar from a box which lay on the table and sank into an easy-chair without speaking.

"What is it to-night, Norman?" he asked at last, as I descended from my stool. "Is it the Elixir of Life or the Philosopher's Stone?"

"Neither," I replied. "I have received some interesting specimens of reduced hæmoglobin, and am experimenting on them. By the way, where have you been all this week?"

"At Eastbourne. The Assizes begin at the Old Bailey, as you know, on Thursday, and I am conducting the defence in the case of the Disney murder. However, I have not come here to talk shop. I had a small adventure at Eastbourne, and have come to tell you about it."

"More developments?" I asked, slightly startled by his tone, which was unusually grave. "Come into the garden; we will have coffee there."

We went through the open French windows and ensconced ourselves in wicker chairs.

"Does it ever occur to you," said Dufrayer, taking his cigar from his mouth as he spoke, "that you and I are in personal danger? It is absurd to lull ourselves into security by saying that such things do not happen in our day, but my only surprise is that Mme. Koluchy has not yet struck a blow at either of us. The thought of her haunts me; she fights with almost omnipotent powers, and we cannot foresee from what quarter the shaft may come."

"You have a reason for saying this?" I interrupted. "Has it anything to do with your visit to the seaside?"

"There is a possibility that it may have something to do with it, but of that I am not certain. In all likelihood, Head, there are no two men in London in such a strange position as ours."

"It is a self-elected one, at any rate," I replied.

"True," he answered. "Well, I will tell you what happened, and the further sequel which occurred this evening. I had been feeling rather done, and as I had a few days to spare, thought I would spend them geologizing along the cliffs at Eastbourne. On Tuesday last I went out for the whole day on a long expedition under the cliffs towards Burling Gap. I was so engrossed in my discovery of some very curious pieces of iron pyrites, for which that part of the coast is noted, that I forgot the time, and darkness set in before I turned for home. The tide was luckily low, so I had nothing to fear. I had just rounded the point on which the lighthouse stands when, to my amazement, I heard a shrill, clear voice call my name. I stopped and turned round, but at first could see nothing. In a moment, however, I observed a figure approaching me—it sprang lightly from rock to rock. As it came nearer it resolved itself into a boy, dressed in a light grey suit and a cloth cap. I was just going to address him when he raised his hand as if in warning, and said quickly, in a low voice: 'Don't return to London—stay here—you are in danger.' 'What do you mean?' I asked. He made no reply, and before I could repeat my question had left me, and was continuing his rapid course toward the promontory. I shouted after him, 'Stop! who are you?' but in another moment I completely lost sight of him in the dark shadow of the cliffs. I ran forward, but not a trace of him could I see. I shouted; there was no answer. I then made up my mind that pursuit was useless, and returned to the town."

"Have you seen or heard anything since of the mysterious youth?" I asked.

"Nothing whatever. What do you think of his warning? Is it possible that I am really in danger? Is Mme. Koluchy mixed up in this affair?"

I paused before replying, then I said slowly:

"As Madame is in existence, and as the youth whoever he was, happened to know your name there is just a possibility that the adventure may wear an ugly aspect. Two conclusions may be arrived at with regard to it: one, that this warning was intended to keep you at Eastbourne for some dangerous object; the other, that it was a friendly warning given for some reason in this strange manner."

"You arrive precisely at my own views on the subject," replied Dufrayer. "I am not a nervous man, and can defend my life if necessary. But that small incident has stuck to me in a curious way. Of course, it is quite impossible for me to leave town. The Disney murder trial comes on this week, and as there are many complications it will occupy some days; but, Head, try as I will, the impression of that boy's warning will not wear off; and now, listen, there is a sequel. See; this came by the last post."

As Dufrayer spoke he drew a letter from his pocket and thrust it into my hands.

I took it to the window, where, by the light of a lamp inside the room, I read the following lines:—

"Meet me inside gates, Marble Arch, at ten to-night. Do not fail. You have disregarded my advice, but I may still be able to do something."

"Your correspondent makes a strange rendezvous," I remarked, as I handed it back to him. "What do you mean to do?"

"What would you do in my place?" asked Dufrayer, shifting the question. He gazed at me earnestly, and with veiled anxiety in his face.

"Take no notice," I said. "The letter is anonymous, and as likely as not may be a trap to lead you into danger. I do not see anything for it but for you to pursue the even tenor of your way, just as if there were no Mme. Koluchy in the world."

It was half-past nine o'clock, the moon was rising, and Dufrayer's grave face, with his dark brows knit, confronted mine. After a time he rose.

"I believe you are right," he said. "I shall disregard that letter as I disregarded the warning of the youth on the sands. My unknown correspondent must keep his rendezvous in vain. I won't stay any longer this evening. I am terribly busy getting up my case for Thursday. Goodnight."

When he was gone I sat out of doors a little longer, pondering much over the two warnings which he had received, and which I had thought best to make little of to him. It was, as he said, impossible for him to leave town, but all the same I by no means liked the aspect of affairs. Whatever the warnings meant, they were at least significant of grave danger ahead, and knowing Mme. Koluchy as I did, I felt certain that no depths of treachery were beyond her powers.

I returned to the house, but felt little inclination to resume my experiments in the laboratory. The night grew more and more sultry, and a thunderstorm threatened.

Between eleven and twelve o'clock I was just preparing to retire for the night, when there came a loud ring at my front door. The servants had all gone to bed. In some surprise, I went to open the door. A woman in a voluminous cloak and old-fashioned bonnet was standing on the threshold. The moment the door was opened, and before I could say a word, she had stepped into the hall.

"Don't keep me out," she said, in a breathless voice; "I am followed, and there is danger. Mr. Dufrayer has failed to keep his appointment, and I was forced to come here. I know you, Mr. Head. I know all about you, and also about Mr. Dufrayer. Let me speak at once. I have something most important to say. Do get over your astonishment, and close the door. I tell you I am closely watched."

The figure of the woman was old, but the voice was young. Without a word, I shut the hall door. As I did so, she removed her bonnet and dropped her cloak. She now stood revealed to me as a slight, handsome, dark-eyed girl. Her skin was of a clear olive, and her eyes black.

"My name is Elsie Fancourt," she said. "My home is at Henley. My mother is the widow of a barrister. Our address is 5, Gloucester Gardens, Albert Road, Henley. Will you remember it?"

I nodded.

"Will you make a note of it?"

"I can remember it without that," I said.

"Very good. You may need that address later on. Now, Mr. Head, you are thinking strange things of me, but I am not, in the ordinary sense of the word, an adventuress. I am a lady—one in sore, sore straits. I have come to you in my desperate need, because I believe you can help me, and because you and also Mr. Dufrayer are in the gravest danger. Will you trust me?"

As she spoke she raised her eyes and looked me full in the face. I read an expression of truth in the depths of her fine eyes. My suspicion vanished; I held out my hand.

"You are a strange girl, and have come here at a strange hour," I said, "but I do trust you. Only extreme circumstances could make you act as you are doing. What is the matter?"

"Take me into one of your sitting-rooms, and I will explain."

I opened the door of my study and asked her to walk in.

"The matter is one of life and death," she began, speaking in a hurried voice. "Mr. Dufrayer has twice disregarded my warning. I warned him at the risk of my liberty, if not my life, and when he failed to keep the appointment which I made for him this evening, I felt there was nothing whatever for it but to come to you and to cast myself on your mercy. Mr. Head, there is not a moment to lose. Our common enemy"—here she lowered her voice—"is Mme. Koluchy. She has done me a great and awful wrong. She has done that which no woman with a woman's wit and intuition can ever forgive. I will avenge myself on her or die."

"Is it possible that you are the person who gave Mr. Dufrayer that strange warning on the beach at Eastbourne?" I asked.

"I am. I dressed myself as a boy for greater safety, but that night I was followed to my lodgings. Had Mr. Dufrayer heeded my advice I should not be here now. Mr. Head, your friend is in imminent danger of his life. I cannot tell you how the blow will fall, for I do not know, but I am certain of what I am saying. Out of London he might have a chance; in London he has practically none. Listen. You are both marked by the Brotherhood, and Mr. Dufrayer is to be the first victim. No human laws can protect him. Even here, in this great and guarded city, he cannot possibly escape. The person who strikes the blow may be caught, may suffer"—here a look of agony crossed her face—"but what is the good of that," she continued, "when the blow has done its work? No one outside the Brotherhood knows its immense resources. I repeat, Mr. Dufrayer has no chance whatever if he remains in London; he must leave immediately."

"That, I fear, is impossible," I replied gravely; "my friend is no coward. He is conducting the defence in an important case at the criminal courts. The life of an accused man hangs on his remaining in town—need I say more?"

She turned white to her lips.

"I know all that," she answered. "Have I not followed the thing step by step? Madame also knows how Mr. Dufrayer is placed, and what he has to do this week. She has made her plans accordingly. Oh! Mr. Head, would I risk my life as I am doing for a mere nothing? Can you not believe in the reality of the danger?"

114

"I can," I answered. "I am certain from your manner that you are speaking the truth, and I know enough of Mme. Koluchy to be sure of the gravity of the situation. Of course, I will tell Mr. Dufrayer what you say, and suggest that he get a substitute to carry on his work in the courts."

"Will you see him to-night?" she asked eagerly.

"Yes."

"Thank you."

"He is certain to refuse to go," I said. "It is right to give him your warning, but he will disregard it."

"Ah! you think so?"

"I am positive."

"In that case something else must be done, and I must know immediately. If your friend refuses, send a letter to E.F., General Post Office, marked 'Poste Restante.' I will go to St. Martin's-le-Grand early to-morrow morning to obtain it. Put nothing within the letter but the word 'No.' Don't sign your name."

"In case my friend decides not to leave town you shall have such a letter," I replied.

"Under those circumstances I must see you again," continued Miss Fancourt.

I made no reply.

"It is better for me not to communicate with you. Even a telegram would scarcely be safe. I have, I believe, managed to elude vigilance in coming here. I feel that I am watched day and night. I dare not risk the chance of meeting you in the ordinary way. Let me think for a moment."

She stood still, leaning her hand against her cheek.

"Are you musical?" she asked suddenly.

"Fairly so," I replied.

"Do you know enough of music to"—she paused and half smiled—"to tune a piano, for instance?"

"What do you mean?" I asked.

"I will soon explain myself. The piano-tuner is expected at our house to-morrow. Will you come in his place? I will send him a line the moment I get home, telling him to postpone his visit, but will let our servant think that he is coming. She has never seen our piano-tuner, and will suppose that you are the man we usually employ for the purpose. Do you mind assuming this rôle?"

"I am perfectly willing to try my hand on your piano," I said.

"Thank you. Then, in case you have to write that letter, come to our house to-morrow about two o'clock. The servant will admit you, believing you to be the tuner, and will show you into our drawing-room—I will join you there in a few moments. You can leave the rest to me."

I promised to do as Miss Fancourt required, and soon afterwards she took her leave.

A few moments later, I was on my way to Dufrayer's flat. He kept late hours, and I was relieved to see lights still burning in his windows. I was quickly admitted by my host himself.

"Come in, Norman," he cried. "That will do, North," he continued, turning to a young man whom I recognized as one of his managing clerks. "You have taken down all those instructions? Murchinson and James Watts must be subpoeFnaed as witnesses. I shall be at the office early to-morrow."

The young man in question, who had a pale, dark face and grey, sensitive eyes, quickly gathered up several papers and, bowing to Dufrayer and myself, took his leave.

"One of the best managing clerks I have ever had," said Dufrayer, as he left the room. "I have been in great luck to secure him. He is a wonderfully well-educated fellow and knows several languages. He has been with me for the last three months. I cannot tell you what a relief it is to have a clerk who really possesses a head on his shoulders. But you have news, Norman; what is it?"

"I have," I answered; "strange news. After all, Dufrayer, I am inclined to believe in your anonymous correspondent. The youth on the Eastbourne beach has merged into a girl. Finding that you would not keep the appointment she made for you, she came straight to me, and has, in fact, only just left me. Strange as it all seems, I believe in that girl. May I tell you what occurred during our interview?"

Dufrayer pulled a chair forward for me without saying a word. He stood facing me while I told my story. When I had finished he gave his shoulders a slight shrug, and then said:

"But, after all, Miss Fancourt has revealed nothing."

"Because at present she only suspects," I replied.

"And she coolly asks you to come to me to request me to throw my client over at the eleventh hour and to leave town?"

"She certainly believes that your danger is real," I answered.

"Well, real or not, I cannot possibly act on her warning," replied Dufrayer. As he spoke he walked to the window and looked out. "Things have come to a pretty pass when a man is hunted in this fashion," he continued. "A respectable London solicitor is converted into a modern Damocles, with the sword of Mme. Koluchy suspended above his head. The thing is preposterous; it cannot go on. My work keeps me here, and here I must stay. I will trust the Criminal Investigation Department against Madame's worst machinations. I shall go to Scotland Yard early to-morrow and see Ford. The thing is a perfect nightmare."

"I told Miss Fancourt you would not leave town," I replied.

"And you did right," he said.

"Nevertheless, I believe in her," I continued.

Dutrayer gave me one of those slow, inscrutable smiles which now and then flitted across his strong face.

"You were always a bit of an enthusiast, Head," he replied, "but the fact is, I have no time to worry over this matter now. All my energies of mind and body must be exerted on behalf of that unfortunate man, the conduct of whose trial has been placed in my hands."

I left Dufrayer, and before I resumed home wrote the single word "No" on a sheet of blank paper, folded it up, and put it into an envelope, and addressed it to E.F., "Poste Restante," St. Martin's-le-Grand.

To think over the enigma which Miss Fancourt had presented to me seemed worse than useless; but, try as I would, I could not banish it from my thoughts; and I even owned to a sense of relief when, on the following day, about two o'clock, I presented myself, as the supposed piano-tuner, at 5, Gloucester Gardens, Albert Road, Henley.

The house was a small one, and a neatly dressed little servant opened the door. She evidently expected the piano-tuner, for she smiled when she saw me, and showed me at once into the drawing-room. She supplied me with the necessary dusters, and opened the piano. I had just struck some chords on the somewhat ancient instrument, when Miss Fancourt came hastily in.

"I am sorry," she said, speaking in a rather loud voice, "but mother has a very bad headache, and has asked me to request you to postpone tuning the instrument to-day; but you must not go before you have had some lunch. I have asked the servant to bring it in."

She had left the door open, and now the girl who had admitted me followed, bearing a tray which contained some light refreshment.

"Put it down on that table, Susan," said Miss Fancourt, "and then please go at once for the medicine for your mistress. I can open the door in case any one calls."

The girl, quite unsuspicious, departed, and Miss Fancourt and I found ourselves alone.

"Susan will be absent for over half an hour," said the girl, "and I have told mother enough to insure her not coming into the room. She has feigned that headache; it was necessary to do so in order to get an excuse for sending our little servant out for some medicine, and so keeping her out of the way. A man was here questioning her only this morning. Oh, you make a first-class piano-tuner, Mr. Head," she continued, looking at me with a smile, which vanished almost as soon as it came. "But now to business. So your friend refuses to leave town."

"He does," I replied. "I told you that it was quite impossible for him to do so."

"I know you said so. Now I am going to give you my full confidence; but before I do so will you give me your word that what I am about to say will never, under any circumstances, pass your lips?"

"I cannot do that," I replied, "but if I find that you are a friend to me, I will be one to you."

She looked at me steadily

"That will not do," she said. "Mr. Dufrayer is an old acquaintance of yours, is he not?"

"My greatest friend," I said.

Her brow cleared, and her dark eyes lightened.

"His life is in danger," she said. "By this time to-morrow he may——" She paused, trembling, her very lips turned white.

"For Heaven's sake, speak out," I cried.

"Yes, I will explain myself. I am certain that when you know all you will give me the promise which is absolutely necessary for my own salvation and the salvation of one dearer to me than myself. Six months ago I became engaged to a man of the name of John North."

another engagement

"North!" I said, "North." I felt puzzled by a memory.

The girl proceeded without noticing my interruption.

"I love John North," she said slowly. "If necessary, I would die for him. I would go to any risk to save him from his present most perilous position."

As she spoke her dark brows were knit, she clasped her hands tightly together, and bent her head.

"There is a managing clerk of the name of North in Dufrayer's office," I said slowly.

"There is," she replied; "he is the man about whom I am speaking. Now please follow me closely. Mr. North, who was educated abroad and spent all his early years in Italy, was articled when still quite a youth to a large firm of solicitors in the City. Early in the spring, Mr. Dufrayer engaged him as one of his managing clerks at a salary of four guineas a week."

"I met North last night," I said. "He looked an intelligent fellow, and my friend spoke very highly of him. I have not the least idea, Miss Fancourt, what this is leading up to, but, as far as I can tell, North seems all right."

"Please let me continue," said the girl; "you will soon see how complicated matters are. Almost immediately after our engagement, John North got into Madame's set. I do not know how he first had an introduction to her, although I sometimes think he must have met her long ago in Italy. She evidently holds the deepest fascination over him, for he was never tired of talking of her, her wonderful house, her fame, her beauty, and the strange power she had over each person with whom she came in contact. One day he told me that through her agency, although her name

120

did not appear in the matter, she had got him an excellent appointment as managing clerk in the office of your friend."

I started. My attention was now keenly aroused.

"This," continued Miss Fancourt, "was three months ago. Mr. Head, during those three months everything has altered, the sun has got behind clouds, the sky is black. I am the most miserable girl on earth."

"You have doubtless a reason for your misery," I said.

"I have. Mr. Head, you tell me you have seen John North?"

"Last night for the first time," I answered.

"And you liked his appearance?"

"I was attracted by his face. I cannot exactly say that I liked it; it seemed clever—he looked intelligent."

"He is wonderfully so. Six months ago, when first we were engaged, his face used to wear the brightest, keenest expression; now it is haggard, restless—each day something of good leaves it and something of evil takes its place. Something, yes, something is eating into his youth, his manhood, and his beauty. He is changed to me—I believe he has almost lost the capacity of loving any one. My love, however, is unaltered, for I know there is a spell over him. When it is removed he will be his own old self again. Three weeks ago, Mr. Head, I swore I would discover what was wrong. Unknown to any one, I followed John North to a house in Mayfair. He went there with a large party, of whom Madame was one. I have found out what that house is. It is an opium den, though few except its frequenters are aware of that fact. It was easy for me, then, to put two and two together, and to know what was wrecking the life of the man I loved. You are a scientist, and understand what the opium vice means. It has ruined my lover, both in body and soul."

"This is terribly sad," I answered, "but I cannot quite understand what it has to do with Dufrayer."

121

"I am coming to that part," she replied. "After I had seen him enter the opium saloon, I began to watch John North more closely than ever, and soon I had strong reason to suspect that he was burdened by a great and very terrible secret. I seemed to read this fact in his eyes, in his manner. He avoided my glance, his gaiety left him, he became more gloomy and depressed hour by hour. My mother lives here, and has done so for years, but my journalistic work keeps me in town during the greater part of the week. I have a small room in Soho, where I sleep whenever necessary, but I always spend from Saturday to Monday at home. I was careful not to give Mr. North the slightest clue that I had guessed his secret, and on the special Sunday evening about which I am going to tell you I asked him to come and visit me at our house. He had neglected me terribly of late, leaving my letters unanswered, seeming indifferent to my presence. He had ceased altogether to speak of our marriage, and the only things which really interested him were his law work and his evenings in Madame's set. When I pressed him, however, he promised faithfully to come to see me on that special Sunday, and I sat for a long time in this room waiting for him. He did not arrive, and I grew restless. I put on my hat, and went along the road to meet him. He did not appear. I felt desperate then, and determined to do a bold thing. I took the next train to town. I arrived in London between six and seven o'clock and took a hansom straight to his rooms. The landlady, whom I had already seen once or twice, told me that he was in. I went upstairs and knocked at his sitting-room door. I heard his voice say, 'Come in,' and I entered. He was sitting on the sofa, and did not show the least surprise at seeing me. He asked me in a low, languid voice what I had come about. I replied that, as he had failed to keep his appointment with me, I had come to him. As I spoke I looked round the room. I noticed that he had in his hand a long pipe, and that there was a peculiar, sickly odour in the air. A small spirit lamp of uncommon shape stood burning on the table. I immediately guessed what was happening. When I interrupted him he was indulging in opium smoke. He was drawing in the pernicious, the awful drug, and did not care that I should interfere with him. I was determined, however, to probe this matter to the bitter end. I resolved at any risk to save him. I knew that there was only one way to do this. I must learn the truth—I must find out what that thing was which was casting its awful shadow over him. Like a flash it occurred to me that in his present condition it would be easy to wrest secrets from his lips. I would, therefore, encourage him to smoke. Instead of blaming him, therefore, for smoking the opium I sat down by him and asked some questions with regard to it. I requested him to continue the pleasure which I had interrupted, and showed him that I was much interested in the effects of opium. Low as he had fallen, he evidently did not like to indulge in the horrible habit in my presence; but I would not hear of his denying himself. I even helped him to put some more of the prepared opium into the bowl of the pipe. I smiled gently at him as the heavy aromatic smoke curled up round his nostrils, soothing and calming him. He began to enter into the fun of the thing, as he called it, and asked me to seat myself by his side. I felt sick and trembling, but never for a moment did my resolution fail me. As he got more and more under the influence of the opium, and I noticed the pin-point pupils of his eyes, I began to question him. My questions were asked with extreme care, and deliberately, step by step, I wormed his secrets from him. A ghastly plot was revealed to me, a plot so horrible, so certain in its issues, that I could scarcely restrain myself while I listened. It had to do with you, Mr. Head, with Mr. Dufrayer, and in especial with my lover himself, John North. Just as he murmured the last words of his awful secret he fell back into complete insensibility.

"I immediately hurried from the room. I knew enough of the effects of opium to be certain that John would have no remembrance of what he had said to me when he awoke in the morning. I saw the landlady, told her enough of my strange position to insure her secrecy, and hurried away.

"That night I spent in town, but I had no rest. Since that dreadful moment I have not had an hour's quiet. The man I love is to be the instrument used by Mme. Koluchy for her terrible purpose. A blow is to be struck, and John North is to strike it. What the blow is in itself, how the fatal deed is to be committed, I have not the slightest idea; but your friend is doomed. Can you not understand my awful position? John North is to execute Madame's vengeance. It matters little to her if eventually he hangs for his crime; for, with her usual cunning, she has so arranged matters that she herself will not be implicated. Mr. Head, you now see what I want to do. I want to save John North. Your friend I should also wish to save, but John North comes first, don't you understand?"

"I understand," I replied, "and I pity you from my heart."

"Then, if you pity, you will help me."

"Undoubtedly I will."

"That is good; that is what I hoped."

"But what is to be done? At present it seems to me that you and I are in the terrible position of knowing that there are rocks ahead without having the slightest idea where they are."

"I know this much at least," she replied. "The fatal deed will be committed in London, hence my entreaty to your friend not to leave Eastbourne. I might have guessed that he would not heed an anonymous warning of that sort. Then I tried what a letter would do, begging him to meet me at the Marble Arch. Little I cared what he thought of me if only I could save John North. Mr. Dufrayer did not come, and as a last resource I fled to you."

"I am glad you did so," I answered. "Have you any plan in your head on which I can immediately act?"

"I have, but first of all I want your promise. You must not only save your friend, but you must save Mr. North. I want your word of honour that you will never give your testimony against him."

"I can only say that I will not be the one to hand him over to the police," I replied; "more it is impossible to promise. Will that content you?"

She hesitated and looked thoughtful.

"I suppose it must," she said at last. "Will Mr. Dufrayer make a similar promise?"

"I think I can answer for him," I said.

"Very well. Now, then, Mr. Head, it is just possible that we may be victorious yet. I have discovered that from time to time Mr. North receives communications from Mme. Koluchy. If we could get hold of some of these we might reach the heart of this ghastly plot."

"But how is that to be done?" I asked.

"I have acquainted myself with all Mr. North's movements," continued the girl. "He goes to his lodgings every evening between ten and eleven o'clock, not leaving them again until the morning. Doubtless, night after night he has recourse to the solace of the opium pipe. It is impossible for me to visit him again, for I am too closely watched, but will you go to him—will you go to him to-night?"

"Do you really mean this?" I asked.

"I do," she replied, "it is the only thing to be done. You can take a message from Mr. Dufrayer. You are Mr. Dufrayer's friend, so a message from him will be natural. When you have got into Mr. North's presence you will know yourself what to do. Your own judgment will guide you. In all probability he will be under the effect of opium, and you can get further secrets from him. At the worst you may be able to find some of Madame's communications."

I stood still, considering.

"I will go," I said; "but success seems more than doubtful."

"I do not agree with you. I am certain that, with your tact, you will succeed. If you can only get hold of some of Madame's letters all may yet be well. By the way, can you read cipher?"

"I understand many ciphers," I replied

"I have discovered that Mme. Koluchy always writes in cipher. Go to-night. Do not fail. This is Mr. North's address. Do not try to communicate with me again. I shall know if you succeed, and if—but I dare not think of the other alternative."

She held out her hand; her face was white her lips trembled.

"You are a brave man," she said. "I feel somehow that you will succeed. Go, you must be out of this house before our little servant returns."

That evening between ten and eleven o'clock I found myself at North's lodgings. The landlady herself opened the door. I inquired if North was in, said that I had come with an urgent message from Dufrayer, and asked to see him at once.

"I do not know whether he is in," replied the woman, "but if you will go upstairs to the sitting-room on the third floor just facing the landing, you can see for yourself."

I nodded to her, and ran upstairs. A moment later I was knocking at the door which the landlady had indicated. There was no reply—I turned the handle and went in. One glance round the room caused my heart to beat with apprehension. The bird had evidently flown. Signs of a speedy departure were all too evident.

Some paper partly torn and partly burnt was lying in the grate, and some more papers completely charred to ashes were near it; the door which opened into the bedroom was flung back on its hinges. I went there, to see drawers and wardrobe open and empty. My next business was to go to the grate, secure the half-burnt paper, thrust it into my pocket, and go downstairs again. The landlady was nowhere in sight, so I let myself out.

About midnight I returned home.

"Now, for one last forlorn hope," I said to myself. "The man has evidently got a fright and has gone off. But like many another clever scoundrel, he did not quite complete his work before his departure. This paper is only half-burnt. Can it be possible that it contains the hidden cipher which may yet save my friend?"

I went straight to my laboratory, and opening the crumpled, torn piece of paper spread it out before me. To my dismay, I saw that it was only an ordinary sheet of a morning daily. I was about to fling it away, when suddenly an old memory returned to me. I knew of a method employed once by a great criminal who communicated with his confederates in the following manner. They received from time to time newspapers, certain of the printed letters of which were pricked with a needle. These prickings, when the paper was held up to the light, could be clearly seen, and the pricked letters, when taken down in consecutive order, formed certain words. Could the torn paper in my hands have been used for a similar purpose? I held it up to the light, but no sign of any pricking appeared.

Pacing to and fro in my laboratory I formulated every conceivable hypothesis that might throw light on the terrible problem. What was to be done?

At last, weary with anxiety, I went to bed, and exhausted as I was, sank into a heavy sleep.

I was roused by my servant calling me at the usual hour the next morning, and almost at once my thoughts flew to our terrible position. I dressed and went again to my laboratory to examine once more the fragment of paper. Without having any definite reason for doing so, I got out my camera, and, placing the paper in a strong light, exposed it to one of my rapid plates; then, going to my dark-room, I proceeded to develop it. As I bent over the dish and rolled the solution to and fro in the plate, I suddenly started, and my heart beat quickly. Was it only imagination, or was something coming out—something beyond and above the mere printed words of the newspaper? In the dim red light I could almost swear that I detected separate dots on the plate, which the paper itself did not show. Could there be a flaw in the negative?

Rapidly fixing it, I took it out and brought it to the light. A cry of joy burst from my lips. Over some of the printed letters something had been put which showed up in the negative, as whiter than the paper, something which would reflect the ultra-violet rays of the spectrum—something fluorescent. Perhaps a solution of quinine was the agent employed. This would, I knew, be quite invisible to the naked eye. Scarcely able to contain the excitement which consumed me, I dried the plate rapidly, and printed off a copy, and without waiting to tone it, took it to the light and examined it with my lens. Great heavens! the awful plot was about to be unveiled. A cipher had really been sent to North in this subtle way. The letters which had been touched with the quinine stood out clearly. As the newspaper was torn and a great part of it burnt, I could not read the full details of the ghastly plot in consecutive order, but the following fragments left little doubt of what the result was meant to be:—-

"Aneroid substituted...thermometer explodes at twenty degrees Réaumur...leave London to-night."

My brain swam. Quick as lightning my thoughts flew to Dufrayer.

"Thermometer explodes at twenty degrees," I found myself repeating.

Twenty degrees on the Réaumur scale in Russia means seventy-seven degrees Fahrenheit on our English scale. For the last few days the thermometer in London had daily recorded as high a temperature as this. Had it done so yet to-day? Dufrayer had an aneroid barometer hanging in his private room at his office. In it I knew was a thermometer. This was enough.

I bolted from the house, and in another moment a hansom was taking me at a hand gallop to Chancery Lane. In half an hour I was at my friend's door. I jumped out of the hansom, and dashed through the clerk's office into his private room. Dufrayer had evidently just come in, and was seated at his desk.

"Is that you, North? How late you are. I want you to go at once," he began. Then he caught sight of my face, and sprang from his chair.

"Norman!" he exclaimed; "what in the world is the matter?"

128

"Get out of this," I shouted. "You will never see that ruffian North again; but no matter, you must save yourself now."

As I spoke, I pushed Dufrayer roughly to the farther end of the room. My eyes were fixed upon the thermometer in the aneroid, which hung on the wall over his desk. The mercury stood at seventy-six degrees. Seizing a jug of cold water, which stood on a table near, I dashed the contents over the instrument. The mercury sank. I was right. I could see it. I was only just in time.

"What in Heaven's name is the matter? Are you mad?" said Dufrayer, gazing at me in astonishment.

"Matter!" I echoed, "the devil's the matter. This thing is an infernal machine."

"That aneroid an infernal machine? My dear Head, you must have lost your senses. I have had it for years."

"This is not the aneroid you have had for years," I answered. "Get a bucket of cold water—don't stand staring like that. Cannot you understand that we may be blown to pieces any moment?"

He paused just to take in the meaning of my words; then the colour left his face, and he rushed from the room.

"There," I said, as I unhooked the instrument and lowered it gently into the bucket which he had got from the housekeeper's kitchen, "we are safe for the present. But look here."

We bent down and examined the aneroid closely. Fused into the glass bore at the line which marked seventy-seven degrees was the tiniest metallic projection.

"But what does it mean? Explain yourself, for Heaven's sake," he said excitedly.

"I will in a moment," I answered, drawing out my heavy knife. With the screw-driver I unscrewed the back and levered it open.

"Good heavens! look here," I said.

The space in the hollow woodwork was literally packed with masses of gun-cotton, and below it lay a small accumulator with its fine connecting wires. I cut the wires and emptied the cotton into the water.

"Don't you see now?" I cried. "This is the most devilishly clever infernal machine that could be contrived. When the mercury rose to seventy-seven degrees the circuit would be completed, the gun-cotton fired, and you and your office blown to kingdom come."

"But who has done it?" said Dufrayer. "Who in the name of Heaven could have changed the aneroid?"

"Your clerk, North. I have a story to tell you, but I must do so in confidence."

"Let us go at once to Scotland Yard, Head. This is unbearable!"

"We cannot do so at present," I replied. "I am under a promise to hold back information."

Dufrayer stared at me as though once more he thought me possessed.

"I will explain matters to-night," I said. "Come now, let us turn the key in the door and go out."

Dufrayer suddenly glanced at his watch.

"In the excitement of this infernal affair I had almost forgotten my unfortunate client," he cried; "his case must be coming on at the Old Bailey about now. I must start at once."

"I will walk with you there," I said.

A moment later we found ourselves in Fleet Street. We passed an optician's—in the window was a thermometer. We stood and looked at it without speaking. The mercury was standing at eighty degrees.

That evening the strange story which Elsie Fancourt had confided to me was told to Dufrayer.

"Once again Madame has scored," was his remark when I had finished, "and that scoundrel North gets off scot-free."

"Madame has not quite scored, for your life has been spared," I said, with feeling.

"The whole thing was planned with the most infernal cunning," said Dufrayer. "Yesterday, North came into my office, pointed out that the aneroid was not working properly, and asked me if he might take it to an optician's in Fleet Street. I very naturally gave him permission. He brought it back in the evening and put it into its place. Yes, the whole plot was timed with the most consummate skill. The thermometer has been daily rising for the last few days, and Madame guessed only too well that it would reach seventy-seven degrees before I went to court this morning. Doubtless, North had informed her that the Disney trial was to come on second in the list, and that I should not be required at the Old Bailey before half-past eleven. Well, I have escaped, and I owe it to you, Head, and to Miss Fancourt. I pity that poor girl; she is too good to be thrown away on a scoundrel like North."

"I wonder what her future history will be," I said. "There is no doubt that North is fast in Madame's toils. Miss Fancourt believes, however, that her mission in life is to reclaim him. The ways of some good women are inexplicable."

Chapter VI

THE STAR SHAPED MARKS

ON a certain Sunday in the spring of 1897, as Dufrayer and I were walking in the Park, we came across one of his friends, a man of the name of Loftus Durham. Durham was a rising artist, whose portrait paintings had lately attracted notice. He invited us both to his studio on the following Sunday, where he was to receive a party of friends to see his latest work, an historical picture for the coming Academy.

"The picture is an order from a lady, who has herself sat for the principal figure," said Durham. "I hope you may meet her also on Sunday. My impression is that the picture will do well; but if so, it will be on account of the remarkable beauty of my model. But I must not add more—you will see what I mean for yourselves."

He walked briskly away.

"Poor Durham," said Dufrayer, when he had left us. "I am glad that he is beginning to get over the dreadful catastrophe which threatened to ruin him body and soul a year back."

"What do you mean?" I asked.

"I allude to the tragic death of his young wife," said Dufrayer. "They were only married two years. She was thrown from her horse on the hunting-field; broke her back, and died a few hours afterwards. There was a child, a boy of about four months old at the time of the mother's death. Durham was so frightfully prostrated from the shock that some of his friends feared for his reason; but I now see that he is regaining his usual calibre. I trust his new picture will be a success; but, notwithstanding his remarkable talent, I own I have my doubts. It takes a man in ten thousand to do a good historical picture."

On the following Sunday, about four o'clock, Dufrayer and I found ourselves at Durham's house in Lanchester Gardens. A number of well-known artists and their wives had already assembled in his studio. We found the visitors all gazing at a life-sized picture in a heavy frame which stood on an easel facing the window.

Dufrayer and I took our places in the background, and looked at the group represented on the canvas in silence. Any doubt of Durham's ultimate success must have immediately vanished from Dufrayer's mind. The picture was a magnificent work of art, and the subject was worthy of an artist's best efforts. It was taken from "The Lady of the Lake," and represented Ellen Douglas in the guard-room of Stirling Castle, surrounded by the rough soldiers of James V. of Scotland. It was named "Soldiers, Attend!"—Ellen's first words as she flung off her plaid and revealed herself in all her dark proud beauty to the wonder of the soldiers. The pose and attitude were superb, and did credit both to Durham and the rare beauty of his model.

I was just turning round to congratulate him warmly on his splendid production, when I saw standing beside him Ellen Douglas herself, not in the rough garb of a Scotch lassie, but in the simple and yet picturesque dress of a well-bred English girl. Her large black velvet hat, with its plume of ostrich feathers, contrasted well with a face of dark and striking beauty, but I noticed even in that first glance a peculiar expression lingering round the curves of her beautiful lips and filling the big brown eyes. A secret care, an anxiety artfully concealed, and yet all too apparent to a real judge of character, spoke to me from her face. All the same, that very look of reserve and sorrow but strengthened her beauty, and gave that final touch of genius to the lovely figure on the canvas.

Just then Durham touched me on the shoulder.

"What do you think of it?" he asked, pointing to the picture.

"I congratulate you most heartily," I responded.

"I owe any success which I may have achieved to this lady," he continued. "She has done me the honour to sit as Ellen Douglas. Mr. Head, may I introduce Lady Faulkner?"

I bowed an acknowledgment, to which Lady Faulkner gravely responded. She stepped a little aside, and seemed to invite me to follow her.

"I am also glad you like the picture," she said eagerly. "For years I have longed to have that special subject painted. I asked Mr. Durham to do it for me on condition that I should be the model for Ellen Douglas. The picture is meant as a present for my husband."

"Has he seen it yet?" I asked

"No, he is in India; it is to greet him as a surprise on his return. It has always been one of his longings to have a really great picture painted on that magnificent subject, and it was also one of his fancies that I should take the part of Ellen Douglas. Thanks to Mr. Durham's genius, I have succeeded, and am much pleased."

A new arrival came up to speak to her. I turned aside, but her face continued to attract me, and I glanced at her from time to time. Suddenly, I noticed that she held up her hand as if to arrest attention, and then flew to the door of the studio. Outside was distinctly audible the patter of small feet, and also the sound of a woman's voice raised in expostulation. This was followed by the satisfied half coo, half cry, of a young child, and the next instant Lady Faulkner reappeared, carrying Durham's baby boy in her arms.

He was a splendid little fellow, and handsome enough in himself to evoke unlimited admiration. A mass of thick, golden curls shadowed his brow; his eyes were large, and of a deep and heavenly blue. He had the round limbs and perfect proportions of a happy, healthy baby. The child had clasped his arms round Lady Faulkner's neck. Seeing a great many visitors in the room, he started in some slight trepidation, but, turning again to Lady Faulkner, smiled in her face.

"Ah! there you are, Robin," said Durham, glancing at the child with a lighting-up of his own somewhat sombre face. "But, Lady

Faulkner, please don't let the little chap worry you—you are too good to him. The fact is, you spoil him dreadfully."

"That is a libel, for no one could spoil you, could they, Robin?" said Lady Faulkner, kissing the boy on his brow. She seated herself on the window-sill. I went up and took a place beside her. She was so altogether absorbed by the boy that she did not at first see me. She bent over him and allowed him to clasp and unclasp a heavy gold chain of antique pattern which she wore round her neck. From time to time she kissed him. Suddenly glancing up, her eyes met mine.

"Is he not a splendid little fellow?" she said. "I don't know how I could have lived through the last few months but for this little one. I have been kept in London on necessary business, and consequently away from my own child; but little Robin has comforted me. We are great friends, are we not, Robin?"

"The child certainly seems to take to you," I said.

"Take to me!" she cried. "He adores me; don't you, baby?"

The boy looked up as she addressed him, opened his lips, as if to utter some baby word, then, with a coy, sweet smile, hid his face against her breast.

"You have a child of your own?" I said.

"Yes, Mr. Head, a boy. Now, I am going to confide in you. My boy is the image of this little one. He is the same age as Robin, and Robin and he are so alike in every feature that the resemblance is both uncommon and extraordinary. But, stay, you shall see for yourself."

She produced a locket, touched a spring, and showed me a painted photograph of a young child. It might have been taken from little Robin Durham. The likeness was certainly beyond dispute.

Dufrayer came near, and I pointed it out to him.

"Is it not remarkable?" I said. "This locket contains a picture of Lady Faulkner's own little boy. You would not know it from little Robin Durham, would you?"

Dufrayer glanced from the picture to the child, then to the face of Lady Faulkner. To my surprise she coloured under his gaze, which was so fixed and staring as to seem almost rude.

Remarking that the picture might assuredly be taken from Durham's boy, he gravely handed back the locket to Lady Faulkner, and immediately afterwards, without waiting for me, took his leave.

Lady Faulkner looked after his retreating form and I noticed that a new expression came into her eyes—a defiant, hard, even desperate, look. It came and quickly went. She clasped her arms more tightly round the boy, kissing him again. I took my own leave soon afterwards, but during the days which immediately followed I often thought with some perplexity of Lady Faulkner, and also of Durham's boy.

I had received a card for the private view of the Academy, and remembering Durham's picture, determined to go there on the afternoon of the great day. I strolled through the rooms, which were crowded, so much so indeed that it was almost impossible to get a good view of the pictures; but by-and-by I caught a sight of Durham's masterpiece. It occupied a place of honour on the line. Beyond doubt, therefore, his success was assured. I had taken a fancy to him, and was glad of this, and now pushed my way into the midst of a knot of admirers, who, arrested by the striking scene which the picture portrayed, and the rare grace and beauty of the central figure, were making audible and flattering remarks. Presently, just behind me, two voices, which I could not fail to recognize, fell on my ears. I started, and then remained motionless. The voices belonged to Lady Faulkner and to Mme. Koluchy. They were together, and were talking eagerly. They could not have seen me, for I heard Lady Faulkner's voice, high and eager. The following words fell on my ears:

"I shall do it to-morrow or next day. My husband returns sooner than I thought, and there is no time to lose. You have arranged about the nurse, have you not?"

"Yes; you can confidently leave the matter in my hands," was Madame's reply.

"And I am safe? There is not the slightest danger of——"

They were pushed on by the increasing crowd, and I could not catch the end of the last sentence, but I had heard enough. The pictures no longer attracted me. I made my way hurriedly from the room. As I descended the stairs my heart beat fast. What had Lady Faulkner to do with Mme. Koluchy? Were the words which unwittingly had fallen on my ears full of sinister meaning? Madame seldom attached herself to any one without a strong reason. Beyond doubt, the beautiful young Scotch woman was an acquaintance of more than ordinary standing. She was in trouble, and Madame was helping her. Once more I was certain that in a new and startling manner Madame was about to make a fresh move in her extraordinary game.

I went straight off to Dufrayer's office, found him in, and told him what had occurred.

"Beyond doubt, Lady Faulkner's manner was that of a woman in trouble," I continued. "From her tone she knows Madame well. There was that in her voice which might dare anything, however desperate. What do you think of it, Dufrayer? Is Durham, by any possible chance in danger?"

"That is more than I can tell you," replied Dufrayer. "Mme. Koluchy's machinations are beyond my powers to cope with. But as you ask me, I should say that it is quite possible that there is some new witchery brewing in her cauldron. By the way, Head, I saw that you were attracted by Lady Faulkner when you met her at Durham's studio."

"Were not you?" I asked.

"To a certain extent, yes, but I was also repelled. I did not like her expression as she sat with the child in her arms."

"What do you mean?"

"I can scarcely explain myself, but my belief is, that she has been subjected by Madame to a queer temptation. What, of course, it is impossible to guess. When you noticed the likeness between Durham's child and her own, I saw a look in her eyes which told me that she was capable of almost any crime to achieve her object."

"I hope you are mistaken," I answered, rising as I spoke. "At least, Durham has made a great success with that picture, and he largely owes it to Lady Faulkner. I must call round to see him, in order to congratulate him."

I did so a few days later. I found the artist busy in his studio working at a portrait of a City magnate.

"Here you are, Head. I am delighted to welcome you," he said, when I arrived. "Pray, take that chair. You will forgive me if I go on working? My big picture having sold so well, I am overpowered with orders. It has taken on; you have seen the reviews, have you not?"

"I have, and I also witnessed the crowds who collected round it on the opening day," I replied. "It is a magnificent work of art, Durham. You will be one of our foremost historical painters from this day out."

He smiled, and, brush in hand, continued to paint in rapidly the background of his picture.

"By the way," I said abruptly, "I am much interested in that beautiful Scotch model who sat for your Ellen Douglas. I have seldom seen a more lovely face."

Durham glanced up at me, and then resumed his work.

"It is a curious story altogether," he said. "Lady Faulkner came to see me in the November of last year. She said that she had met my little boy in Regent's Park, was struck by the likeness between her child and mine; on account of this asked the name of the child, discovered that I was his father (it seems that my fame as a portrait painter had already reached her ears), and she ventured to visit me to know if I would care to undertake an historical picture. I had done nothing so ambitious before, and I hesitated. She pressed the matter, volunteered to sit for the central figure, and offered me £2,000 for the picture when completed.

"I am not too well off, and could not afford to refuse such a sum. I begged of her to employ other and better-known men, but she would not hear of it—she wanted my work, and mine alone. She was convinced that the picture would be a great success. In the end her enthusiasm prevailed. I consented to paint the picture, and set to work at once. For such a large canvas the time was short, and Lady Faulkner came to sit to me three or four times a week. She made one proviso—the child was to be allowed to come freely in and out of the room. She attracted little Robin from the first, and was more than good to him. The boy became fond of her, and she never looked better, nor more at her ease, than when she held him in her arms. She has certainly done me a good service, and for her sake alone I cannot be too pleased that the picture is appreciated.

"Is Lady Faulkner still in town?" I asked.

"No, she left for Scotland only this morning. Her husband's place, Bram Castle, in Inverness, is a splendid old historical estate dating from the Middle Ages."

"How is your boy?" I asked. "You keep him in town, I see; but you have good air in this part of London."

"Yes, capital; he spends most of his time in Regent's Park. The little chap is quite well, thank you. By the way, he ought to be in now. He generally joins me at tea. Would it worry you if he came in as usual, Head?"

"Not at all: on the contrary, I should like to see him," I said.

Durham rang the bell. A servant entered.

"You can get tea, Collier," said his master. "By the way, is baby home yet?"

"No, sir," was the reply. "I cannot understand it," added the man; "Jane is generally back long before now."

Durham made no answer. He returned to his interrupted work. The servant withdrew. Tea was brought in, but there was no sign of the child. Durham handed me a cup, then stood abstracted for a moment, looking straight before him. Suddenly he went to the bell and rang it.

"Tell nurse to bring Master Robin in," he said.

"But nurse and baby have not returned home yet, sir."

Durham glanced at the clock.

"It is just six," he exclaimed. "Can anything be wrong? I had better go out and look for them."

"Let me go with you," I said. "If you are going into Regent's Park, it is on my way home."

"Nurse generally takes the child to the Broad Walk," said Durham; "we will go in that direction."

We entered the park. No sign of nurse or child could we see, though we made several inquiries of the park-keepers, who could tell us nothing.

"I have no right to worry you with all this," said Durham suddenly.

I glanced at him. He had expressed no alarm in words, but I saw now that he was troubled and anxious, and his face wore a stern expression. A nameless suspicion suddenly visited my heart. Try as I would, I could not shake it off.

"We had better go back," I said; "in all probability you will find the little fellow safe at home."

I used cheerful words which I did not feel. Durham looked at me again.

"The child is not to me as an ordinary child," he said, dropping his voice. "You know the tragedy through which I have lived?"

"Dufrayer has told me," I replied.

"My whole life is wrapped up in the little fellow," he continued. "Well, I hope we shall find him all right on our return. Are you really coming back with me?"

"Certainly, if you will have me. I shall not rest easy myself until I know that the boy is safe."

We turned in the direction of Durham's house. We ran up the steps.

"Have you seen them, sir?" asked the butler, as he opened the door.

"No. Are they not back yet?" asked Durham.

"No, sir; we have heard nor seen nothing of either of them."

"This is quite unprecedented," said the artist. "Jane knows well that I never allow the boy to be out after five o'clock. It is nearly seven now. You are quite certain," he added, turning to the man, "that no message has come to account for tile child's delay?"

"No, sir, nothing."

"What do you think of it, Head?" He looked at me inquiringly.

"It is impossible to tell you," I replied; "a thousand things may keep the nurse out. Let us wait for another hour. If the child has not returned by then, we ought certainly to take some action."

I avoided looking at Durham as I spoke, for Lady Faulkner's words to Mme. Koluchy returned unpleasantly to my memory:

"I shall do it to-morrow or next day—you have arranged about the nurse?"

We went into the studio, and Durham offered me a cigarette. As he did so I suddenly heard a commotion in a distant part of the house; there was the sound of hurrying feet and the noise of more than one voice raised in agitation and alarm. Durham's face turned ghastly.

"There has been an accident," he said. "I felt that there was something wrong. God help me!"

He rushed to the door. I followed him. Just as he reached it, it was flung open, and the nurse, a comely-looking woman, of between thirty and forty years of age, ran in and flung herself at Durham's feet.

"You'll never forgive me, sir," she gasped. "I feel fit to kill myself."

"Get up, Jane, at once, and tell me what has happened. Speak! Is anything wrong with the child?"

"Oh, sir, he is gone—he is lost! I don't know where he is. Oh, I know you'll never forgive me. I could scarcely bring myself to come home to tell you."

"That was folly. Speak now. Tell the whole story at once."

Durham's manner had changed. Now that the blow had really fallen, he was himself once again—a man of keen action, resolute, resolved.

The woman stared at him, then she staggered to her feet, a good deal of her own self-control restored by his manner.

"It was this way, sir," she began. "Baby and I went out as usual early this afternoon. You know how fond baby has always been of Lady Faulkner?"

"Lady Faulkner has nothing to do with this matter," interrupted Durham. "Proceed with your story."

"Her ladyship is in Scotland; at least, it is supposed so, sir," continued the woman. "She came here late last night, and bade us all good-bye. I was undressing baby when she entered the nursery. She took him in her arms and kissed him many times. Baby loves her very much. He always called her 'Pitty lady.' He began to cry when she left the room."

"Go on! go on!" said Durham.

"Well, sir, baby and I went into the park. You know how active the child is, as merry as a lark, and always anxious to be down on his legs. It was a beautiful day, and I sat on one of the seats and baby ran about. He was very fond of playing hide-and-seek round the shrubs, and I used to humour him. He asked for his usual game. Suddenly I heard him cry out, 'Pitty lady! Pitty lady,' and run as fast as ever he could round to the other side of a big clump of rhododendrons. He was within a few feet of me, and I was just about to follow him—for half the game, sir, was for me to peep round the opposite side of the trees and try to catch him—when a gentleman whose acquaintance I had made during the last two days came up and began to speak to me. He was a Mr. Ivanhoe, and a very gentlemanly person, sir. We talked for a minute or two, and I'll own I forgot baby. The moment I remembered him I ran round the rhododendrons to look for him, but from that hour to now, sir, I have seen nothing of the child. I don't know where he is—I don't know what has happened to him. Some one must have stolen him, but who, the Lord only knows. He must have fancied that he saw a likeness to Lady Faulkner in somebody else in the park, for he did cry out, 'Pitty lady,' just as if his whole heart was going out to some one, and away he trotted as fast as his feet could carry him. That is the whole story, sir. I'd have come back sooner, but I have been searching the place, like one distracted."

"You did very wrong not to return at once. Did you by any chance happen to see the person the child ran to?"

"I saw no one, sir; only the cry of the child still rings in my ears and the delight in his voice. 'Pitty lady,' he said, and off he went like a flash."

"You should have followed him."

"I know it, sir, and I'm fit to kill myself; but the gentleman was that nice and civil, and I'll own I forgot everything else in the pleasure of having a chat with him."

"The man who spoke to you called himself Ivanhoe?"

"Yes, sir."

"I should like you to give me some particulars with regard to this man's appearance," I said, interrupting the conversation for the first time.

The woman stared at me. I doubt if she had ever seen me before.

"He was a dark, handsome man," she said; then, slowly, "but with something peculiar about him, and he spoke like a foreigner."

I glanced at Durham. His eyes met mine in the most hopeless perplexity. I looked away. A thousand wild fears were rushing through my brain.

"There is no good in wasting time over unimportant matters," said the poor father impatiently. "The thing to do is to find baby at once. Control yourself, please, Jane; you do not make matters any better by giving way to undue emotion. Did you mention the child's loss to the police?"

"Yes, sir, two hours back."

"Durham," I said suddenly? "you and I had better go at once to Dufrayer. He will advise us exactly what is to be done."

Durham glanced at me, then without a word went into the hall and put on his hat. We both left the house.

"What do you think of it, Head?" he said presently, as we were bowling away in a hansom to Dufrayer's flat.

"I cannot help telling you that I fear there is grave danger ahead," I replied; "but do not ask me any more until we have consulted Dufrayer."

The lawyer was in, and the whole story of the child's disappearance was told to him. He listened gravely. When Durham had finished speaking, Dufrayer said slowly:

"There is little doubt what has happened."

"What do you mean?" cried Durham. "Is it possible that you have got a solution already?"

"I have, my poor fellow, and a grave one. I fear that you are one of the many victims of the greatest criminal in London. I allude to Mme. Koluchy."

"Mme. Koluchy!" said Durham, glancing from one of us to the other. "What can you mean? Are you dreaming? Mme. Koluchy! What can she have to do with my little boy? Is it possible that you allude to the great lady doctor?"

"The same," cried Dufrayer. "The fact is Durham, Head and I have been watching this woman for months past. We have learned some grave things about her. I will not take up your time now relating them, but you must take our word for it that she is not to be trusted—that to know her is to be in danger—to be her friend is to be in touch with some monstrous and terrible crime. For some reason she has made a friend of Lady Faulkner. Head saw them standing together under your picture. Head, will you tell Durham the exact words you overheard Lady Faulkner say?"

I repeated them.

Durham, who had been listening attentively, now shook his head.

"We are only wasting time following a clue of that sort," he said. "Nothing would induce me to doubt Lady Faulkner. What object

146

could she possibly have in stealing my child? She has a child of her own exactly like Robin. Head, you are on a wrong track—you waste time by these conjectures. Some one has stolen the child hoping to reap a large reward. We must go to the police immediately, and have wires sent to every station round London."

"I will accompany you, Durham, if you like, to Scotland Yard," said Dufrayer.

"And I will go back to Regent's Park to find out if the keepers have learned anything," I said.

We went our separate ways.

The next few days were spent in fruitless endeavours to recover the missing child. No stone was left unturned; the police were active in the search—large rewards were freely offered Durham, accompanied by a private detective; spent his entire time rushing from place to place. His face grew drawn and anxious, his work was altogether neglected. He slept badly, and morning after morning awoke feeling so ill that his friends became alarmed about him.

"If this fearful strain continues much longer I shall fear for his life," said Dufrayer, one evening, to me. This was at the end of the first week.

On the next morning there was a fresh development in the unaccountable mystery. The nurse, Jane Cleaver, who had been unfeignedly grieving for the child ever since his disappearance, had gone out and had not returned. Inquiries were immediately set on foot with regard to what had become of her, but not a clue could be obtained as to her whereabouts.

On the evening of that day I called to see Durham, and found the poor fellow absolutely distracted.

"If this suspense continues much longer, I believe I shall lose my reason," he said. "I cannot think what has come to me. It is not only the absence of the child. I feel as if I were under the weight of some terrible illness. I cannot explain to you what my nights are. I have horrible nightmares. I suffer from a sensation as if I were being scorched by fire. In the morning I awake more dead than alive. During the day I get a little better, but the following night the same thing is repeated. The image of the child is always before my eyes. I see him everywhere. I hear his voice crying to me to come and rescue him."

He turned aside, so overcome by emotion that he could scarcely speak.

"Durham," I said suddenly, "I have come here this evening to tell you that I have made up my mind."

"To do what?" he asked.

"I am going to Scotland to-morrow. I mean to visit Lady Faulkner at Bram Castle. It is quite possible that she knows something of the fate of the child. One thing, at least, is certain, that a person who had a strong likeness to her beguiled the little fellow round the rhododendron clump."

Durham smiled faintly.

"I cannot agree with you," he said. "I would stake my life on the honour of Lady Faulkner."

"At least you must allow me to make inquiries," I replied. "I shall be away for a few days. I may return with tidings. Keep up your heart until you see me again."

On the following evening I found myself in Inverness-shire. I put up at a small village just outside the estate of Bram. The castle towering on its beetling cliffs hung over the rushing waters of the River Bramley. I slept at the little inn, and early on the following morning made my way to the castle. Lady Faulkner was at home, and showed considerable surprise at seeing me. I noticed that her colour changed, and a look of consternation visited her large, beautiful eyes.

"You startled me, Mr. Head," she said; "is anything wrong?"

"Wrong? Yes," I answered. "Is it possible you have not heard the news?"

"What news?" she inquired. She immediately regained her self-control, sat down on the nearest chair, and looked me full in the face.

"I have news which will cause you sorrow, Lady Faulkner. You were fond of Durham's boy, were you not?"

"Mr. Durham's boy—sweet little Robin?" she cried. "Of course. Has anything happened to him?"

"Is it possible that you have not heard? The child is lost."

I then related all that had occurred. Lady Faulkner looked at me gravely, with just the right expression of distress coming and going on her face. When I had finished my narrative there were tears in her eyes.

"This will almost send Mr. Durham to his grave," she cried; "but surely—surely the child will be found?"

"The child must be found," I said. As I spoke I looked at her steadily. Immediately my suspicions were strengthened. She gazed at me with that wonderful calm which I do not believe any man could adopt. It occurred to me that she was overdoing it. The slight hardening which I had noticed before round her lovely lips became again perceptible. In spite of all her efforts, an expression the reverse of beautiful filled her eyes.

"Oh, this is terrible!" she said, suddenly springing to her feet. "I can feel for Mr. Durham from my very heart. My own little Keith is so like Robin. You would like to see my boy, would you not, Mr. Head?"

"I shall be glad to see him," I answered. "You have spoken before of the extraordinary likeness between the children."

"It is marvellous," she cried; "you would scarcely know one from the other."

She rang the bell. A servant appeared.

"Tell nurse to bring baby here," said I Faulkner.

A moment later the door was opened—the nurse herself did not appear, but a little boy, dressed in white, rushed into the room. He ran up to Lady Faulkner, clasping his arms ecstatically round her knees.

"Mother's own little boy," she said. She lifted him into her arms. Her fingers were loaded with rings, and I noticed as she held the child against her heart that they were trembling. Was all this excessive emotion for Durham's miserable fate?

"Lady Faulkner," I said, jumping to my feet and speaking sternly, "I will tell you the truth. I have come here in a vain hope. The loss of the child is killing the poor father—can you do anything for his relief?"

"I?" she said. "What do you mean?"

My words were unexpected, and they startled her.

"Can you do anything for his relief?" I repeated. "Let me look at that boy. He is exactly like the child who is lost."

"I always told you there was an extraordinary likeness," she answered. "Look round, baby, look at that gentleman—tell him you are mother's own, own little boy."

"Mummy's boy," lisped the baby. He looked full up into my face. The blue eyes, the mass of golden hair, the slow, lovely smile—surely I had seen them before.

Lady Faulkner unfastened her locket, opened it and gave it to me.

"Feature for feature," she said. "Feature for feature the same. Mr. Head, this is my child. Is it possible—-" She let the child drop from her arms and stood up confronting me. Her attitude reminded me of Ellen Douglas. "Is it possible that you suspect me?" she cried.

"I will be frank with you, Lady Faulkner," I answered. "I do suspect you."

She seated herself with a perceptible effort.

"This is too grave a matter to be merely angry about," she said; "but do you realize what you are saying? You suspect me—me of having stolen Robin Durham from his father?"

"God help me, I do," I answered.

"Your reasons?"

She took the child again on her knee. He turned towards her and caught hold of her heavy gold chain. As he did so I remembered that I had seen Durham's boy playing with that chain in the studio at Lanchester Gardens.

I briefly repeated the reasons for my fears. I told Lady Faulkner what I had overheard at the Academy. I said a few strong words with regard to Mme. Koluchy.

"To be the friend of that woman is to condemn you," I said, at last. "Do you know what she really is?"

Lady Faulkner made no answer. During the entire narrative she had not uttered a syllable.

"When my husband returns home," she said at last, faintly, "he will protect me from this cruel charge."

"Are you prepared to swear that the boy sitting on your knee is your own boy?" I asked.

She hesitated, then said boldly, "I am."

"Will you take an oath on the Bible that he is your child?"

Her face grew white.

"Surely that is not necessary," she said.

"But will you do it?" I repeated.

She looked down again at the boy. The boy looked up at her.

"Pitty lady," he said, all of a sudden.

The moment he uttered the words I noticed a queer change on her face. She got up and rang the bell. A grave-looking, middle-aged woman entered the room.

"Take baby, nurse," said Lady Faulkner.

The woman lifted the boy in her arms and conveyed him from the room

"I will swear, Mr. Head," said Lady Faulkner. "There is a Bible on that table—I will swear on the Bible."

She took the Book in her hands, repeated the usual words of the oath, and kissed the Book.

"I declare that that boy is my own son, born of my body," she said, slowly and distinctly.

"Thank you," I answered. I laid the Bible down on the table.

"What else do you want me to do?" she said.

"There is one test," I replied, "which, in my opinion, will settle the matter finally. The test is this. If the boy I have just seen is indeed your son, he will not recognize Durham, for he has never seen him. If, on the other hand, he is Durham's boy, he cannot fail to know his father, and to show that he knows him when he is taken into his presence. Will you return with me to town to-morrow, bringing the child with you? If little Robin's father appears as a stranger to the boy, I will believe that you have spoken the truth."

Before Lady Faulkner could reply, a servant entered the room bearing a letter on a salver. She took it eagerly and tore it open, glanced at the contents, and a look of relief crossed her face as her eyes met mine. They were bright now and full of a curious defiance.

"I am willing to stand the test," she said. "I will come with you to-morrow."

"With the boy?"

"Yes, I will bring the boy."

"You must allow him to enter Durham's presence without you."

"He shall do so."

"Good," I answered. "We can leave here by the earliest train in the morning."

I left the castle a few minutes later, and wired to Dufrayer, telling him that Lady Faulkner and I would come up to town early on the following day, bringing Lady Faulkner's supposed boy with us. I asked Dufrayer not to prepare Durham in any way.

Late in the evening I received a reply to my telegram.

"Come by first possible train," were its contents. "Durham is seriously ill."

I thought it best to say nothing of the illness to Lady Faulkner, and at an early hour on the following day we started on our journey. No nurse accompanied the child. He slept a good part of the day—Lady Faulkner herself was almost silent. She scarcely addressed me. Now and then I saw her eyes light upon the child with a curious expression. Once, as I was attending to her comfort, she looked me full in the face.

"You doubt me, Mr. Head," she said. "It is impossible for me to feel friendly towards you until your doubts are removed."

"I am more grieved than I can say," I answered; "but I must, God helping me, at any cost see justice done."

She shivered.

At 7 p.m. we steamed into King's Cross. Dufrayer was on the platform, and at the carriage door in a second. From the grave expression on his face I saw that there was bad news. Was it possible that the worst had happened to Durham, and that now there would never be any means of proving whether the child were Lady Faulkner's child or not?

"Be quick," he exclaimed, when he saw me. "Durham is sinking fast; I am afraid we shall be too late as it is."

"What is the matter with him?" I asked.

"That is what no one can make out. Langley Chaston, the great nerve specialist, has been to see him this afternoon. Chaston is completely non-plussed, but he attributes the illness to the shock and strain caused by the loss of the child."

Dufrayer said these words eagerly, and as he imagined into my ear alone. A hand touched me on the shoulder. I turned and confronted Lady Faulkner.

"What are you saying?" she exclaimed. "Is it possible that Mr. Durham is in danger, in danger of his life?"

"He is dying," said Dufrayer brusquely.

Lady Faulkner stepped back as though some one had shot her. She quivered all over.

"Take the child," she said to me, in a faint voice.

I lifted the boy in my arms. A brougham awaited us; we got in. The child, weary with the journey, lay fast asleep.

In another moment we were rattling along the Marylebone Road towards Lanchester Gardens.

As we entered the house, Dr. Curzon, Durham's own physician, received us in the hall.

"You are too late," he said, "the poor fellow is unconscious. It is the beginning of the end. I doubt if he will live through the night."

The doctor's words were interrupted by a low cry. Looking round, I saw that Lady Faulkner had flung off her cloak, had lifted her veil, and was staring at Dr. Curzon as though she were about to take leave of her senses.

"Say those words again," she cried.

"My dear madam, I am sorry to startle you. Durham is very ill; quite unconscious; sinking fast."

"I must see him," she said eagerly; "which is his room?"

"The bedroom facing you on the first landing," was the doctor's reply.

She rushed upstairs, not waiting for any one. We followed her slowly. As we were about to enter the room, the child being still in my arms, Lady Faulkner came out, and confronted me.

"I have seen him," she said. "One glance at his face was sufficient. Mr. Head, I must speak to you, and alone, at once—at once! Take me where I can see you all alone."

I opened the door of another room on the same landing, and switched on the electric light.

"Put the child down," she said, "or take him away. This is too horrible; it is past bearing. I never meant things to go as far as this."

"Lady Faulkner, do you quite realize what you are saying?"

"I realize everything. Oh, Mr. Head, you were right. Madame is the most terrible woman in all the world. She told me that I might bring the boy to London in safety—that she had arranged matters so that his father should not recognize him—so that he would not recognize his father. I was to bring him straight here, and trust to her to put things right. I never knew she meant this. I have just looked at his face, and he is changed; he is horrible to look at now. Oh, my God! this will kill me."

"You must tell me all, Lady Faulkner," I said. "You have committed yourself now—you have as good as confessed the truth. Then the child—this child—is indeed Durham's son?"

"That child is Loftus Durham's son. Yes, I am the most miserable woman in the universe. Do what you will with me. Oh yes, I could bring myself to steal the boy, but not, not to go to this last extreme step. This is murder, Mr. Head. If Mr. Durham dies, I am guilty of murder. Is there no chance of his life?"

"The only chance is for you to tell me everything as quickly as you can," I answered.

"I will," she replied. She pulled herself together, and began to speak hurriedly.

"I will tell you all in as few words as possible; but in order that you should understand why I committed this awful crime, you must know something of my early history.

"My father and mother died from shock after the death of three baby brothers in succession. Each of these children lived to be a year old, and then each succumbed to the same dreadful malady, and sank into an early grave. I was brought up by an aunt, who treated me sternly, suppressing all affection for me, and doing her utmost to get me married off her hands as quickly as possible. Sir John Faulkner fell in love with me when I was eighteen, and asked me to be his wife. I loved him, and eagerly consented. On the day when I gave my consent I met our family doctor. I told him of my engagement and of the unlooked for happiness which had suddenly dawned on my path. To my astonishment old Dr. Macpherson told me that I did wrong to marry.

"'There is a terrible disease in your family,' he said; 'you have no right to marry.'

"He then told me an extraordinary and terrible thing. He said that in my family on the mother's side was a disease which is called pseudo-hypertrophic muscular paralysis. This strange disease is hereditary, but only attacks the male members of a house, all the females absolutely escaping. You have doubtless heard of it?"

I bowed. "It is one of the most terrible hereditary diseases known," I replied.

Her eyes began to dilate.

"Dr. Macpherson told me about it that dreadful day," she continued. "He said that my three brothers had died of it, that they had inherited it on the mother's side—that my mother's brothers had also died of it, and that she, although escaping herself, had communicated it to her male children. He told me that if I married, any boys who were born to me would in all probability die of this disease.

"I listened to him shocked. I went back and told my aunt. She laughed at my fears, told me that the doctor was deceiving me, assured me that I should do very wrong to refuse such an excellent husband as Sir John, and warned me never to repeat a word of what I had heard with regard to my own family to him. In short, she forced on the marriage.

"I cannot altogether blame her, for I also was only too anxious to escape from my miserable life, and but half-believed the doctor's story.

"I married to find, alas, that I had not entered into Paradise. My husband, although he loved me, told me frankly, a week after our marriage, that his chief reason for marrying me was to have a healthy heir to his house. He said that I looked strong, and he believed my children would be healthy. He was quite morbid on this subject. We were married nearly three years before our child was born. My husband was almost beside himself with rejoicing when this took place. It was not until the baby lay in my arms that I suddenly remembered what I had almost forgotten—old Dr. Macpherson's warning. The child however, looked perfectly strong, and I trusted that the dreadful disease would not appear in him.

"When the baby was four months old my husband was suddenly obliged to leave home in order to visit India. He was to be absent about a year. Until little Keith was a year old he remained perfectly healthy, then strange symptoms began. The disease commenced in the muscles of the calves of the legs, which became much enlarged. The child suffered from great weakness—he could only walk by throwing his body from side to side at each step.

"In terror I watched his symptoms. I took him then to see Dr. Macpherson. He told me that I had neglected his warning, and that my punishment had begun. He said there was not the slightest hope for the child—that he might live for a few months, but would in the end die.

"I returned home, mad with misery. I dared not let my husband know the truth. I knew that if I did he would render my life a hell, for the fate which had overtaken my first child would be the fate of every other boy born to me. My misery was beyond any words. Last winter, when baby's illness had just begun, I came up to town. I brought the child with me—he grew worse daily. When in town, I heard of the great fame of Mme. Koluchy and her wonderful cures. I went to see her, and told her my pitiful story. She shook her head when I described the features of the case, said that no medicine had ever yet been discovered for this form of muscular paralysis, but said she would think over the case, and asked me to call upon her again.

"The next day, when in Regent's Park, I saw Loftus Durham's little boy. I was startled at the likeness, and ran forward with a cry, thinking that I was about to embrace my own little Keith. The child had the same eyes, the same build. The child was Keith to all intents and purposes, only he was healthy—a splendid little lad. I made friends with him on the spot. I went straight then to Mme. Koluchy, and told her that I had seen a child the very same as my own child. She then thought out the scheme which has ended so disastrously. She assured me it only needed courage on my part to carry it through. We discovered that the child was the only son of a widower, a rising artist of the name of Durham. Mr. Head, you know the rest. I determined to get acquainted with Mr. Durham, and in order to do so gave him a commission to paint the picture called 'Soldiers, Attend!'

"You can scarcely understand how I lived through the past winter. Madame had persuaded me to send my dying child to her. A month ago I saw my boy breathe his last. I smothered my agony and devoted every energy to the kidnapping of little Robin. I took him away as planned, the nurse's attention being completely engrossed by a confederate of Mme. Koluchy's. It was arranged that in a week's time the nurse was also to be kidnapped, and removed from the country. She is now, I believe, on her way to New Zealand. Having removed the nurse, the one person we had to dread in the recognizing of the child was the father himself. With great pains I taught the boy to call me 'Mummy,' and I believed he had learned the name and had forgotten his old title of 'Pitty lady.' But he said the words yesterday in your presence, and I have not the slightest doubt by so doing confirmed your suspicions. When I had taken the dreadful oath that the child was my own, and so perjured my soul, a letter from Mme. Koluchy arrived. She had discovered that you had gone to Scotland, and guessed that your suspicions were aroused. She said that you were her most terrible enemy, that more than once you had circumvented her in the moment of victory, but she believed that on this occasion we should win, and she further suggested that the very test which you demanded should be acceded to by me. She said that she had arranged matters in such a way that the father would not recognize the child, nor would the child know him; that I was to trust to her, and boldly go up to London, and bring the boy into his father's presence. The butler, Collier, who of course also knew the child, had, owing to Madame's secret intervention, been sent on a fruitless errand into the country, and so got out of the way. I now see what Madame really meant. She would kill Mr. Durham and so insure his silence for ever; but, oh! Mr. Head, bad as I am, I cannot commit murder. Mr. Head, you must save Mr. Durham's life."

"I will do what I can," I answered. "There is no doubt, from your confession, that Durham is being subjected to some slow poison. What, we have to discover. I must leave you now Lady Faulkner."

I went into the next room, where Dufrayer and Dr. Curzon were waiting for me. It was darkened. At the further end, in a bed against the wall, lay Durham. Bidding the nurse bring the lamp, I went across, and bent over him. I started back at his strange appearance. I scarcely recognized him. He was lying quite still, breathing so lightly that at first I thought he must be already dead. The skin of the face and neck had a very strange appearance. It was inflamed and much reddened. I called the poor fellow by name very gently. He made no sign of recognition.

"What is all this curious inflammation due to?" I asked of Dr. Curzon, who was standing by my side.

"That is the mystery," he replied; "it is unlike anything I have seen before."

I took up my lens and examined it closely. It was certainly curious. Whatever the cause, the inflammation seemed to have started from many different centres of disturbance. I was at once struck by the curious shape of the markings. They were star-shaped, and radiated as if from various centres. As I still examined them, I could not help thinking that I had seen similar markings somewhere else not long ago, but when and connected with what I could not recall. This was, however, a detail of no importance. The terrible truth which confronted me absorbed every other consideration. Durham was dying before my eyes, and from Lady Faulkner's confession, Mme. Koluchy was doubtless killing him by means unknown. It was, indeed, a weird situation.

I beckoned to the doctor, and went out with him on to the landing.

"I have no time to tell you all," I said. "You noticed Lady Faulkner's agitation? She has made a strange and terrible confession. The child who has just been brought back to the house is Durham's own son. He was stolen by Lady Faulkner for reasons of her own. The woman who helped her to kidnap the child was the quack doctor, Mme. Koluchy."

160

"Mme. Koluchy?" said Dr. Curzon.

"The same," I answered; "the cleverest and the most wicked woman in London—a past-master in every shade of crime. Beyond doubt, Madame is at the bottom of Durham's illness. She is poisoning him—we have got to discover how. I thought it necessary to tell you as much, Dr. Curzon. Now, will you come back with me again to the sick-room?"

The doctor followed me without a word.

Once more I bent over Durham, and as I did so the memory of where I had seen similar markings returned to me. I had seen them on photographic plates which had been exposed to the induction action of a brush discharge of high electro-motive force from the positive terminal of a Plante Rheostatic machine. An eminent electrician had drawn my attention to these markings at the time, had shown me the plates, and remarked upon the strange effects. Could there be any relationship of cause and effect here?

"Has any kind of electrical treatment been tried?" I asked, turning to Dr. Curzon.

"None," he answered. "Why do you ask?"

"Because," I said, "I have seen similar effects produced on the skin by prolonged exposure to powerful X-rays, and the appearance of Durham's face suggests that the skin might have been subjected to a powerful discharge from a focus tube."

"There has been no electricity employed, nor has any stranger been near the patient."

He was about to proceed, when I suddenly raised my hand.

"Hush!" I cried, "stay quiet a moment."

There was immediately a dead silence in the room.

The dying man breathed more and more feebly. His face beneath the dreadful star-like markings looked as if he were already dead.

Was I a victim to my own fancies, or did I hear muffled, distant and faint the sound I somehow expected to hear—the sound of a low hum a long way off? An ungovernable excitement seized me.

"Do you hear? Do you hear?" I asked grasping Curzon's arm.

"I hear nothing. What do you expect to hear?" he said, fear dawning in his eyes.

"Who is in the next room through there?" I asked, bending over the sick man and touching the wall behind his head.

"That room belongs to the next house, sir," said the nurse.

"Then, if that is so, we may have got the solution," I said. "Curzon, Dufrayer, come with me at once."

We hurried out of the room.

"We must get into the next house without a moment's delay," I said.

"Into the next house? You must be mad," said the doctor.

"I am not. I have already told you that there is foul play in this extraordinary case, and a fearful explanation of Durham's illness has suddenly occurred to me. I have given a great deal of time lately to the study of the effect of powerful cathode and X-rays. The appearance of the markings on Durham's face are suspicious. Will you send a messenger at once to my house for my fluorescent screen?"

"I will fetch it," said Dufrayer. He hurried off.

"The next thing to be done is to move the bed on which the sick man lies to the opposite side of the room," I said.

Curzon watched me as I spoke, with a queer expression on his face.

"It shall be done," he said briefly. We returned to the sick-room.

In less than an hour my fluorescent screen was in my hand. I held it up to the wall just where Durham's bed had been. It immediately became fluorescent, but we could make nothing out. This fact, however, converted my suspicions into certainties.

"I thought so," I said. "Who owns the next house?"

I rushed downstairs to question the servants. They could only tell me that it had been unoccupied for some time, but that the board "To let" had a month ago been removed. They did not believe that the new occupants had yet taken possession.

Dufrayer and I went into the street and looked at the windows. The house was to all appearance the counterpart of the one in which Durham lived. Dufrayer, who was now as much excited as I was, rushed off to the nearest fire-engine station, and quickly returned with an escape ladder. This was put up to one of the upper windows and we managed to get in. The next instant we were inside the house, and the low hum of a "make and break" fell on our ears. We entered a room answering to the one where Durham's bedroom was situated, and there immediately discovered the key to the diabolical mystery.

Close against the wall, within a few feet of where the sick man's bed had been, was an enormous focus tube, the platinum electrode turned so as to direct the rays through the wall. The machine was clamped in a holder, and stood on a square deal table, upon which also stood the most enormous induction coil I had ever seen. This was supplied from the main through wires coming from the electric light supplied to the house. This induction coil gave a spark of at least twenty-four inches. Insulated wires from it ran across the room, to a hole in the farther wall into the next room, where the "make and break" was whirring. This had evidently been done in order that the noise of the hum should be as far away as possible.

"Constant powerful discharges of cathode and X-rays, such as must have been playing upon Durham for days and nights continuously, are now proved to be so injurious to life, that he would in all probability have been dead before the morning," I cried. "As it is, we may save him." Then I turned and grasped Dufrayer by the arm.

"I believe that at last we have evidence to convict Mme. Koluchy," I exclaimed. "What with Lady Faulkner's confession, and——"

"Let us go back at once and speak to Lady Faulkner," said Dufrayer.

We returned at once to the next house, but the woman whom we sought had already vanished. How she had gone, and when, no one knew.

The next day we learned that Mme. Koluchy had also left London, and that it was not certain when she would return. Doubtless, Lady Faulkner, having confessed, in a moment of terrible agitation, had then flown to Mme. Koluchy for protection. From that hour to now we have heard nothing more of the unfortunate young woman. Her husband is moving Heaven and earth to find her, but in vain.

Removed from the fatal influence of the rays Durham has recovered, and the joy of having his little son restored to him has doubtless been his best medicine.

Chapter VII

THE IRON CIRCLET

MADAME had left London, and my first wild hope was that she might not return; but this was quickly doomed to disappointment, for two months after the events related in the last story, as I was walking down Welbeck Street I noticed that the blinds in her house were up, that there were fresh curtains to the windows, and that the place bore all the usual marks of habitation. With a sinking heart I was just commenting on this fact when I saw the hall door open, and a slender, dark-eyed young woman run down the steps. She glanced at me, raised her brows very slightly as if she recognized me, half paused as if about to speak, then changed her mind and walked rapidly just a few paces in front of me down the street. I had certainly never seen her before, and pitying her as in all probability one of Madame's victims, went on my own way.

In the course of the same afternoon I visited Dufrayer at his office. A glance at his face showed me that he had something to say. He drew me aside with a certain eagerness, and began to speak.

"I really believe," he cried, "that the tide has turned at last. Madame is so emboldened by her success that she is certain to do something foolish."

"She is back in town," I interrupted. "I passed her house this morning and——"

"She returned about a fortnight ago," interrupted Dufrayer. "Now, listen, Head, I have something to tell you. You know that for a long time Tyler's agents have been following Mme. Koluchy? It was only yesterday morning that Tyler drew my attention to a matter which looks uncommonly suspicious. But read this advertisement for yourself."

As he spoke, Dufrayer handed me the Times of a week back. Under the heading "Situations Vacant," he pointed to the following words:——

WANTED a first-rate Bacteriologist to advise on a matter of a very private nature. Handsome remuneration to any one possessing the necessary knowledge. Apply, in strict privacy by letter only to K.K., 350, Times Office, E.C.

I put the paper down.

"What is there suspicious about that?" I asked.

"At first sight one would think nothing," was the answer; "but Tyler is so alert that not a single thing escapes him now. The 'K.K.' first aroused his sense of inquiry."

"Katherine Koluchy!" I cried. "Surely, if this were an advertisement put in by Madame, she would not, knowing how she is wanted, use her own initials?"

"It seems scarcely likely," he answered, "but I will tell you exactly what has happened. On seeing the advertisement Tyler at once posted a man in the Times advertisement office, explaining his business to the clerks. Tyler's man was instructed how to proceed. About eleven o'clock on the morning after the advertisement was first published a person arrived, received two letters, and went away. Tyler's clerk immediately followed this man, who went straight to Mme. Koluchy's house. It was a lucky shot of Tyler's, and they are following up the scent closely. He has further discovered that they have engaged no less a person than the well-known bacteriologist, James Lockhart, to undertake this very mysterious business. His private laboratory is in Devonshire Street. The question now arises: What steps are we to take?"

"I see that you have an idea," I replied.

"Well, I have; or, rather, it is Tyler's—he suggests a bold step. He thinks that you and I ought to call on Lockhart. There is no question with regard to his position and knowledge. He has done more original work during the last two years in bacteriology than any one else in the country, and if this terrible Brotherhood should worm some secret out of him on a plausible pretext, they may use it to deadly effect, making him the unsuspecting agent of a terrible crime. Knowing all that we do, Head, I think we are bound to see him."

I thought over Dufrayer's suggestion.

"I am puzzled to know what to say," was my reply. "Lockhart may not like our interfering."

"Very possibly; but, nevertheless, the duty of warning him remains the same."

"If you feel so, Dufrayer, I have no doubt you are right," I said. "When will you go to see Lockhart? I shall, of course, be willing to accompany you."

"I cannot look him up to-day, for I am unfortunately busy at the courts to the last moment; but I suggest that you and I go to his house to-morrow morning at ten."

"Very well," I answered; "I will meet you outside his door at that hour."

A few minutes later I left Dufrayer. Absorbed in anxious thought, I presently found myself in Piccadilly, and then in Bond Street. I walked on slowly—my thoughts were so anxious that they seemed to impede my movements.

Madame had returned. Once again she was at work on some hideous machination. Once again Dufrayer and I held our lives in our hands. Knowing the woman as I did, I could scarcely agree with Dufrayer that, emboldened by success, she was becoming less cautious. Never yet was she known to allow her vigilance to sleep, and not even in the hour of victory would it fail her. On the face of it, this very open advertisement looked queer, but surely there was more behind. Yes, we must warn Lockhart. He would resent our interfering, but what matter? He was a strong man in every sense of the word, and I rather wondered at Madame selecting him to do her deadly work. I had seen him more than once during the last couple of years. His remarkable genius and the brilliancy of some of his lectures before the Royal Society returned vividly to my memory.

The hour was now between four and five. I suddenly remembered that I had promised to meet a man in some tea-rooms which had lately been opened in Bond Street. I found the right place, and walked down a long, narrow passage, which opened into a small courtyard surrounded by coffee—and tea-rooms of different descriptions. The seclusion and unexpected quiet of the place were refreshing; the soft notes of distant music took my steps upstairs to the first floor, and the next instant I had entered a tea-room, as still and peaceful as if London were miles away. Some girls, tastefully dressed and looking like ladies, were waiting on the visitors. I seated myself at a small table and waited for my friend. I looked at my watch—he was late. I resolved to wait for him for a few moments, but before many had passed, one of the young waitresses approached me with a telegram, asking if my name was Head. I replied in the affirmative, and tore it open. It was from my friend. He had suddenly been called out of town, and could not keep his appointment. I ordered tea for myself, and leaning back in my chair looked around me. The room was tastefully decorated with a certain aiming after simplicity, which produced a most inviting effect. My tea was brought on a small tray, and at the same time a girl, very quietly dressed, took the place opposite to mine. My first glance caused me to look at her again. She was the dark-eyed girl whom I had seen that morning coming down Mme. Koluchy's steps. I observed that her eyes, larger than those of most Englishwomen, wore a strained expression; otherwise she was fresh and young-looking.

I poured out a cup of tea and was just raising it to my lips, when she suddenly bent forward.

"I am addressing Mr. Norman Head, am I not?" she said, in a low, hurried voice.

I bowed coldly in acknowledgement.

"Forgive me," she said again. "I know that you are very much surprised at my addressing you, but I must tell you the simple truth. I meant to speak to you this morning outside Mme. Koluchy's house, but I could not summon courage. I happened to be in Bond Street just now, and saw you passing. You entered here, and I followed you. I know I have taken a very bold step, but I cannot rest until I tell you something: it is not a message of any sort, but it is a word of warning."

I made an impatient exclamation.

"If you have anything to say I must, of course, listen," I replied; "but, remember, you are a total stranger to me."

"I will tell you my name," she said eagerly. "Valentia Ward. I am Mr. Lockhart's secretary. You know Mr. Lockhart, of 205, Devonshire Street, do you not?"

"By name, well. You allude to the great bacteriologist?"

"Yes," she answered; "I have been his secretary for over a year. I work with him every morning in his laboratory. It is about him, and also about you, Mr. Head, that I want to speak."

"Well, say what you have to say as quickly as possible," I replied.

"I will do so. Bend forward a little, so that others may not overhear."

She poured herself out a cup of tea as she uttered the last words. Her hand shook slightly. It was a delicate and very small white hand, the blue veins showing under the skin.

"I happen to know," she continued, "no matter how or why, that you, Mr. Head, and a certain Mr. Dufrayer, a well-known criminal solicitor, intend to follow up an advertisement which appeared in the Times of this day week. The advertisement was to the effect that a first-rate bacteriologist was required to advise on a matter of a private nature. Mr. Dufrayer has learned, no matter how, that Mr. James Lockhart, of 205, Devonshire Street, has been appointed to undertake the work. It is your intention, and also Mr. Dufrayer's, to call upon him in order to warn him with regard to some hidden danger. Am I not right?"

"You must forgive me, but I cannot reply to your question."

She smiled very faintly.

"You are a wise man to guard your lips, but your face is my answer," she said. "Now I will tell you why I have ventured to speak to you. I want you to give up your intention of calling on Mr. Lockhart."

"And by what right do you, a complete stranger, interfere with my movements?"

"By the right of my superior knowledge," she answered at once. "My reasons I cannot explain, but they are of the gravest character. You and your friend will implicate yourselves most seriously if you do what you intend to do. You will run into danger if you meddle in this matter. In giving you this warning I risk much myself, and I earnestly beseech of you to believe me and to attend to my words. Do not see Mr. Lockhart. Let the advertisement alone. By so doing you will circumvent—you will circumvent—-" Her lips trembled, fire shone in her big eyes, she rose to her feet.

"I can do no more," she said. "If you fail to understand me I am sorry, but I have at least performed a very painful and necessary duty."

She drew down her veil, went to a little table near the door, where an accountant sat, paid for her tea, and left the room.

I sat on where she had left me, feeling puzzled and shaken. The girl's face bore the impress of truth, and yet it seemed hard not to believe that she was one of Madame's agents. Had I not actually seen her coming down the steps of Madame's house? She seemed troubled when she spoke. When she pleaded with me, her voice shook with the extreme and passionate eagerness of her words. But all these signs might only be put on in order to prevent an interference, which Madame, from long experience, had learned to dread.

When I met Dufrayer on the following morning outside Lockhart's house, I took his arm, and walked with him for a moment or two up and down the street. I then related briefly the incident of the day before. He listened to my words with marked attention.

"What do you think?" I said, when I had concluded.

"That beyond doubt the girl has been employed to warn you," was his reply. "Lockhart's danger is even greater than I was at first inclined to suspect. If he is not very careful he will find himself in a hornet's nest. Yes, we must warn him immediately. It is past ten—let us ring the bell; he will probably be at home."

In reply to our summons, we were told that Mr. Lockhart was within, and were shown at once into a private room next to his laboratory. He joined us almost immediately. His appearance was already well known to me, but when he entered the room I was struck once again by his remarkable personality. He was a tall and very heavily built man, standing quite six feet, with broad shoulders, and a jovial red face, as unlike the typical scientist as man could be. His manner was bluff and hearty, and he had a merry smile, suggestive more of a country squire than of one who spent most of his time over culture plates.

"What can I do for you, sir?" he asked genially, extending his hand to me. "Your name, Mr. Head, is not unfamiliar to me; and if I remember aright, we were once antagonists in print in a discussion on Nitrifying Bacteria. I am afraid in the end I had to yield to your superior knowledge, but I should like now to show you a little thing which may change your views."

"Thank you," I answered, "but I have not called to discuss your work. May I introduce my friend, Mr. Dufrayer? He and I have come here this morning on a matter which we believe to be of the utmost importance. It is of a strictly private nature, and when you have heard what we have both got to say, you will, I am sure, pardon what must seem an unwarrantable espionage."

He raised his eyebrows, and looked from Dufrayer to me in some astonishment.

I drew a copy of the Times from my pocket, and pointed to the advertisement. As I did so I noticed for the first time that the door between this room and the next was open, and at the same instant the distinct noise of breaking glass came to my ears.

"Pardon me a moment," said Lockhart; "my secretary is in the next room, and you would rather that no one overheard us. I will just go to her, and ask her to do some work in my study."

Still retaining the copy of the Times in his hand, he entered a large laboratory, where doubtless his own important discoveries were made.

"Ah! Miss Ward," he exclaimed, "so you have broken that culture tube. Well, never mind now; don't wait to pick up the fragments, I am particularly engaged. There are letters which I want you to copy in my study; you can go there until I send for you."

The light steps of a young woman were heard leaving the room; a door was opened at the farther end and closed again softly. Lockhart returned to us.

"I am fortunate," he said, "in having secured as my secretary a most intelligent and clever girl, one in a thousand. At one time she thought of embracing the medical profession, and has studied bacteriology a little herself; but what possessed her to break a valuable culture tube just now is more than I can understand. Poor girl, she was quite white and trembling when I went into the room, and yet I am never harsh to her. Her name is Valentia Ward, a pretty creature, and a better secretary than any man I have ever come across. But there, gentlemen, you must pardon my alluding to my own private affairs. The loss of that culture tube has upset me a trifle, but I shall soon put matters right, and Miss Ward need not have looked so stricken. Now let us attend to business. You speak of an advertisement in this paper—where is it? Is it to-day's edition?"

"No, the edition of a week back," I replied. "I have reason to know, Mr. Lockhart, that you have answered this advertisement. Pray glance your eye over it again—it is in your own interests that my friend and I have come here to-day."

"I fail to understand," said Lockhart, a trifle coldly.

"I will gladly explain," I said. "We have the strongest reasons for suspecting that these words were inserted by a well-known lady doctor called Mme. Koluchy."

"Still, I do not perceive your meaning," he replied. "Even granted that such is the case, may I ask what business this is of yours?"

"You certainly may. Our business is to warn you against any dealings with that woman."

"Indeed! But the lady in question is well known, and her scientific attainments are respected by every scientist in the kingdom. I think we must either close our present interview, or I must beg of you to give me a further explanation."

"As honourable men we can speak quite plainly," I replied. "However impossible it may seem to you, I am now prepared to tell you that Mme. Koluchy is the head of a gang, or secret society, whose head-quarters are at present in London. This society is perpetrating some of the most terrible crimes the century has known. I could mention half a dozen which would be familiar to you. Up till now Madame has eluded justice with a most remarkable ingenuity, but she cannot do so much longer. All my friend and I beg of you is to have nothing to do with her, and, beyond all other things, not to put into her hands or into the hands of any of her confederates one or more of the great secrets of bacteriology. You know as well as I do how omnipotent such powers would be in the hands of the unscrupulous."

While I was speaking Lockhart's red face became troubled. He wrinkled his forehead and knit his brows.

"What you have told me sounds almost incredible," he said, at last. "I suppose I ought to be obliged to you, but I scarcely know that I am. You have upset my confidence, and sown doubt where I must frankly say I had absolute faith. Since, however, you have spoken to me so frankly, it is but fair that I should tell you what I know of this matter. It is true that I did see that advertisement in the Times, and replied to it. Famous bacteriologist as I doubtless am, I am also a poor man. Pure science, as you know, Mr. Head,

173

brings riches to none. I answered the advertisement, and received almost immediately afterwards a letter from Mme. Koluchy asking me to call upon her at her house in Welbeck Street. She received me in her consulting-room, and put a few questions to me. I found her frank and agreeable, and there was nothing in the least sinister, either in her manner or in the disclosures which she was obliged to make to me. She soon perceived that I was admirably adapted to carry out her requirements, said that she would give me the work if I cared to undertake it, and on my promising to do so proceeded at once to business. I cannot divulge the nature of the research which I am about to make on her behalf, as I am under a solemn vow not to do so, but I can at least assure you that it is a perfectly honourable matter, and the pay—well, the pay is so good that I cannot afford to lose it. Mme. Koluchy is prepared to give me what may mean a small fortune. But I will tell you this, Mr. Head: if I find out that what you have just said is really the case, and I see the smallest likelihood of my information being used for dishonourable purposes, I shall withdraw."

"You cannot do more," I answered, "and I am much obliged to you for listening to us so patiently."

"I respect the honesty of your purpose," he said.

"May I also beg that you will regard what I have just said as strictly confidential?"

The ghost of a smile flitted across his face; it passed almost immediately.

"I will," he replied.

"It seems hard to press you still further," said Dufrayer; "but, short of abusing any confidence you may have made with Mme. Koluchy, would it be possible for you to keep us posted in what goes on?"

"I think I may promise that also, and, as a preliminary, I may as well say that I expect to leave town at a moment's notice on this very business. I do not know where I am going, for I have not yet received full instructions. It occurs to me, that if matters are really as serious as you think them to be, it would be as well for me to go, in order to make Mme. Koluchy show her hand."

"Yes," replied Dufrayer, "you are right there, Mr. Lockhart. The interests involved are so enormous that we shall only be able to defeat our enemies on their own ground; but if you happen to be going to a lonely part of the country, do not, I beg of you, go unarmed, and also communicate freely with Mr. Head or myself. You need have no fear, as our agents and detectives will be ready and alert, and will follow you anywhere."

Again that almost imperceptible smile passed across his face. Certainly, to look at him, he did not appear to be a man to want much protection in case of a personal encounter. His huge frame-towered above Dufrayer and myself as he rose and conducted us to the door.

"Well," said Dufrayer, when we got outside, "what do you think of it all? My own opinion is," he added, without waiting for me to speak, "that we shall have them this time. Madame has not conducted this matter with half of her usual acumen. Her successes have rendered her thoroughly contemptuous of us. Depend upon it, she will soon learn her lesson."

"And what about Miss Valentia Ward?" I cried. "From Lockhart's manner he seems to place absolute trust in her, and yet either there is grave mischief ahead, of which we know nothing or the girl is in Madame's pay."

"I have not the slightest doubt which way the balance lies," said Dufrayer; "but Lockhart has been warned by us, and he is quite capable of looking after himself. We could not well betray Miss Ward. Having neglected her advice, we show her very plainly that we do not believe the cock-and-bull story she tried to tempt you with."

"And yet the girl looked as if she spoke the truth," I answered.

"Ah, Head, you were always influenced by a pretty face," said Dufrayer. "Had Miss Ward been old and wrinkled, you would have treated her cool attempt to impose upon you with the harshness it deserves."

"She was agitated and upset to-day, at any rate," I replied. "Beyond doubt, it was nervousness at suddenly hearing our voices which caused her to break that culture tube."

Dufrayer said nothing further, and I went to my own house.

All during the day which followed I could not get either Lockhart or his secretary out of my head, and more than once I congratulated myself upon having acted so promptly on Dufrayer's advice. Having opened Lockhart's eyes, it was scarcely likely that he would be hoodwinked now; and if Madame herself did not fall into our hands, in all probability some of her gang would.

Between four and five on the afternoon of that same day, to my great astonishment, Lockhart was shown into my laboratory. His fat face was redder than ever, and he was panting with excitement.

"Ah!" he said, when he saw me, "I hope I am in time. Get ready quickly, Mr. Head." He took out his handkerchief and began to mop his face.

"I have suddenly received orders to go down from Waterloo by the 5.10 to Lymington, in Hampshire, and to bring three broth cultures of a certain bacillus with me. I am to be met at Lymington by a boat. Beyond this I know nothing. During the day which has passed I have thought more than once of what you have told me, and I will confess that my suspicions are aroused. On receiving this sudden summons, it occurred to me that if you were to accompany me we could see for ourselves what the matter really means, and perhaps be able to frustrate Madame's plans. Can you manage to come? If so, we have not a single moment to lose—my cab is waiting at the door."

"By Jove! this looks really like business," I said; "but I ought to let Dufrayer know."

"You have no time to do so now. We can barely manage to get the train by going straight off. If we reach Waterloo in time, we can send your friend a telegram from there."

"True," I answered; "I will go with you at once."

Lockhart glanced impatiently at his watch.

"It is more than half-past four," he said; "it will be a gallop to the station as it is."

I considered for a moment. There was no time to pack anything, and I dared not lose what might be the opportunity that I had so longed to meet. I ran upstairs, put on a Norfolk suit and travelling cap, and thrust a revolver into my pocket. I then joined my companion.

"Is there any chance of your being watched to see if you come down alone?" I said, as our cab dashed along the Marylebone Road.

Lockhart turned and stared at me without replying.

"I have not thought of that," he said, at last.

"It is a possible contingency," I answered. "I know the wariness of my enemy. Had we not better go down to Lymington in separate carriages? When we get there it will be dark, and we can start off together without being observed."

"That would be a good plan," he replied. "I will go third-class, you can go first."

The clock pointed to eight minutes past five as we dashed up the incline to Waterloo. We rushed for our tickets, and just as the doors were being closed were running up the platform towards the train. As I flew past the third-class compartments to my own more luxurious carriage, I fancied I saw in one, marked "Ladies only," a face pressed against the window and watching me. It was the face of a woman with dark eyes. It appeared for a flash, and then disappeared behind a curtain. My heart sank with sick apprehension. If Valentia Ward were indeed following us to Lymington there was no doubt whatever that she was one of Madame's accomplices. She knew that I had met Lockhart contrary to her warning, and was now, doubtless, hurrying to Yarmouth to reveal the truth to Madame.

The train sped on, and my thoughts continued to be both busy and anxious. The face with its dark eyes pursued me, turn where I would. I now regretted that a certain sense of honour had forbade my telling Lockhart of my suspicions that morning, and I determined to do so when we reached Lymington.

There was no change at Brockenhurst, and at half-past eight we drew up at Lymington Pier. Pulling the collar of my Norfolk jacket well up, and drawing down my cap over my eyes, I stepped out. Lockhart passed me, pushed slightly against me in doing so, and slipped a note into my hand. I glanced at this at once.

"Go in the boat to Yarmouth, and then on to Freshwater. I am coming over in a private boat," he wrote.

I looked up quickly. Already he was lost in the throng of passengers who had left the train. I had no opportunity to give him any warning; there was nothing for it but to obey his directions—take a ticket to Yarmouth and hasten on board. In a few moments I found myself steaming down the river and out into the Solent. The sun had set, and the moon would not rise for an hour or two. I stood on deck looking back at the lights of Lymington as they were reflected in the water. Suddenly I felt some one touch me. I looked round, and Miss Ward was by my side.

"You have disregarded my advice," she said; "you are in great danger. Don't land at Yarmouth. Take the return boat to Lymington."

Her voice was so earnest, and there was such a ring of real distress in it, that, try as I would, I could scarcely treat her with the harshness which I thought her conduct deserved.

"You are a woman," I began, "but—-"

"Oh, I know all that you think of me," she answered, "but the risk is too terrible, and my duty too plain, for any harsh judgment of yours to influence me. Go back, go back while there is time."

"I cannot understand you," I said. "You warn me of some vague danger, and yet you allow Lockhart, the man who employs you, to run into what, according to your own showing, is a trap for his destruction. How can I respect you or believe your words when you act in such a manner?"

"I dare not tell you the whole truth," she answered. "I wish I had courage, but it means too much. Mr. Lockhart is in no danger; you are. Won't you go back—won't you be guided by me?"

"No," I said; "where he goes, I will go; his danger is mine also. Miss Ward, you are implicating yourself in the queerest way; you are showing me all too plainly that you are on the side of—-"

"You think that I am Mme. Koluchy's agent?" she answered. "Well, there is only one way of saving you! I tried yesterday to do what I could; you would not be warned. When I heard your voice, and that of your friend, in Mr. Lockhart's dining-room this morning, my agitation was so great that I almost betrayed myself. On your behalf I have listened, and watched, and acted the spy all day. You can scarcely realize what my awful position is. But, if you will not yield to my entreaties, I must tell you everything."

Just then, a friend whom I happened to know, and who lived at Yarmouth, came up, uttered an exclamation of astonishment, and drew me aside. He invited me to spend the night with him, but knowing that Lockhart expected me at Freshwater, I declined his invitation. I was glad of the interruption, and kept by his side until we reached the pier at Yarmouth. I then looked round for Miss Ward, but she had disappeared.

I now hoped that I had escaped her altogether. I took a carriage and drove to the hotel at Freshwater, where I intended staying until Lockhart communicated with me. I knew the place well, having spent many a summer holiday there in my young days.

The hotel was nearly empty, the season not having yet begun, and I found myself the only occupant of the coffee-room. I ordered a hasty meal, and was just beginning to eat when a lady dressed in black entered the room and sat down at a distant table. A waiter came up and asked if she wanted anything. She ordered a cup of coffee, which was presently brought to her. I do not think she touched it. I saw her slowly stirring it with her teaspoon; she raised her eyes and encountered mine. She was Miss Ward. I perceived she had followed me. My dinner became instantly distasteful. I took up a paper and pretended to read. In a few moments a waiter brought me a note. I tore it open. It ran as follows:

"I am staying here at a big house called the Towers, where the work is to be done. Come up path by cliff towards the golf links. Will meet you there. We can talk alone and arrange our plans. This is a matter of life and death."

I thrust the note into my coat-pocket and, raising my eyes, saw that Miss Ward had left her seat and come up to my table.

"You are to meet Mr. Lockhart on the path by the cliff towards the golf links?" she said, in an interrogative voice.

I made no reply.

"If you go I shall go also," she continued. "By so doing I put myself into the most deadly peril. Will not the thought of my danger influence you?"

"It is not necessary for you to go, and it is for me," I replied. "Miss Ward, I cannot understand your motive, nor why you persist in harassing me as you are doing, but I can only act on my own judgment and as I think best Leave me now to my fate, whatever it is. I have my work to do and must do it."

"Then it will be as I said," she answered. "You are imperilling your life and mine, but I have spoken—I can add no more."

She left the room, closing the door after her.

Making a great effort, I tried to banish her words and her strange persistency from my mind. I put on my hat and started off. I went down the lawn, crossed the little front parade, and began to ascend the pathway. I walked on for about half a mile, along the edge of the cliff, looking to right and left for Lockhart. My mind was torn with conflicting thoughts. Should I tell Lockhart about Miss Ward, or should I forbear? Was there by any possibility some truth in the wild words of this girl, who had followed me down to this lonely place on a quest of such evident peril? I had always prided myself on reading character well, and the straight glance of those dark and troubled eyes added now to my perplexity. She looked like one who was speaking the truth. Still, to believe her was impossible, for to believe her was to doubt Lockhart.

I walked on, wondering that he had not yet put in an appearance. I was now close to the golf links. Suddenly I heard to my right, and not a long way off, the sharp cry of a woman. It came on the night breeze, once, twice, then there was no further sound. I rushed in the direction from which the cry had come, and the next moment stumbled up against Lockhart. He spoke in an eager voice—there was a tremble in it.

"They have got me down here on some cock-and-bull idea of analyzing the water supply," he exclaimed.

"But," I interrupted, "did you not hear that cry, a woman in some sort of trouble—did you not hear it?"

"No, I can't say I did," he answered. "What is the matter with you, Head—you look quite overcome?"

"There was a sound just beyond you as if a woman was in trouble," I continued. "She cried out twice; are you certain you did not hear her?"

"Quite certain," he replied. "But let us listen for a moment. If we hear it again, we must of course go to the rescue."

We both stood still. The huge form of the bacteriologist was between me and the sea. Not a sound broke the stillness. The night was dark but quite calm, the moon had not yet risen, only the distant roar of the waves came up to us as we listened.

"You mistook the cry of one of the numerous sea-birds about here for that of a woman," said Lockhart; "but, be it woman or not, I am afraid we have no time to attend to it any longer. Do you know that the tubes I brought with me have been stolen? But I was too clever for my foes, whoever they are. I suspected mischief, and threw the real culture away while we were crossing the Solent, and substituted plain broth in its stead. Now, what are we to do? This is a very ill-protected place, and I believe there is only one policeman."

"We must stay quiet until the morning," I answered, "and then get help from Newport. With our evidence they have not the ghost of a chance. But, Lockhart, I have something painful to tell you. Your secretary——"

"Valentia Ward! What do you mean? Oh, don't worry about her now—she is safe in London. We shall catch the whole gang by the first light, if we are wary."

We continued to walk on and to talk in low voices. Now and then I observed that Lockhart glanced behind him. It was evident to me that he was in a state of extreme nervous tension. As for me, I could not get that startled and anguished cry out of my ears. I wished now that I had insisted on making a more thorough search when I had first heard it.

Suddenly, as we walked, I caught sight of a low shed in a hollow. It was partly surrounded by broken-down trees.

"Let us make for that old golf-house," said Lockhart. "It has been long unoccupied; we shall be safe from any observation there, and can discuss our plans in quiet."

I instantly acquiesced. I had made up my mind to tell Lockhart all about Miss Ward. I thought that I could do so best there.

We entered the dark shadow of the trees, and as we did so I detected a light between the chinks in the walls. I started back.

"Look!" I whispered, "the house is not unoccupied—they suspect us already. Let us go back."

"No time for that now," he answered, hardly breathing the words, they were uttered so low; "it is true there is some one there—some one you would like to meet."

Before I could move a step or utter a single cry he had flung me on the grass, his great hands clutched at my throat like a vice, and with all the weight of his huge body he knelt upon my chest and pinned me to the ground. The sudden violence of the attack, the awful conviction that Valentia Ward had indeed warned me of a terrible danger, and that I myself was the duped victim of some hideous plot, completely stunned me and paralyzed resistance. The cruel hands crushed my throat and light swam before my eyes. I felt dimly, without comprehending it, that my last hour had come. The earth seemed to recede away, and I remembered no more.

When I returned to consciousness I was lying on a rough deal table inside the shed. I tried to move, but quickly discovered that I was both gagged and bound. By the dim light I could further see that I was surrounded by four men. They were all masked. Yes, at last I was in the clutch of the Brotherhood. As I watched, too stunned to realize all the awful meaning of the scene in which I found myself, another figure also masked—slowly entered the room. It came forward and stood over me. My blood froze, for a pair of eyes of terrible power and Satanic beauty looked into mine. I had seen them before, and even through the disguise of the mask I knew them. It was the voice of Mme. Koluchy herself that spoke. The words which now fell upon my ears I had heard from those same lips years ago in Naples.

"For a traitor to this Brotherhood there is but one penalty. Death!"

Then followed clear and concise the words of the sentence. They were spoken in Italian, but the last words were English.

"And neither earth nor sea shall hold his body, but it shall be rent asunder between them."

A dead silence followed the uttering of this sentence. Without a word, two of the men lifted me in their arms and carried me out. One of them I felt certain by his size and bulk must be Lockhart himself.

The little procession moved slowly down the path to Compton Bay, just below. I now abandoned all hope. Mme. Koluchy had won, and I had lost. I had, indeed, been the victim of the cruellest and the most astute foe in the world. But Lockhart—Lockhart, whom I had trusted! His name was well known in the scientific world. All men sang his praises, for was he not by his recent discoveries one of the benefactors of the race; and yet—and yet—my dizzy brain almost turned at the thought—he was in reality one of Madame's own satellites, a member of the Brotherhood of the Seven Kings. I saw, when too late, the whole deadly trap into which I had walked. The advertisement had been meant to arouse my attention. I had been inveigled down to Freshwater by means which only Mme. Koluchy could devise. Lockhart was my decoy. Why had I not listened to the words of the brave girl who had truly risked her life for me? That twice-repeated cry must have come from her lips. Without doubt, in trying to follow me she had been captured by our deadly enemy. Lockhart himself, in all probability, had done the deed. Had I not met him coming up the path in the direction from which the cry had sounded? What ghastly doom was even now hanging over her head?

While my heart beat wildly in my ears, and my brain swam, and my eyes were dizzy, wild thoughts such as the above came and flashed before me. Then there came a dizzy moment when all was blank, and then again the cloud was lifted, and Madame's sentence as she bent over me filled the entire horizon.

"Neither earth nor sea shall hold his body, but it shall be rent asunder between them," she had said. Death awaited me beyond doubt, but I had yet to learn what a lingering death was to be mine.

We reached the sands, and I perceived lying at anchor within half a mile of the shore a small steam yacht. So this was the way Madame and her satellites had come here. Doubtless, when they had sealed the doom of their victims, they would sail away and never return. But where was the girl? She was certainly not in the old golf-house; what had they done with her?

I was lifted into a boat. Four men took the oars, and Madame Koluchy, still wearing her mask, sat in the stern and steered. Were we going to the yacht? No. The men pulled the boat rapidly along, beneath the white chalk cliffs that towered above us. It was high tide, and the water rose in crested waves against the face of the cliffs. Suddenly we headed sharply round, and the men, shipping their oars, shot the boat beneath an overhanging lip into one of the chalk caverns that abound along the coast. I knew that I was entering my tomb. One of the oarsmen now lit a torch, and I at once saw something floating on the water, which looked like some heavy balks of timber lashed together to form a sort of raft. From the roof of the cave a chain was dangling. At the end of the chain was an iron circlet.

Rapidly, and without a word, the ruffians seized me and placed me standing upright on the raft. They quickly lashed my feet to the heavy block of wood with a strong rope. Another man snapped the iron ring round my neck, and the next instant they had pushed the boat back out of the cave. As they did so, I distinctly heard Lockhart's voice address Mme. Koluchy.

"The other boat is ready," he said.

"How long will it float?" asked Madame.

"From two to three hours," was the reply. "We shall lash her to the bottom, and—-"

The boat turned the corner, and I lost the remainder of the sentence. For a moment or two I thought of it, but the awful scene through which I had just passed confused my thoughts, and soon all feeling was concentrated on my own awful position.

My neck was fixed to the chain above, my feet to the timber in the sea below. The words of my terrible sentence burst upon me now with all their fiendish meaning. As the tide went down the whole weight of the raft would gradually drag my body from my head. The horror of such a fearful doom almost benumbed my faculties, and I stood as one already dead, being swayed up and down by the light swell that found its way into the cave.

"The moon rose presently, and its pale beams struck across my dungeon."

The moon rose presently, and its pale beams struck across my dungeon with a weird light. The moon that ruled the tide was to be a witness of her own work that night. I wondered vaguely how long I had to live; but Lockhart must have given me a violent blow when he felled me to the ground, and I was still more or less stunned. Gradually, however, the cool air which blew into the cave revived me, and I was able more thoroughly to realize the position. I now perceived that the chain had at least two feet of slack. Thus the Brotherhood had arranged to prolong my tortures. Was there the most remote possibility of escape? I laughed to myself, a horrible laugh, as the hopelessness of the whole thing rushed over me. And yet there was a mad passionate desire to make up to Miss Ward for my want of faith in her, which brought sudden fire to my heart and awoke each intellectual faculty to its fullest. She also was doomed. In what way and how, I had but the vaguest idea; but that her death was certain, I felt sure. If I could escape myself I might yet save her. To rescue her now seemed to be the one important thing left to me in the world. I could only manage it by setting myself free. My hands were lashed behind me, but not, I noticed, very tightly. This was, my conquerors knew, unnecessary, for even with them free I could neither, on account of the ring of iron which held my neck, bend down sufficiently far to release my feet, nor drag myself up by the chain, as my feet were secured to the raft, and the effort would be too tremendous—I should soon have to let go. I determined, however, to free my hands if I could, and at last, with great pain and difficulty, worked off the cords that bound my wrists. I then instantly removed the gag from my lips, and felt

186

a momentary sense of freedom. I stretched out my hands impotently. Could they not in some way help me?

My long scientific training enabled me now to think clearly and consecutively. The knowledge that on my life another in all probability depended spurred each endeavour to the highest point. This much at least was obvious. I could not stop the tide, nor release the iron ring from my neck, nor free my feet from the raft; but there was one thing just possible. Could it by any means be done? I grew cold with excitement as the thought struck me. Could I by any known means connect the raft with the slack of the chain above my head, and so let this connection, instead of my body, take the strain as the tide sank? If I could manage this, it might give time for possible relief to come. Surely it seemed a hopeless task, for I could not reach down my hands to the raft. But still, I determined to make the effort, herculean though it was. It would at any rate be better than the inaction of slowly waiting my doom. Each second the tide was sinking—each second therefore would render my task harder, as it would diminish the slack of the chain.

I rapidly unbuckled the strong leather belt from my waist, and tried to stoop down sufficiently far to slip the end of the belt underneath the ropes that bound my feet. It was useless. At my utmost stretch I could not reach the ropes. But, stay, if only a big swell would come, I might just slip the belt through the rope. I crouched as low as I could, waiting and ready. The precious time sped on. Suddenly I felt the raft dip deeply. I rose up to save my neck, and as the next wave lifted the raft high I crouched quickly down again, and just managed to slip the strap under the rope and through the buckle before the swell subsided. It was touch and go, but I had done it.

To connect the belt to the chain above my head was the next thing to try. I had still the cord that had bound my hands. One end of this I now lashed securely to the slack of the chain, but when I had done so I found that it was not quite long enough to reach the belt. I tore my strong silk scarf from my neck and fastened it to the cord, and thus managed at last to bind cord and belt together.

As I looked at the extraordinary rope which I had made for my deliverance my hope sank within me, for I felt certain that it was far too flimsy. The strain on it would become greater and greater each moment as the weight of the raft was thrown upon it. I seized the chain above my head with my hands, but I knew well that directly the connection gave way I should not be able to bear the strain on my arms for more than a moment, and when I released them I should be instantly strangled.

The terrible time dragged on, and the tide sank steadily lower and lower. I saw the silk scarf stretch, and could hear the belt below creaking with the weight at each fall of the swell. In a few seconds I knew it must go, and then all would be over. I closed my eyes. My hour had come. Madame had indeed won, and I had lost. But what was that? What had happened?

There was a loud crack, and I was sprawling on the raft. One glance showed me what had taken place. The iron ring in the rock, which would have been amply strong enough to bear the strain of strangling me, had yielded to the combined weight of myself and the raft, which had been half drawn out of the water. The ring had been suddenly torn from the rock. It was indeed a miraculous deliverance, for I did not believe the extempore rope would have held another second. Yes, the worst danger was over, but I was still in an evil plight. I quickly unlashed my feet, and then, with the ring of iron round my neck and the chain attached, sprang on to a projecting ledge of rock at the mouth of the cave. I saw to my joy that the fall of the tide was now on my side, for it had left me a means of regaining the sandy bay.

Plunging and stumbling, sometimes neck-deep in water, I at last reached the sands and fell down, trembling with exhaustion.

A dark bank of clouds had crept up and blotted out the moon. I struggled to my feet and looked out to sea. Where was Miss Ward? To go to her rescue now was my first and only duty. I gathered the long chain in my hand, and ran up the winding pathway to the summit of the cliff. My intention was to make my way with all possible speed across the Downs to Freshwater. I had gone about two hundred yards on the top of the cliff when I saw a man coming to meet me. I hurried up to him, and saw to my joy that he was one of the coastguards. I quickly told him my story, pointing as I spoke to my dripping clothes and to the chain about my neck.

The man was aghast, and stared at me with absolute amazement and horror.

"Well, sir," he replied, "and you think the young lady is in a similar plight?"

I told him what I had overheard Mme. Koluchy and Lockhart say.

"Then they have put her in a boat and allowed her to drift with the tide," said the man. "The tide is running out, and what wind there is is from the east. I have been a coastguard here for more than twenty years, but I'm blessed if ever I heard such a tale as this before."

"We must save her," I said. "What is the quickest way in which we can get a boat? If anything is to be done, there is not a moment to lose."

The man considered for a moment, without speaking.

"There's a gent down here for the summer," he said. "His name is Captain Oldham, and there's his yacht lying out yonder in the bay. Maybe he would let her go out again for such a thing as this. It's no use trying with a rowing boat. Captain Oldham has got a search-light on board, too."

"Is he on the yacht now?" I asked.

"Yes, sir; he's sleeping on board to-night, for he has only just come in from a cruise. The luck is on your side now."

"The very thing!" I cried. "Don't let us lose a single moment."

We ran down the road to the bay, and a few moments later my new friend and I were pulling rapidly out to Captain Oldham's yacht.

As we approached my companion hailed the man on watch, and the owner himself appeared as we scrambled up the ladder.

In the presence of the coastguard, I repeated my extraordinary story. The emphasis of my words, and the iron ring round my neck, carried conviction.

"And the girl risked her life for you?" said the old seaman, his eyes almost starting from his head in his excitement.

"That she did," I replied, "and I treated her brutally—I refused to believe in her."

"And you have good cause to think they set her adrift in a leaky boat?"

"I fear so, and I want to search these waters without an instant's delay."

"It shall be done," he cried. "My God! I never heard of such devilish cruelty."

He turned, and shouted his orders to the astonished engineer and crew. All possible haste was made, and I tried to control my own growing impatience in getting the search-light ready. I saw, with satisfaction, that it was one of the latest Admiralty pattern, such as the steamers use in the Suez Canal. There was a powerful arc-light supplied from an accumulator. The moon had sunk and it was quite dark now, but with this light not a speck on the sea would escape us within a radius of a mile.

I went forward, holding the light in its projecting apparatus, and in about ten minutes we were steaming out to sea. Regulating the apparatus with the hand-gear, I began to play the great light to and fro in front of us. Two of the crew stood beside me sharply on the look-out. We had already passed the Needles, but still there was nothing to be seen. Captain Oldham was at the wheel, and he now turned the yacht's head more determinedly out to sea. Mile after mile we went, without success. A hopeless despair began to creep over me. If that girl died, I felt that I could never hold up my head again. Suddenly one of the men beside me sang out:

"Skiff on the port beam, sir. Hard a starboard!"

The engine bell rang to "full speed," and in a short time I saw that we were quickly bearing down on what appeared to be an empty boat, aimlessly drifting with its gunwale nearly down to the water line. What did it mean? Was the girl really in the boat? Were we in time to save her?

The yacht stopped, a boat was lowered, and the coastguard and I and two of the men pulled for all we were worth towards her.

Lying at the bottom of the boat was the motionless form of a woman. Her head was just above water, her eyes were shut; she looked like one dead. One glance at her face was sufficient to show me who she was. Was I in time to save her?

We quickly released the thongs which bound the poor girl, and lifted her into our boat. From there we brought her quickly to the yacht.

"Take the boat in tow," I cried to one of the men; "we may get some evidence from her that will help us."

This was quickly done, and we were soon steaming back to Freshwater Bay.

Alas! however, my worst fears were confirmed. I was too late. All that was possible was done, but Valentia Ward never recovered. The shock and exposure had killed her. Thus my efforts on her behalf had proved unavailing. She had risked and lost her life for mine.

I telegraphed to Dufrayer early on the following morning, and he arrived at Freshwater at noon. To him I told my extraordinary and awful adventure.

One of our first cares was to examine the boat. We then perceived what Madame's fiendish cruelty really meant. A hole had been made in the bottom in such a way that the boat would take several hours to sink. Thus Valentia was also to be the victim of a lingering death. The name of the yacht to which the boat belonged had been carefully scraped off the side, thus obliterating any chance of obtaining evidence against Madame.

Chapter VIII

THE MYSTERY OF THE STRONG ROOM

LATE in the autumn of that same year Mme. Koluchy was once more back in town. There was a warrant out for the arrest of Lockhart, who had evidently fled the country; but Madame, still secure in her own invincible cunning, was at large. The firm conviction that she was even now preparing a mine for our destruction was the reverse of comforting, and Dufrayer and I spent many gloomy moments as we thought over the possibilities of our future.

On a certain evening towards the latter end of October I went to dine with my friend. I found him busy arranging his table, which was tastefully decorated, and laid for three.

"An unexpected guest is coming to dine," he said, as I entered the room. "I must speak to you alone before he arrives. Come into the smoking-room; he may be here at any moment."

I followed Dufrayer, who closed the door behind us.

"I must tell you everything and quickly," he began, "and I must also ask you to be guided by me. I have consulted with Tyler, and he says it is our best course."

"Well?" I interrupted.

"The name of the man who is coming here to-night is Maurice Carlton," continued Dufrayer. "His mother was a Greek, but on the father's side he comes of a good old English stock. He inherited a place in Norfolk, Cor Castle, from his father; but the late owner lost heavily on the turf, and in consequence the present man has endeavoured to retrieve his fortunes as a diamond merchant. I met him some years ago in Athens. He has been wonderfully successful, and is now, I believe—or, at least, so he says—one of the richest men in Europe. He called upon me with regard to some legal business, and in the course of conversation referred incidentally to Mme. Koluchy. I drew him out, and found that he knew a good deal about her, but what their actual relations are I cannot say. I was very careful not to commit myself, and after consideration decided to ask him to dine here to-night in order that we both might see him together. I have thought over everything carefully, and am quite sure our only course now is not to mention anything we know about Madame. We may only give ourselves away in doing so. By keeping quiet we shall have a far better chance of seeing what she is up to. You agree with me, don't you?"

"Surely we ought to acquaint Carlton with her true character?" I replied.

Dufrayer shrugged his shoulders impatiently.

"No," he said, "we have played that game too often, and you know what the result has been. Believe me, we shall serve both his interests and ours best by remaining quiet. Carlton is living now at his own place, but comes up to London constantly. About two years ago he married a young English lady, who was herself the widow of an Italian. I believe they have a son, but am not quite sure. He seems an uncommonly nice fellow himself, and I should say his wife was fortunate in her husband; but, there, I hear his ring—let us go into the next room."

We did so, and the next moment Carlton appeared. Dufrayer introduced him to me, and soon afterwards we went into the dining-room. Carlton was a handsome man, built on a somewhat massive scale. His face was of the Greek type, but his physique that of an Englishman. He had dark eyes, somewhat long and narrow, and apt, except when aroused, to wear a sleepy expression. It needed but a glance to show that in his blood was a mixture of the fiery East, with the nonchalance and suppression of all feeling which characterize John Bull. As I watched him, without appearing to do so, I came to the conclusion that I had seldom seen more perfect self-possession, or stronger indications of suppressed power.

As the meal proceeded, conversation grew brisk and brilliant. Carlton talked well, and, led on by Dufrayer, gave a short resumé of his life since they had last met.

194

"Yes," he said, "I am uncommonly lucky, and have done pretty well on the whole. Diamond dealing, as perhaps you know, is one of the most risky things that any man can take up, but my early training gave me a sound knowledge of the business, and I think I know what I am about. There is no trade to which the art of swindling has been more applied than to mine; but, there, I have had luck, immense luck, such as does not come to more than one man in a hundred."

"I suppose you have had some pretty exciting moments," I remarked.

"No, curiously enough," he replied; "I have personally never had any very exciting times. Big deals, of course, are often anxious moments, but beyond the natural anxiety to carry a large thing through, my career has been fairly simple. Some of my acquaintances, however, have not been so lucky, and one in particular is just going through a rare experience."

"Indeed," I answered; "are you at liberty to tell us what it is?"

He glanced from one of us to the other.

"I think so," he said. "Perhaps you have already heard of the great Rocheville diamond?"

"No," I remarked; "tell us about it, if you will."

Dinner being over, he leant back in his chair and helped himself to a cigar.

"It is curious how few people know about this diamond," he said, "although it is one of the most beautiful stones in the world. For actual weight, of course, many of the well-known stones can beat it. It weighs exactly eighty-two carats, and is an egg-shaped stone with a big indented hollow at the smaller end; but for lustre and brilliance I have never seen its equal. It has had a curious history. For centuries it was in the possession of an Indian Maharajah—it was bought from him by an American millionaire, and passed through my hands some ten years ago. I would have given anything to have kept it, but my finances were not so prosperous as they are now, and I had to let it go. A Russian baron bought it and took it to Naples, where it was stolen. This diamond was lost to the world till a couple of months ago, when it turned up in this country."

When Carlton mentioned Naples, the happy hunting-ground of the Brotherhood, Dufrayer glanced at me.

"But there is a fatality about its ownership," he continued; "it has again disappeared."

"How?" I cried.

"I wish I could tell you," he answered. "The circumstances of its loss are as follows: A month ago my wife and I were staying with an old friend, a relation of my mother's, a merchant named Michael Röden, of Röden Frères, Cornhill, the great dealers. Röden said he had a surprise for me, and he showed me the Rocheville diamond. He told me that he had bought it from a Cingalese dealer in London, and for a comparatively small price."

"What is its actual value?" interrupted Dufrayer.

"Roughly, I should think about fifteen thousand pounds, but I believe Röden secured it for ten. Well, poor chap, he has now lost both the stone and his money. My firm belief is that what he bought was an imitation, though how a man of his experience could have done such a thing is past knowledge. This is exactly what happened. Mrs. Carlton and I, as I have said, were staying down at his place in Staffordshire, and he had the diamond with him. At my wife's request, for she possesses a most intelligent interest in precious stones, he took us down to his strong room, and showed it to us. He meant to have it set for his own wife, who is a very beautiful woman. The next morning he took the diamond up to town, and Mrs. Carlton and I returned to Cor Castle. I got a wire from Röden that same afternoon, begging me to come up at once. I found him in a state of despair. He showed me the stone, to all appearance identically the same as the one we had looked at on the previous evening, and declared that it had just been proved to be an imitation. He said it was the most

196

skilful imitation he had ever seen. We put it to every known test, and there was no doubt whatever that it was not a diamond. The specific gravity test was final on this point. The problem now is: Did he buy the real diamond which has since been stolen or an imitation? He swears that the Rocheville diamond was in his hands, that he tested it carefully at the time; he also says that since it came into his possession it was absolutely impossible for any one to steal it, and yet that the theft has been committed there is very little doubt. At least one thing is clear, the stone which he now possesses is not a diamond at all."

"Has anything been discovered since?" I asked.

"Nothing," replied Carlton, rising as he spoke, "and never will be, I expect. Of one thing there is little doubt. The shape and peculiar appearance of the Rocheville diamond are a matter of history to all diamond dealers, and the maker of the imitation must have had the stone in his possession for some considerable time. The facsimile is absolutely and incredibly perfect."

"Is it possible," said Dufrayer suddenly, "that the strong room in Röden's house could have been tampered with?"

"You would scarcely say so if you knew the peculiar make of that special strong room," replied Carlton. "I think I can trust you and your friend with a somewhat important secret. Two strong rooms have been built, one for me at Cor Castle, and one for my friend Röden at his place in Staffordshire. These rooms are constructed on such a peculiar plan that the moment any key is inserted in the lock electric bells are set ringing within. These bells are connected in each case with the bedroom of the respective owners. Thus you will see for yourselves that no one could tamper with the lock without immediately giving such an alarm as would make any theft impossible. My friend Röden and I invented these special safes, and got them carried out on plans of our own. We both believe that our most valuable stones are safer in our own houses than in our places of business in town. But stay, gentlemen, you shall see for yourselves. Why should you not both come down to my place for a few days' shooting? I shall then have the greatest possible pleasure in showing you my strong room. You may be interested, too, in seeing some of my collection—I flatter myself, a unique one. The weather is perfect just now for shooting, and I have plenty of pheasants, also room enough and to spare. We are a big, cheerful party, and the lioness of the season is with us, Mme. Koluchy."

As he said the last words both Dufrayer and I could not refrain from starting. Luckily it was not noticed—my heart beat fast.

"It is very kind of you," I said. "I shall be charmed to come."

Dufrayer glanced at me, caught my eye, and said quietly:

"Yes, I think I can get away. I will come, with pleasure."

"That is right. I will expect you both next Monday, and will send to Durbrook Station to meet you, by any train you like to name."

We promised to let him know at what time we should be likely to arrive, and soon afterwards he left us. When he did so we drew our chairs near the fire.

"Well, we are in for it now," said Dufrayer. "Face to face at last—what a novel experience it will be! Who would believe that we were living in the dreary nineteenth century? But, of course, she may not stay when she hears we are coming."

"I expect she will," I answered; "she has no fear. Halloa! who can this be now?" I added, as the electric bell of the front door suddenly rang.

"Perhaps it is Carlton back again," said Dufrayer; "I am not expecting any one."

The next moment the door was opened, and our principal agent, Mr. Tyler himself, walked in.

"Good evening, gentlemen," he said. "I must apologize for this intrusion, but important news has just reached me, and the very last you would expect to hear." He chuckled as he spoke. "Mme. Koluchy's house in Welbeck Street was broken into a month ago. I am told that the place was regularly sacked. She was away in

198

her yacht at the time, after the attempt on your life, Mr. Head; and it is supposed that the place was unguarded. Whatever the reason, she has never reported the burglary, and Ford at Scotland Yard has only just got wind of it. He suspects that it was done by the same gang that broke into the jeweller's in Piccadilly some months ago. It is a very curious case."

"Do you think it is one of her own gang that has rounded on her?" I asked.

"Hardly," he replied; "I do not believe any of them would dare to. No, it is an outside job, but Ford is watching the matter for the official force."

"Mr. Dufrayer and I happen to know where Madame Koluchy is at the present moment," I said.

I then gave Tyler a brief résumé of our interview with Carlton, and told him that it was our intention to meet Madame face to face early in the following week.

"What a splendid piece of luck!" he cried, rubbing his hands with ill-suppressed excitement.

"With your acumen, Mr. Head, you will be certain to find out something, and we shall have her at last. I only wish the chance were mine."

"Well, have yourself in readiness," said Dufrayer; "we may have to telegraph to you at a moment's notice. Be sure we shall not leave a stone unturned to get Madame to commit herself. For my part," he added, "although it seems scarcely credible, I strongly suspect that she is at the bottom of the diamond mystery."

It was late in the afternoon on the following Monday, and almost dark, when we arrived at Cor Castle. Carlton himself met us at the nearest railway station, and drove us to the house, which was a fine old pile, with a castellated roof and a large Elizabethan wing. The place had been extensively altered and restored, and was replete with every modern comfort.

Carlton led us straight into the centre hall, calling out in a cheerful tone to his wife as he did so.

A slender, very fair and girlish-looking figure approached. She held out her hand, gave us each a hearty greeting, and invited us to come into the centre of a circle of young people who were gathered round a huge, old-fashioned hearth, on which logs of wood blazed and crackled cheerily. Mrs. Carlton introduced us to one or two of the principal guests, and then resumed her place at a table on which a silver tea-service was placed. It needed but a brief glance to show us that amongst the party was Mme. Koluchy. She was standing near her hostess, and just as my eye caught hers she bent and said a word in her ear. Mrs. Carlton coloured almost painfully, looked from her to me, and then once more rising from her seat came forward one or two steps.

"Mr. Head," she said, "may I introduce you to my great friend, Mme. Koluchy? By the way, she tells me that you are old acquaintances."

"Very old acquaintances, am I not right?" said Mme. Koluchy, in her clear, perfectly well-bred voice. She bowed to me and then held out her hand. I ignored the proffered hand and bowed coldly. She smiled in return.

"Come and sit near me, Mr. Head," she said; "it is a pleasure to meet you again; you have treated me very badly of late. You have never come once to see me."

"Did you expect me to come?" I replied quietly. There was something in my tone which caused the blood to mount to her face. She raised her eyes, gave me a bold, full glance of open defiance, and then said, in a soft voice, which scarcely rose above a whisper:

"No, you are too English."

Then she turned to our hostess, who was seated not a yard away.

"You forget your duties, Leonora. Mr. Head is waiting for his tea."

200

"Oh, I beg a thousand pardons," said Mrs. Carlton. "I did not know I had forgotten you, Mr. Head." She gave me a cup at once, but as she did so her hand shook so much that the small, gold-mounted and jewelled spoon rattled in the saucer.

"You are tired, Nora," said Mme. Koluchy; "may I not relieve you of your duties?"

"No, no, I am all right," was the reply, uttered almost pettishly. "Do not take any notice just now, I beg of you."

Madame turned to me.

"Come and talk to me," she said, in the imperious tone of a sovereign addressing a subject. She walked to the nearest window, and I followed her.

"Yes," she said, at once, "you are too English to play your part well. Cannot you recognize the common courtesies of warfare? Are you not sensible to the gallant attentions of the duellist? You are too crude. If our great interests clash, there is every reason why we should be doubly polite when we do meet."

"You are right, Madame, in speaking of us as duellists," I whispered back, "and the duel is not over yet."

"No, it is not," she answered.

"I have the pertinacity of my countrymen," I continued. "It is hard to rouse us, but when we are roused, it is a fight to grim death."

She said nothing further. At that moment a young man of the party approached. She called out to him in a playful tone to approach her side, and I withdrew.

At dinner that night Madame's brilliancy came into full play. There was no subject on which she could not talk—she was at once fantastic, irresponsible, and witty. Without the slightest difficulty she led the conversation, turning it into any channel she chose. Our host hung upon her words as if fascinated; indeed, I do not think there was a man of the party who had eyes or ears for any one else.

I had gone down to dinner with Mrs. Carlton, and in the intervals of watching Mme. Koluchy I could not help observing her. She belonged to the fair-haired and Saxon type, and when very young must have been extremely pretty—she was pretty still, but not to the close observer. Her face was too thin and too anxious, the colour in her cheeks was almost fixed; her hair, too, showed signs of receding from the temples, although the fashionable arrangement of the present day prevented this being specially noticed.

While she talked to me I could not help observing that her attention wandered, that her eyes on more than one occasion met those of Madame, and that when this encounter took place the younger woman trembled quite perceptibly. It was easy to draw my own conclusions. The usual thing had happened. Madame was not spending her time at Cor Castle for nothing—our hostess was in her power. Carlton himself evidently knew nothing of this. With such an alliance, mischief of the usual intangible nature was brewing. Could Dufrayer and I stop it? Beyond doubt there was more going on than met the eye.

As these thoughts flashed through my brain, I held myself in readiness, every nerve tense and taut. To play my part as an Englishman should I must have, above all things, self-possession. So I threw myself into the conversation. I answered Madame back in her own coin, and presently, in an argument which she conducted with rare brilliance, we had the conversation to ourselves. But all the time, as I talked and argued, and differed from the brilliant Italian, my glance was on Mrs. Carlton. I noticed that a growing restlessness had seized her, that she was listening to us with feverish and intense eagerness, and that her eyes began to wear a hunted expression. She ceased to play her part as hostess, and looked from me to Mme. Koluchy as one under a spell.

Just before we retired for the night Mrs. Carlton came up and took a seat near me in the drawing-room. Madame was not in the room, having gone with Dufrayer, Carlton, and several other members of the party to the billiard-room. Mrs. Carlton looked eagerly and nervously round her. Her manner was decidedly embarrassed. She made one or two short remarks, ending them abruptly, as if she wished to say something else but did not dare. I resolved to help her.

"Have you known Mme. Koluchy long?" I asked.

"For a short time, a year or two," she replied. "Have you, Mr. Head?"

"For more than ten years," I answered. I, stooped a little lower and let my voice drop in her ear.

"Mme. Koluchy is my greatest enemy," I said.

"Oh, good heavens!" she cried. She half started to her feet, then controlled herself and sat down again.

"She is also my greatest enemy, she is my direst foe—she is a devil, not a woman," said the poor lady, bringing out her words with the most tense and passionate force. "Oh, may I, may I speak to you and alone?"

"If your confidence relates to Mme. Koluchy, I shall be only too glad to hear what you have got to say," I replied.

"They are coming back—I hear them," she said. "I will find an opportunity to-morrow. She must not know that I am taking you into my confidence."

She left me, to talk eagerly, with flushed cheeks, and eyes bright with ill-suppressed terror, to a merry girl who had just come in from the billiard-room.

The party soon afterwards broke up for the night, and I had no opportunity of saying a word to Dufrayer, who slept in a wing at the other end of the house.

The next morning after breakfast Carlton took Dufrayer and myself down to see his strong room. The ingenuity and cleverness of the arrangement by which the electric bells were sounded the moment the key was put into the lock struck me with amazement. The safe was of the strongest pattern; the levers and bolts, as well as the arrangement of the lock, making it practically impregnable.

"Röden's safe resembles mine in every particular," said Carlton, as he turned the key in the lock and readjusted the different bolts in their respective places. "You can see for your—selves that no one could rob such a safe without detection."

"It would certainly be black magic if he did," was my response.

"We have arranged for a shooting party this morning," continued Carlton; "let us forget diamonds and their attendant anxieties, and enjoy ourselves out of doors. The birds are plentiful, and I trust we shall have a good time."

He took us upstairs, and we started a few moments later on our expedition.

It was arranged that the ladies should meet us for lunch at one of the keepers' cottages. We spent a thoroughly pleasant morning, the sport was good, and I had seldom enjoyed myself better. The thought of Mme. Koluchy, however, intruded itself upon my memory from time to time; what, too, was the matter with Mrs. Carlton? It needed but to glance at Carlton to see that he was not in her secret. In the open air, and acting the part of host, which he did to perfection, I had seldom seen a more genial fellow.

When we sat down to lunch I could not help owning to a sense of relief when I perceived that Mme. Koluchy had not joined us.

Mrs. Carlton was waiting for us in the keeper's cottage, and several other ladies were with her. She came up to my side immediately.

"May I walk with you after lunch, Mr. Head?" she said. "I have often gone out with the guns before now, and I don't believe you will find me in the way."

"I shall be delighted to have your company," I replied.

"Madame is ill," continued Mrs. Carlton, dropping her voice a trifle; "she had a severe headache, and was obliged to go to her room. This is my opportunity," she added, "and I mean to seize it."

I noticed that she played with her food, and soon announcing that I had had quite enough, I rose. Mrs. Carlton and I did not wait for the rest of the party, but walked quickly away together. Soon the shooting was resumed, and we could hear the sound of the beaters, and also an occasional shot fired ahead of us.

At first my companion was very silent. She walked quickly, and seemed anxious to detach herself altogether from the shooting party. Her agitation was very marked, but I saw that she was afraid to come to the point. Again I resolved to help her.

"You are in trouble," I said; "and Mme. Koluchy has caused it. Now, tell me everything. Be assured that if I can help you I will. Be also assured of my sympathy. I know Mme. Koluchy. Before now I have been enabled to get her victims out of her clutches."

"Have you, indeed?" she answered. She looked at me with a momentary sparkle of hope in her eyes; then it died out.

"But in my case that is impossible," she continued. "Still, I will confide in you; I will tell you everything. To know that some one else shares my terrible secret will be an untold relief."

She paused for a moment, then continued, speaking quickly:

"I am in the most awful trouble. Life has become almost unbearable to me. My trouble is of such a nature that my husband is the very last person in the world to whom I can confide it."

I waited in silence.

"You doubtless wonder at my last words," she continued, "but you will see what I mean when I tell you the truth. Of course, you will regard what I say as an absolute secret?"

"I will not reveal a word you are going to tell me without your permission," I answered.

"Thank you; that is all that I need. This is my early history. You must know it in order to understand what follows. When I was very young, not more than seventeen, I was married to an Italian of the name of Count Porcelli. My people were poor, and he was supposed to be rich. He was considered a good match. He was a handsome man, but many years my senior. Almost immediately after the marriage my mother died, and I had no near relations or friends in England. The Count took me to Naples, and I was not long there before I made some terrible discoveries. My husband was a leading member of a political secret society, whose name I never heard. I need not enter into particulars of that awful time. Suffice it to say that he subjected me to almost every cruelty.

"In the autumn of 1893, while we were in Rome, Count Porcelli was stabbed one night in the Forum. He had parted from me in a fury at some trifling act of disobedience to his intolerable wishes, and I never saw him again, either alive or dead. His death was an immense relief to me. I returned home, and two years afterwards, in 1895, I married Mr. Carlton, and everything was bright and happy. A year after the marriage we had a little son. I have not shown you my boy, for he is away from home at present. He is the heir to my husband's extensive estates, and is a beautiful child. My husband was, and is, devotedly attached to me—indeed, he is the soul of honour, chivalry, and kindness. I began to forget those fearful days in Naples and Rome; but, Mr. Head, a year ago everything changed. I went to see that fiend in human guise, Mme. Koluchy. You know she poses as a doctor. It was the fashion to consult her. I was suffering from a trifling malady, and my husband begged me to go to her. I went, and we quickly discovered that we both possessed ties, awful ties, to the dismal past. Mme. Koluchy knew my first husband, Count Porcelli, well. She told me that he was alive and in England, and that my marriage to Mr. Carlton was void.

"You may imagine my agony. If this were indeed true, what was to become of my child, and what would Mr. Carlton's feelings be? The shock was so tremendous that I became ill, and was almost delirious for a week. During that time Madame herself insisted on nursing me. She was outwardly kind, and told me that my sorrow was hers, and that she certainly would not betray me. But she said that Count Porcelli had heard of my marriage, and would not keep my secret if I did not make it worth his while. From that moment the most awful blackmailing began. From time to time I had to part with large sums of money Mr. Carlton is so rich and generous that he would give me anything without question. This state of things has gone on for a year. I have kept the awful danger at bay at the point of the sword."

"But how can you tell that Count Porcelli is alive?" I asked. "Remember that there are few more unscrupulous people than Mme. Koluchy. How do you know that this may not be a fabrication on her part in order to wring money from you?"

"I have not seen Count Porcelli," replied my companion; "but all the same, the proof is incontestable, for Madame has brought me letters from him. He promises to leave me in peace if I will provide him with money; but at the same time he assures me that he will declare himself at any moment if I fail to listen to his demands."

"Nevertheless, my impression is," I replied, "that Count Porcelli is not in existence, and that Madame is playing a risky game; but you have more to tell?"

"I have. You have by no means heard the worst yet. My present difficulty is one to scare the stoutest heart. A month ago Madame came to our house in town, and sitting down opposite to me, made a most terrible proposal. She took a jewel-case from her pocket, and, touching a spring, revealed within the largest diamond that I had ever seen. She laid it in my hand—it was egg-shaped, and had an indentation at one end. While I was gazing at it, and admiring it, she suddenly told me that it was only an imitation. I stared at her in amazement.

"'Now, listen attentively,' she said. 'All your future depends on whether you have brains, wit, and tact for a great emergency. The stone you hold in your hand is an imitation, a perfect one. I had it made from my knowledge of the original. It would take in the greatest expert in the diamond market who did not apply tests to it. The real stone is at the house of Monsieur Röden. You and your husband, I happen to know, are going to stay at the Rödens' place in the country to-morrow. The real stone, the great Rocheville diamond, was stolen from my house in Welbeck Street six weeks ago. It was purchased by Monsieur Röden from a Cingalese employed by the gang who stole it, at a very large figure, but also at only a third of its real value. For reasons which I need not explain, I was unable to expose the burglary, and in consequence it was easy to get rid of the stone for a large sum—but those who think that I will tamely submit to such a gigantic loss little know me. I am determined that the stone shall once more come into my possession, either by fair means or foul. Now, you are the only person who can help me, for you will be unsuspected, and can work where I should not have a chance. It is to be your task to substitute the imitation for the real stone.'

"'How can I?' I asked.

"'Easily, if you will follow my guidance. When you are at the Rödens', you must lead the conversation to the subject of diamonds, or rather you must get your husband to do so, for he would be even less suspected than you. He will ask Monsieur Röden to show you both his strong room where his valuable jewels are kept. You must make an excuse to be in the room a moment by yourself. You must substitute the real for the unreal as quickly, as deftly as if you were possessed of legerdemain. Take your opportunity to do this as best you can—all I ask of you is to succeed—otherwise'—her eyes blazed into mine—they were brighter than diamonds themselves.

"'Otherwise?' I repeated faintly.

"'Count Porcelli is close at hand—he shall claim his wife. Think of Mr. Carlton's feelings, think of your son's doom.' She paused, raising her brows with a gesture peculiarly her own. 'I need not say anything further,' she added.

"Well, Mr. Head, I struggled against her awful proposal. At first I refused to have anything to do with it, but she piled on the agony, showing me only too plainly what my position would be did I not accede to her wishes. She traded on my weakness; on my passionate love for the child and for his father. Yes, in the end I yielded to her.

"The next day we went to the Rödens. Despair rendered me cunning; I introduced the subject of the jewels to my husband, and begged of him to ask Monsieur Röden to show us his safe and its contents. Monsieur Röden was only too glad to do so. It is one of his fads, and that fad is also shared by my husband, to keep his most valuable stones in a safe peculiarly constructed in the vaults of his own house. My husband has a similar strong room. We went into the vaults, and Monsieur Röden allowed me to take the Rocheville diamond in my hand for a moment. When I had it in my possession I stepped backward, made a clumsy movement by intention, knocked against a chair, slipped, and the diamond fell from my fingers. I saw it flash and roll away. Quicker almost than thought I put my foot on it, and before any one could detect me had substituted the imitation for the real. The real stone was in my pocket and the imitation in Monsieur Röden's case without any one being in the least the wiser.

"With the great Rocheville diamond feeling heavier than lead in my pocket, I went away the next morning with my husband. I had valuable jewels of my own, and have a jewel-case of unique pattern. It is kept in the strong room at the Castle. I obtained the key of the strong room from my husband, went down to the vaults, and under the pretence of putting some diamonds and sapphires away, locked up the Rocheville diamond in my own private jewel-case. It is impossible to steal it from there, owing to the peculiar construction of the lock of the case, which starts electric bells ringing the moment the key is put inside. Now listen, Mr. Head. Madame knows all about the strong room, for she has wormed its secrets from me. She knows that with all her cleverness she cannot pick that dock. She has, therefore, told me that unless I give her the Rocheville diamond to-night she will expose me. She declares that no entreaties will turn her from her purpose. She is like adamant, she has no heart at all. Her sweetness and graciousness, her pretended sympathy, are all on the surface. It is useless appealing to anything in her but her avarice. Fear!—she does not know the meaning of the word. Oh, what am I to do? I will not let her have the diamond, but how mad I was ever to yield to her!"

I gazed at my companion for a few moments without speaking. The full meaning of her extraordinary story was at last made abundantly plain. The theft which had so completely puzzled Monsieur Röden was explained at last. What Carlton's feelings would be when he knew the truth, it was impossible to realize; but know the truth he must, and as soon as possible. I was more than ever certain that Count Porcelli's death was a reality, and that Madame was blackmailing the unfortunate young wife for her own purposes. But although I believed that such was assuredly the case, and that Mrs. Carlton had no real cause to dread dishonour to herself and her child, I had no means of proving my own belief. The moment had come to act, and to act promptly. Mrs. Carlton was overcome by the most terrible nervous fear, and had already got herself into the gravest danger by her theft of the diamond. She looked at me intently, and at last said, in a whisper:

"Whatever you may think of me, speak. I know you believe that I am one of the most guilty wretches in existence, but you can scarcely realize what my temptation has been."

"I sympathize with you, of course," I said then; "but there is only one thing to be done. Now, may I speak quite plainly? I believe that Count Porcelli is dead. Madame is quite clever enough to forge letters which you would believe to be bonâ-fide. Remember that I know this woman well. She possesses consummate genius, and never yet owned to a scruple of any sort. It is only too plain that she reaps an enormous advantage by playing on your fears. You can never put things right, therefore, until you confide in your husband. Remember how enormous the danger is to him. He will not leave a stone unturned to come face to face with the Count. Madame will have to show her hand, and you will be saved. Will you take my advice: will you go to him immediately?"

"I dare not, I dare not."

"Very well; you have another thing to consider. Monsieur Röden is determined to recover the stolen diamond. The cleverest members of the detective force are working day and night in his behalf. They are quite clever enough to trace the theft to you. You will be forced to open your jewel-case in their presence just think of your feelings. Yes, Mrs. Carlton, believe me I am right: your husband must know all, the diamond must be returned to its rightful owner immediately."

She wrung her hands in agony.

"I cannot tell my husband," she replied. "I will find out some other means of getting rid of the diamond—even Madame had better have it than this. Think of the wreck of my complete life, think of the dishonour to my child. Mr. Head, I know you are kind, and I know your advice is really wise, but I cannot act on it. Madame has faithfully sworn to me that when she gets the Rocheville diamond she will leave the country for ever, and that I shall never hear of her again. Count Porcelli will accompany her."

"Do you believe this?" I asked.

"In this special case I am inclined to believe her. I know that Madame has grown very anxious of late, and I am sure she feels that she is in extreme danger—she has dropped hints to that effect. She must have been sure that her position was a most unstable one when she refused to communicate the burglary in Welbeck Street to the police. But, hark! I hear footsteps. Who is coming?"

Mrs. Carlton bent forward and peered through the brushwood.

"I possess the most deadly fear of that woman," she continued; "even now she may be watching us—that headache may have been all a presence. God knows what will become of me if she discovers that I have confided in you. Don't let it seem that we have been talking about anything special. Go on with your shooting. We are getting too far away from the others."

She had scarcely said the words before I saw in the distance Mme. Koluchy approaching. She was walking slowly, with that graceful motion which invariably characterized her steps. Her eyes were fixed on the ground, her face looked thoughtful.

"What are we to do?" said Mrs. Carlton.

"You have nothing to do at the present moment," I replied, "but to keep up your courage. As to what you are to do in the immediate future, I must see you again. What you have told me requires immediate action. I swear I will save you and get you out of this scrape at any cost."

"Oh, how good you are," she answered; "but do go on with your shooting. Madame can read any one through, and my face bears signs of agitation."

Just at that moment a great cock pheasant came beating through the boughs overhead. I glanced at Mrs. Carlton, noticed her extreme pallor, and then almost recklessly raised my gun and fired. This was the first time I had used the gun since luncheon. What was the matter? I had an instant, just one brief instant, to realize that there was something wrong—there was a deafening roar—a flash as if a thousand sparks came before my eyes—I reeled and fell, and a great darkness closed over me.

Out of an oblivion that might have been eternity a dawning sense of consciousness came to me. I opened my eyes. The face of Dufrayer was bending over me.

"Hush!" he said, "keep quiet, Head. Doctor," he added, "he has come to himself at last."

A young man, with a bright, intelligent face, approached my side. "Ah! you feel better?" he said. "That is right, but you must keep quiet. Drink this."

He raised a glass to my lips. I drank thirstily. I noticed now that my left hand and arm were in a splint, bandaged to my side.

"What can have happened?" I exclaimed. I had scarcely uttered the words before memory came back to me in a flash.

"You have had a bad accident," said Dufrayer; "your gun burst."

"Burst!" I cried. "Impossible."

"It is only too true; you have had a marvellous escape of your life, and your left hand and arm are injured."

"Dufrayer," I said at once, and eagerly, "I must see you alone. Will you ask the doctor to leave us?"

"I will be within call, Mr. Dufrayer," said the medical man. He went into the ante-room. I was feverish, and I knew it, but my one effort was to keep full consciousness until I had spoken to Dufrayer.

"I must get up at once," I cried. "I feel all right, only a little queer about the head, but that is nothing. Is my hand much damaged?"

"No. Luckily it is only a flesh wound," replied Dufrayer.

"But how could the gun have burst?" I continued. "It was one of Riley's make, and worth seventy guineas."

I had scarcely said the last words before a hideous thought flashed across me. Dufrayer spoke instantly, answering my surmise.

"I have examined your gun carefully—at least, what was left of it," he said, "and there is not the slightest doubt that the explosion was not caused by an ordinary cartridge. The stock and barrels are blown to fragments. The marvel is that you were not killed on the spot."

"It is easy to guess who has done the mischief," I replied.

"At least one fact is abundantly clear," said Dufrayer: "your gun was tampered with, probably during the luncheon interval. I have been making inquiries, and believe that one of the beaters knows something, only I have not got him yet to confess. I have also made a close examination of the ground where you stood, and have picked up a small piece of the brasswork of a cartridge. Matters are so grave that I have wired to Tyler and Ford, and they will both be here in the morning. My impression is that we shall soon have got sufficient evidence to arrest Madame. It goes without saying that this is her work. This is the second time she has tried to get rid of you; and, happen what may, the thing must be stopped. But I must not worry you any further at present, for the shock you have sustained has been fearful."

"Am I badly hurt?" I asked.

"Fortunately you are only cut a little about the face, and your eyes have altogether escaped. Dynamite always expends its force downwards."

"It is lucky my eyes escaped," I answered. "Now, Dufrayer, I have just received some important information from Mrs. Carlton. It was told to me under a seal of the deepest secrecy, and even now I must not tell you what she has confided to me without her permission. Would it be possible to get her to come to see me for a moment?"

"I am sure she will come, and gladly. She seems to be in a terrible state of nervous prostration. You know she was on the scene when the accident happened. When I appeared I found her in a half-fainting condition, supported, of course, by Mme. Koluchy, whom she seemed to shrink from in the most unmistakable manner. Yes, I will send her to you, but I do not think the doctor will allow you to talk long."

"Never mind about the doctor or any one else," I replied; "let me see Mrs. Carlton—there is not an instant to lose."

Dufrayer saw by my manner that I was frightfully excited. He left the room at once, and in a few moments Mrs. Carlton came in.

Even in the midst of my own pain I could not but remark with consternation the look of agony on her face. She was trembling so excessively that she could scarcely stand.

"Will you do something for me?" I said, in a whisper. I was getting rapidly weaker, and even my powers of speech were failing me.

"Anything in my power," she said, "except—-"

"But I want no exceptions," I said. "I have nearly lost my life. I am speaking to you now almost with the solemnity of a dying man. I want you to go straight to your husband and tell him all."

"No, no, no!" She turned away. Her face was whiter than the white dress which she was wearing.

"Then if you will not confide in him, tell all that you have just told me to my friend Dufrayer. He is a lawyer, well accustomed to hearing stories of distress and horror. He will advise you. Will you at least do that?"

"I cannot." Her voice was hoarse with emotion, then she said, in a whisper:

"I am more terrified than ever, for I cannot find the key of my jewel-case."

"This makes matters still graver, although I believe that even Mme. Koluchy cannot tamper with the strong room. You will tell your husband or Dufrayer—promise me that, and I shall rest happy."

"I cannot, Mr. Head; and you, on your part, have promised not to reveal my secret."

"You put me in a most cruel dilemma," I replied.

Just then the doctor came into the room, accompanied by Carlton.

"Come, come," said the medical man, "Mr. Head, you are exciting yourself. I am afraid, Mrs. Carlton, I must ask you to leave my patient. Absolute quiet is essential. Fortunately the injuries to the face are trivial, but the shock to the system has been considerable, and fever may set in unless quiet is enforced."

"Come, Nora," said her husband; "you ought to rest yourself, my dear, for you look very bad."

As they were leaving the room I motioned Dufrayer to my side.

"Go to Mrs. Carlton," I said; "she has something to say of the utmost importance. Tell her that you know she possesses a secret, that I have not told you what it is, but that I have implored her to take you into her confidence."

"I will do so," he replied.

Late that evening he came back to me.

"Well?" I cried eagerly.

"Mrs. Carlton is too ill to be pressed any further, Head; she has been obliged to go to her room, and the doctor has been with her. He prescribed a soothing draught. Her husband is very much puzzled at her condition. You look anything but fit yourself, old man," he continued. "You must go to sleep now. Whatever part Madame has played in this tragedy, she is keeping up appearances with her usual aplomb. There was not a more brilliant member of the dinner party to-night than she. She has been inquiring with apparent sympathy for you, and offered to come and see you if that would mend matters. Of course, I told her that the doctor would not allow any visitors. Now you must take your sleeping draught, and trust for the best. I am following up the clue of the gun, and believe that it only requires a little persuasion to get some really important evidence from one of the beaters; but more of this to-morrow. You must sleep now, Head, you must sleep."

The shock I had undergone, and the intense pain in my arm which began about this time to come on, told even upon my strong frame. Dufrayer poured out a sleeping draught which the

216

doctor had sent round—I drank it off, and soon afterwards he left me.

An hour or two passed; at the end of that time the draught began to take effect, drowsiness stole over me, the pain grew less, and I fell into an uneasy sleep, broken with hideous and grotesque dreams. From one of these I awoke with a start, struck a match, and looked at my watch. It was half-past three. The house had of course long ago retired to rest, and everything was intensely still. I could hear in the distance the monotonous ticking of the great clock in the hall, but no other sound reached my ears. My feverish brain, however, was actively working. The phantasmagoria of my dream seemed to take life and shape. Fantastic forms seemed to hover round my bed, and faces sinister with evil appeared to me—each one bore a likeness to Mme. Koluchy. I became more and more feverish, and now a deadly fear that even at this moment something awful was happening began to assail me. It rose to a conviction. Madame, with her almost superhuman knowledge, must guess that she was in danger. Surely, she would not allow the night to go by without acting? Surely, while we were supposed to sleep, she would steal the Rocheville diamond, and escape?

The horror of this thought was so over-powering that I could stay still no longer. I flung off the bed-clothes and sprang from the bed. A delirious excitement was consuming me. Putting on my dressing-gown, I crept out on to the landing, then I silently went down the great staircase, crossed the hall, and, turning to the left, went down another passage to the door of the stone stairs leading to the vault in which was Carlton's strong room. I had no sooner reached this door than my terrors and nervous feats became certainties.

A gleam of light broke the darkness. I drew back into a recess in the stonework. Yes, I was right. My terrors and convictions of coming peril had not visited me without cause, for standing before the iron door of the strong room was Mme. Koluchy herself. There was a lighted taper in her hand. My bare feet had made no noise, and she was unaware of my presence. What was she doing? I waited in silence—my temples were hot and throbbing with overmastering horror. I listened for the bells which would give the alarm directly she inserted the key in the iron door. She was doing something to the safe—I could tell this by the noise she was making—still no bells rang.

The next instant the heavy door slipped back on its hinges, and Madame entered. The moment I saw this I could remain quiet no longer. I sprang forward, striking my wounded arm against something in the darkness. She turned and saw me—I made a frantic effort to seize her—then my brain swam and every atom of strength left me. I found myself falling upon something hard. I had entered the strong room. For a moment I lay on the floor half stunned, then I sprang to my feet, but I was too late. The iron door closed upon me with a muffled clang. Madame had by some miraculous means opened the safe without a key, had taken the diamond from Mrs. Carlton's jewel-case which stood open on a shelf, and had locked me a prisoner within. Half delirious and stunned, I had fallen an easy victim. I shouted loudly, but the closeness of my prison muffled and stifled my voice.

How long I remained in captivity I cannot tell. The pain in my arm, much increased by my sudden fall on the hard floor, rendered me, I believe, partly delirious—I was feeling faint and chilled to the bone when the door of the strong room at last was opened, and Carlton and Dufrayer entered. I noticed immediately that there was daylight outside; the night was over.

"We have been looking for you everywhere," said Dufrayer. "What in the name of fortune has happened? How did you get in here?"

"In pursuit of Madame," I replied. "But where is she? For Heaven's sake, tell me quickly."

"Bolted, of course," answered Dufrayer, in a gloomy voice; "but tell us what this means, Head. You shall hear what we have to say afterwards."

I told my story in a few words.

"But how, in the name of all that's wonderful, did she manage to open the safe without a key?" cried Carlton. "This is black art with a vengeance."

"You must have left the strong room open," I said.

"That I will swear I did not," he replied. "I locked the safe as usual, after showing it to you and Dufrayer yesterday. Here is the key."

"Let me see it," I said.

He handed it to me. I took it over to the light.

"Look here," I cried, with sudden excitement, "this cannot be your original key—it must have been changed. You think you locked the safe with this key. Carlton, you have been tricked by that arch-fiend. Did you ever before see a key like this?"

I held the wards between my finger and thumb, and turned the barrel from left to right. The barrel revolved in the wards in a ratchet concealed in the shoulder.

"You could unlock the safe with this key, but not lock it again," I exclaimed. "See here."

I inserted the key in the keyhole as I spoke. It instantly started the bells ringing.

"The barrel turns, but the wards which are buried in the keyhole do not turn with it, and the resistance of the ratchet gives exactly the impression as if you were locking the safe. Thus, yesterday morning, you thought you locked the safe with this key, but in reality you left it open. No one but that woman could have conceived such a scheme. In some way she must have substituted this for your key."

"Well, come to your room now, Head," cried Dufrayer, "or Madame will have achieved the darling wish of her heart, and your life will be the forfeit."

I accompanied Carlton upstairs, dressed, and though still feeling terribly ill and shaken, presently joined the rest of the household in one of the sitting-rooms. The utmost excitement was apparent on every face. Mrs. Carlton was standing near an open window. There were traces of tears on her cheeks, and yet her eyes, to my astonishment, betokened both joy and relief. She beckoned me to her side.

"Come out with me for a moment, Mr. Head."

When we got into the open air she turned to me.

"Dreadful as the loss of the diamond is," she exclaimed, "there are few happier women in England than I am at the present moment. My maid brought me a letter from Mme. Koluchy this morning which has assuaged my worst fears. In it she owns that Count Porcelli has been long in his grave, and that she only blackmailed me in order to secure large sums of money."

I was just about to reply to Mrs. Carlton when Dufrayer hurried up.

"The detectives have arrived, and we want you at once," he exclaimed.

I accompanied him into Carlton's study. Tyler and Ford were both present. They had just been examining the strong room, and had seen the false key. Their excitement was unbounded.

"She has bolted, but we will have her now," cried Ford. "We have got the evidence we want at last. It is true she has the start of us by three or four hours; but at last—yes, at last—we can loose the hounds in full pursuit."

220

Chapter IX

THE BLOODHOUND

THE aspect of matters had now completely changed. Mme. Koluchy had at last put herself under the power of the law, and her arrest at the worst was only a question of days. She had, it is true, a good start of her enemy, but an early wire to Scotland Yard would limit her movements by every conceivable device. Each railway terminus in England would be watched, as well as every port all over the country; for in all probability she would try to make straight back to Italy, where, even if she were arrested for crimes committed in England, according to international law the Italian authorities would not be bound to deliver her up to an English tribunal.

Yes, we felt that circumstances were at last pointing to a crisis, and the arrest of the greatest criminal of her day was all but accomplished. Nevertheless, one knew that with such resources as Madame possessed she might surround herself with unexpected defences, for she had many friends in the country, and some of these moved in the highest and most influential circles.

By an early train the two detectives, Dufrayer and myself returned to town. Madame had, of course, avoided the railways, and had doubtless gone off by road on a pre-arranged plan with some of her confederates.

On the way up, Tyler, who had been silent for some little time, leant across to the official inspector and said: "Ford, I shall put Miss Beringer on to this case now. I have more faith in her intuition and skill where a woman is to be hunted down than in any of my own men, or yours either."

The inspector smiled.

"Just as you like," he said. "I am well aware of Miss Beringer's skill. There is not a cleverer lady detective in the whole of London; but, whether she is employed in the case or not,

Madame cannot keep out of our clutches much longer. She has probably got back to London by now, and when once there I'll swear she won't get out. What we have to do when we arrive is to go straight to Bow Street and get the warrant drawn up."

"You look terribly knocked up, Head," said Dufrayer, glancing at me.

"I have not quite got over the shock I received yesterday," was my reply; "but my hand and arm are not nearly so painful as they were, and I am far too excited to think of rest at present. When I reach town I shall go straight off to Monkhouse, in Wimpole Street, and take his advice. My impression is that the arm will be all right in a week or so; and now, happen what may, I intend to be in at the death."

Dufrayer gave me one of his steady, long glances, but he did not shake his head or attempt to oppose me, for he knew that on this point my resolution was firm.

On reaching London I left my companions, who promised to call at my house about one o'clock, and went straight off to see Monkhouse. He dressed my arm and hand carefully, and said that I had had a miraculous escape.

I then went home and waited anxiously for the arrival of Dufrayer and the police officers. They came soon after the hour arranged, having obtained the warrant for the arrest of Mme. Koluchy. To my surprise I saw that they were accompanied by a stranger, a tall, well-made girl of about five-and-twenty years of age. Tyler introduced her to me as Miss Anna Beringer, and added, in a whisper, that we were all right now, as we had secured her services.

I glanced at her with some curiosity. She was a good-looking girl, with a keen, clever face. Her grey eyes were very bright, and all her features small and well formed, but there was a certain hardness about her lips which struck me even at the first glance. Those lips alone gave indication of her character, for there was nothing else in her appearance at all out of the common, and to an ordinary person she would appear simply as a bright, well-set-up young girl, with high spirits and a somewhat off-hand manner. Her usual expression was both frank and open, and her voice was very pleasant to listen to.

"Mr. Tyler has already given me the outline of the case," she said, turning to me. "I know exactly what occurred yesterday. By the way, Mr. Head, I hope you are feeling better. Mme. Koluchy acted in a most dastardly way towards you, and you escaped as by a miracle. I need not say that Madame is very well known to me. It has been the most earnest wish of my life for several years now to be connected with her capture. I look upon such a capture as the blue ribbon of my profession. She shall not escape me now."

As Miss Beringer spoke the hard lines round her mouth grew still harder, and the womanly element in her face faded out, giving place to a strong, masculine look of determination and resolution.

"Well," said Ford, "we have got the warrant at last, so it is all comparatively plain sailing. The first thing is to go at once to Madame's house. She will scarcely have arrived there yet, but we can at least search the place and put a man on guard. Do you feel up to coming with us, Mr. Head?" he added, turning to me.

"Certainly," I replied.

"Well, then, we had better lose no time. I have a carriage at the door, and also a hansom."

Miss Beringer, Dufrayer, and myself a moment later entered the landau which was in waiting for us, and the two detectives followed in the hansom. We all drove straight to Welbeck Street. As we approached Madame's house we saw that it bore the usual marks of being shut up and comparatively deserted. The window-boxes were destitute of flowers, the blinds were down, the steps had not been cleaned, and an air of desolation hung over the place. Dufrayer and I ascended the steps and rang the bell. Ford, Tyler, and Miss Beringer remained in the street.

"Suppose we cannot get in?" I said, after a moment's pause, for no one had yet come to answer our summons.

"With this warrant in my possession we can, if necessary, break down the door," replied Ford, laughing. "But here comes some one at last."

We heard shuffling footsteps approaching, they reached the door, the chain inside was undone, and some bolts drawn back. The door was then opened, and a tall, old woman stood on the threshold.

"What do you want?" she said, speaking in a mumbling voice.

"We want Mme. Koluchy," said Ford; "is she within?"

The woman started back quite perceptibly. When Ford came up and spoke to her I saw that she trembled all over.

"Madame is not at home," she began.

Ford interrupted hastily.

"Look here, missus. I have a warrant here for the arrest of Mme. Koluchy, and I demand an entrance, as I wish to search the house immediately."

The woman drew back, apparently paralyzed with fear, and we immediately entered the hall in a body.

"I tell you Madame is not here," she whimpered. "Madame has not been here since Saturday last."

Ford pushed her aside unceremoniously, and we began our search. We began with the magnificent reception-rooms on the ground-floor.

This was the first time I had been inside Madame's house in Welbeck Street, but the splendour of the great rooms and the extraordinary luxury of their decorations scarcely astonished me, for I knew the tastes of their owner only too well. Had I not seen Mme. Koluchy's palace in Naples? Had not her reception-rooms there been all too familiar to me in those early days, when she exercised so fatal a charm over my life, and by so doing ruined all my future?

The English house bore many marks of its foreign ownership. Treasures of priceless value from all parts of the globe were scattered here and there. The most valuable curios of every sort abounded; while carvings of strange heathen deities and frescoes, executed with all the skill of which modern art is capable, decorated the ceilings. Magnificent pictures by English as well as foreign painters, both old masters and more recent productions, were to be found on the walls.

We entered the consulting-room, the door of which was hung with a splendid specimen of Gobelins tapestry. The same magnificence and wealth of detail were to be found here. Madame's own special desk was an Italian one in walnut wood. It was inlaid with scroll work and figures of the cardinal virtues and the pagan deities. Close by its side was the chair in which she must have sat to receive her many patients. This was of antique oak lined with old tapestry, the back and arms profusely set with enamelled medallions. There was also, not far from the desk and chair, a handsome Louis XV. escritoire, inlaid with various woods and heavy mountings of chased ormolu. The rest of the furniture of the room was in keeping with that portion which immediately surrounded Madame's chair.

The walls from floor to ceiling were formed of inlaid woods, and the ceiling itself was in the shape of a dome, which gave a sort of colossal effect to the great room. But, splendid as everything was, the place wore a strange air of desolation. It was only to stand within these walls to know that the animating and dominant spirit was no longer present to give life and significance to the whole.

Having finished searching the ground-floor we went upstairs. The upper part of the house was furnished in a less heavy and more cheerful style, but it was also quite deserted. We were just coming down again when a ladder, leading to the roof, attracted Ford's attention. He ran up and opened a trap-door. We followed him and found, secured in a sheltered part of the roof between two gables, a pigeon-cote, which was now open and empty.

"There is nothing to be found here," I said, somewhat impatiently. "Had we not better go at once and search the vaults and the laboratories?"

As I said the words I little knew that our apparently unimportant discovery on the roof of the house was destined to be brought home to us in a remarkable manner. We went down to the basement and continued our exhaustive search. The old woman now came forward and said, in a whining, agitated voice, that she was the only person in the house, all the other servants having been dismissed.

"Can you show us the way to the laboratories?" I asked of her.

She looked uneasy, but did not hesitate to comply. She pointed with her finger, and we went down a dim passage. The door of the outer laboratory was open, and we entered. There was another beyond this also with its door ajar. Both rooms were fitted up with every modern device, and excited my curiosity as well as envy. But search as we would we could get no clue to Madame's whereabouts.

"She is not in the house, that is certain," said Ford; "and now there is nothing whatever for us to do but to keep a sharp watch in case she should venture to return."

As he spoke my attention was attracted by the attitude of the old woman. Hitherto she had followed us about something like a snarling and ill-conditioned cur, who protested, but had not courage to attack. Now she came boldly into the room, and stood facing us, leaning up against the wall. Her eyes were dark and piercing, and shone out on us from beneath heavy, overhanging brows. Her mouth was almost toothless, and she had a nutcracker chin.

"You won't find her," she muttered. "Ah, you may look as long as you like, but you'll never find her. The likes of her ain't for the likes of you. She ain't like other women. She's more spirit than woman, and the Evil One himself is a friend to her. You won't find her, never, never!"

She laughed in a hollow and exultant manner as she spoke.

"Would it not be well to arrest this old crone?" I said, turning to Ford.

He shook his head. "I don't believe she has anything to do with the conspiracy," he said, dropping his voice to a whisper, "beyond the fact that she is Madame's paid servant; but even if we wished to arrest her, we could not do so on vague suspicion. We can but watch her closely."

"Then there is nothing more to be done at present?" I queried, in a tone of disappointment.

"As far as you are concerned, Mr. Head, there is nothing more," answered Tyler. "I should recommend you to go home and have a good rest. We will let you know the instant anything happens."

We parted outside the house, where an officer in plain dress was already standing on duty. Dufrayer said he would look me up in the evening, and the detectives and Miss Beringer went on their way.

I hailed a hansom and returned to my own house. As I have already said, I was far too excited to rest. The old woman's words had affected me more strongly than I cared to allow, and as I paced up and down in my study, I could not help feeling anything but certain of the final result. I knew that Dufrayer, Miss Beringer, Tyler, and Ford were each and all absolutely sure that Madame would soon be captured, but I was possessed by uneasy fears. In this moment of extremity, would not the great criminal bring all the strength of her magnificent genius to bear on the situation?

As I thought over these things I was suddenly possessed by a sense of comfort. This was caused by my recollection of Miss Beringer's face. Ordinary as that face looked to the casual observer, it was by no means so to those who watched it more

Miss
Beringer

narrowly. To such a watcher its strange look of power could not but appeal. So contemplated, the face was the reverse of pleasant—the hardness round the lips became its dominant feature. There was also an insistence in the grey eyes which might on emergency amount to absolute cruelty. But it was the strange look of strength which I now remembered with a feeling of satisfaction. If Madame ever met her match, it would be in the person of that slight girl, for she possessed, I knew well, a grip of her subject which neither Ford nor Tyler, with all their intelligence and long practice, could own to. Miss Beringer could do work which they could not even attempt, for to her belonged the delicate intuition which is so essentially a woman's province. I longed to see her again, and also alone, that I might talk over matters more freely with her. Tyler had furnished me with her private address, and I now resolved to telegraph to her. I did so, asking permission to call upon her that evening. The reply came within an hour.

"Don't come to-night, but expect me to call on you early to-morrow."

Dufrayer came in as I was reading the telegram.

"What have you got there?" he asked.

"A wire from Miss Beringer," I replied. I put it into his hand.

"You are impressed, then, by our new detective?" he said slowly.

"Very much so," I answered. I gave a few of my reasons, and he favoured me with a grave smile.

"I never felt so hopeful," he continued; "we are in a position we were never in yet. It is, as Tyler says, merely a question of days. Where so many are on the watch, Madame cannot long escape us."

"Remember that the person we want to get is Mme. Koluchy," I answered, "and do not be too sure. For my part, I shall never be certain of her until she is absolutely our prisoner."

228

He did not remain with me much longer, and I spent the night as best I could.

Between ten and eleven o'clock on the following morning Miss Beringer arrived. She entered my room quickly, came close to my side, and fixed her eyes on my face.

I was startled by the change in her appearance. The grey eyes had a curious bright glitter in them, and her face was pale and drawn.

"Yes, Mr. Head," she said; as she took the chair offered her, "these cases take it out of me. When once on the track, I never rest day or night. I have never failed yet. If I did, I think it would kill me."

She shivered as she spoke, and her thin lips were drawn back to show her teeth. She had somewhat the expression of a tigress about to spring.

"You have news, Miss Beringer?" I said; "I hope good news?"

"I have news," she replied gravely, "and I trust it is good. It was because of what I am about to tell you that I was unable to call to see you last evening. Are you strong enough and well enough to go down at once with Ford to Hastings?"

"Certainly," I replied.

"I will give you my reasons for asking you to do so. There is a yacht cruising off the coast. It is said to belong to a Captain Marchant. I have had my suspicions from the first that it is subsidized by Madame. It was on account of these suspicions that I went to Hastings last night."

"To Hastings?" I said.

"Yes; I spent several hours of the night and evening in one of the low quarters of the town by the fish-market. There is no doubt that several members of the gang are hiding in the neighbourhood of Hastings, and their object is, of course, to get to the yacht. It is all-important to take immediate steps to prevent this."

"But how could you find out about the yacht in the first instance?" I asked.

"I obtained a slight clue," she replied, "no matter how obtained, and just when your telegram reached me was on my way to Hastings, disguised as a fisher-woman. I possess many disguises in my rooms, and am seldom taken aback when I want to act a good part. I went third-class to Hastings, and immediately visited the vicinity of the fish-market. I have a friend there, a fishwife, who does not know my real character, and who is always glad to see me. I can act the part admirably, and when I asked her to accompany me to a large gin-palace she was all too willing. I was in reality following two men, but she knew nothing of that. While these men were drinking at the bar, I drew near and was fortunate enough to hear a few words of their conversation. They spoke for the most part in Italian, which I happen to know. The name of Captain Marchant's yacht, the Snowflake, dropped from the lips of one. There was also a woman mentioned, but not by name. The Snowflake was waiting for the woman. Meanwhile, the men were hiding in an old disused Martello tower on the Pevensey Marshes. This I learned scrap by scrap, but it was enough for my purpose. I returned to town by the first train this morning. Ford and Tyler have received all the information I have just told you, and are certain that the yacht belongs to Madame. Ford and Tyler go to Hastings by the twelve o'clock train. And now the question is, Can you go with them, and will Mr. Dufrayer be induced to accompany you? Knowing as much as you must do about the Society, your help will be invaluable."

"I will go," I said, "and I will send a wire to Dufrayer."

"Very well," she replied; "it is scarcely eleven o'clock yet—you will find the detectives at Charing Cross at noon."

"But won't you come with us?" I said.

She turned a little pale.

"No," she answered, "my work obliges me to remain in town."

"Do you mind telling me what your next step is?" I asked.

"I would rather not," she answered, "for even here walls may have ears."

As she spoke she glanced round her with a nervous flash in her eyes, which left them almost as soon as it appeared.

"I never confide my plan of operations to any one in advance," she continued. "I have much to do and not a moment to lose. I believe now, between us, Madame has little chance of escape; but one false step, the smallest indiscretion, would be fatal. Good-bye, Mr. Head. I am glad that you have confidence in me."

"The utmost," I replied, as I wrung her hand.

A moment later she left the house. I packed a few things, sent a wire to Dufrayer, and at the right moment drove off to Charing Cross, where I met my friend, and also the two detectives. We took our seats in the train and it moved out of the station. We happened to have the carriage to ourselves, and Ford was in such a state of excitement that he could scarcely sit still.

"Did I not say that Miss Beringer was the one person in all London to help us?" he cried. "She is like a bloodhound when she scents the prey, and never lets go of the scent. From what she tells me, there is little or no doubt that most of the gang are hiding down in the Pevensey Marshes, and have taken possession of one of the old, disused Martello towers. There are a good many of them along the south coast."

Dufrayer asked one or two questions, and Ford continued: "That's a cute idea about using the old tower, and I believe the one which we are to watch is No. 59. It stands on the beach by the marshes of Pevensey Bay. The gang are only waiting till the steam yacht now being closely watched can take them off. Of course, we could quite easily go straight to the tower and catch those members of the gang who are there, but we want Mme. Koluchy, and my impression is, that she is quite certain to come down to-night or to-morrow. Our present work, however, will be to watch the tower day and night, so that when she does arrive we can catch her. Miss Beringer is under the strong impression that at present Madame is hiding in London. We may have a rough and tumble with the gang when it comes to the point, but I have taken steps to secure lots of assistance."

On arriving at Hastings station we were met by a couple of Tyler's agents.

"Has anything fresh occurred?" asked Ford, as we alighted.

"Nothing," answered one of the men, "but there is no doubt that several members of the gang are in No. 59 tower, and the steam yacht has drawn off down Channel."

"Just as I expected," said Ford; "well, the sooner we mount guard the better. We will start as soon as it is dark."

The next few hours we spent in making preparations. It was arranged that we should go as if we intended shooting wild duck. This would give us the excuse of carrying guns, which we knew we might possibly want for bigger game if the gang offered any serious resistance.

At six o'clock our little band, consisting of Dufrayer, Ford, Tyler, myself, and a couple of policemen in plain clothes, drove westwards out of the town to a lonely part of the shore. Here a boat awaited us, and, entering it, we pulled out into the bay. The moon had risen, and we could see the row of Martello towers dotted along the beach, and the dark waste of the marshes behind them.

Ford steered, and, after an hour's hard pulling, turned the boat's head towards the beach, where one of the dykes ran into the marshes from the sea. This we silently entered, and in a few moments the tall bulrushes that grew on either side completely concealed us. Ford raised his hand, and we quietly shipped our sculls.

"That's where they are," he whispered, pointing to one of the towers about two hundred yards off. "There is not a light visible, but they are there and no mistake. Now, what we have to do is this. We will leave the boat here, and crawl up under cover of the shingle ridge. We shall be quite close to the tower there, and we can lie in wait, unseen by the gang. How Madame will come, if to-night at all, by boat or otherwise, it is impossible to say; but at any rate, whenever she arrives she cannot escape us. There is the steam yacht now," he added, pointing out to sea.

I looked up and saw two red and green lights moving slowly along a mile or so from the shore.

Taking our guns and the provisions and flasks we had brought with us, we crept through the rushes and out on to the shingle, till we were within twenty yards of the tower. So close were we that I could see every detail. The ladder leading up to the door of the tower half-way up the wall was plainly visible; as was, also, the old, rusty 24-pounder, pointing uselessly out to sea. The tower itself was almost in ruins, and here and there the brickwork of the walls showed through the stucco which had worn off by time.

It was a calm night, and only the wash of the sea broke the stillness. I stretched myself on the rough, loose boulders and shingle, and laid my gun by my side. Hour after hour crept by. The vigil we were all keeping was sufficiently strange and exciting to keep us wakeful and attentive. Presently a night breeze arose and sighed among the bulrushes in the marshes behind us. But all within the tower was absolutely silent—not a light showed through the chinks of windows, not a footfall came to our ears. From where I lay, I could watch the lights of the yacht move to and fro in the black darkness. The slow hours dragged on, and still nothing happened. At last the dawn began to break—it grew brighter each moment. I was just turning towards Ford for our signal to go back to the boat, when suddenly I saw him leap up, raise his gun, and a loud report rang out on the still morning air I leapt to my feet also, as did the others. The little window of the tower opened, and two revolver shots rang through it as Tyler, Dufrayer, and three of the men rushed up the ladder. I followed them immediately, at a loss to know what this sudden change of plan meant. In a few moments we had smashed down the flimsy wooden door and had come in contact with four men, who, armed with revolvers, greeted us from within. Our onslaught, however, was so sudden and unexpected, that after a short but desperate resistance we had taken them all prisoners. They were immediately handcuffed, and Ford and Tyler with the other police-officers led them out of the tower on to the beach. Ford's eyes were blazing with excitement, and to my surprise I saw a dead pigeon at his feet.

"A messenger to Welbeck Street, Mr. Head," he exclaimed, handing me what looked like a piece of cigarette paper.

"A carrier pigeon!" I cried, the meaning of his first shot now bursting upon me.

"Yes, and I had a lucky shot at it in this half light," he continued; "but to tell you the truth, I half expected something of the kind, and, so to speak, lay in wait for that pigeon. Last night things came back to me, and I remembered that empty pigeon-cote on the roof of the house in Welbeck Street. From the fact that a message was about to be sent to her, there is no doubt whatever that Madame has returned to her town residence. We will catch her for certain now, though how she has contrived to get into her house with our man watching it is more than I can say. Can you read this?"

As he spoke he put the cigarette paper into my hand. I scrutinized it closely. Written in very tiny letters I read the following words: "Stay in London. Don't come here. Danger."

"Yes," went on Ford, "they spied us directly it began to get light, and seeing their game was up, dispatched this to Madame. But for that shot of mine she would probably have escaped us again. Now we have her safe."

"But how?" I answered. "The pigeon is dead, so she won't get the message, and in all probability will come down to Hastings to-day or to-night."

"We will keep her in London," said Ford, looking extremely knowing and much excited. "Oh yes, she will have her message all right, and in two hours from the present time. Bring them along, Tom."

One of the men was now seen descending the ladder with a wooden cage in his hands, in which were fluttering two more pigeons.

"By Jove!" I cried, seeing what he meant, "this is splendid."

"Yes, it is about the smartest bit of work I have ever done," he replied, "and we owe it all to Miss Beringer; she has given us the clue."

As he spoke he handed me another piece of cigarette paper, exactly like the one on which the first message had been written.

"You might make things a bit stronger, Mr. Head," he said.

I thought a moment, and then wrote: "Stay in Welbeck Street until one of us comes to you. Important. Danger if you stir."

Ford's eyes glittered as he read my words. He attached the little note deftly to the neck of one of the birds.

"There, off you go," he exclaimed, "it's lucky birds can't talk."

He tossed the pigeon into the air: the bird rose rapidly in gradually increasing circles, and then shot off in a straight line for the north, and so was lost to view bearing my message to Mme. Koluchy.

As the pigeon darted up into the air I heard one of the prisoners utter an exclamation, and saw him turn to his fellow. This action of ours had evidently taken him completely by surprise. The man at whom he looked made no reply, even by a glance, but folding his arms across his breast stood motionless as if at attention. A glance showed me all too plainly that, desperate as the men were, they were at least true to Madame. Even death by torture, did such await them, would not induce any one of the Brotherhood to betray their chief. They were all well dressed, and had the appearance of gentlemen. They took their apparently hopeless fate with stoicism, and did not attempt any escape.

By this time the sun had well risen, and a glorious morning had chased away the gloom of the night. Placing our prisoners in the boat, we pulled round to a lower part of the shore. Here a trap met us by appointment, and in less than an hour we were all on our way to London. Success had at last rewarded our efforts. We had secured Madame's gang, and now it would be an easy feat to make Madame herself our prisoner.

Ford had wired to Miss Beringer to meet us at the station, and he whispered to me from time to time as we ran up to town his keen sense of satisfaction.

"Trust Miss Beringer not to have been idle while we were busy down here!" he exclaimed. "She may probably be able to account for the way in which Mme. Koluchy has got back to her house. Ah, we have done for Mme. Koluchy at last. She has got the message of the carrier pigeon by now, but she little guesses who are coming to pay her a visit."

He laughed as he spoke. The train began to approach its destination, and slowed down preparatory to coming into the station.

"The first thing to be done," said Ford, "is to take our prisoners to Bow Street and have them formally charged, then we will all go and visit Madame in a party. Ah! here we are: I'll just jump out first, and have a look round for Miss Beringer."

He was the first to spring on to the platform, but look as he would he could not find the lady detective. He came back presently to the rest of us with a crestfallen expression of face.

"It's odd," he said, "but it only shows that she's precious busy with our business. In all probability we will find her in the vicinity of the house. Now, then, to look after the prisoners."

We took our men in a couple of cabs to Bow Street, and having seen them safe in the cells, drove straight to Madame's house. We had our last great capture to make in order to complete our work.

As we neared the house a strange and almost ungovernable excitement took possession of me. Dufrayer and the two detectives were also silent. This was no time for speech. My heart beat hard and fast—the stirring events of the last twenty-four hours had kept my brain going at fever heat, and, weak after the shock I had recently undergone, the strain began to tell. Once or twice I had to shake myself as a man in a dream. Truly, it was almost impossible to believe that in a few moments now Mme. Koluchy, the invincible, the daring, the all-powerful, would be our prisoner.

We drew up at last at the well-known entrance, and spoke a few words to the man on duty.

"Oh yes," he replied, "it's all right, and there's little or no news. The old woman has gone out once or twice to a shop to get some food, but no one has entered the house."

"What about Miss Beringer? Has she been here?" I asked.

"She was here yesterday evening," he answered, "but I've not seen her since."

Telling him to be in readiness without informing him of our convictions, we knocked loudly and rang imperiously at the door. After a very short delay the same old woman appeared. She wore a sort of night-cap with a deep frill, and her piercing eyes confronted us from under the shaggy brows. She would only now vouchsafe to open the door a few inches.

The place showed dimly in the half light, for every blind was down and every shutter up. We could not even see the bent form of the old woman distinctly.

"Now, look here," said Ford, "your mistress is in this house somewhere. We happen to know it for an absolute fact. Will you take us to her or not, for find her we will?"

The woman gave a low laugh, suppressed as soon as uttered.

"You may look all you can," she exclaimed, "but Madame is not here. You are welcome to search the house to your hearts' content."

After saying the last words she mumbled something more to herself, and then shuffled off down the passage.

We all entered the house.

"Now, then," said Ford, "we'll search from cellar to garret, and we'll start this time downstairs."

We descended to the basement, and made a careful search through the various domestic offices, until once more we found ourselves in the first of Mme. Koluchy's magnificent laboratories. Ford switched on the electrics, and we looked around us. The place was in perfect order, but a curious ethereal distillate familiar to my nostrils hung in the air. I could not account for this at the time, although it filled me with a vague fear. We went on into the second laboratory, which was also in order, but was pervaded even more strongly by the same smell. At the farther end of this room was a very low doorway studded with nails and iron bands. It looked as if it led into some cellar, and I suddenly remembered that we had not explored beyond its portals on the occasion of our first visit. The old woman had followed us into the laboratories, keeping well in the background. Ford, who seemed to observe the door at the same moment that I had, turned upon her eagerly.

"Where is the key of this door?" he said.

"I don't know," she answered.

"Go and find it immediately."

"My mistress keeps the key of that room, and until she returns you can't get in," was the low reply.

"We'll soon see about that," cried Ford.

He turned to one of his men.

"Just go out," he said, "and tell the man on duty outside to get me an axe and crowbar, and bring them here as soon as possible. Hurry as fast as you can, Johnson; there's not a moment to lose."

The man left us immediately.

"I think we shall find a clue at the other sit of this locked door," continued Ford, glancing at me. "I hope Johnson will look sharp."

In less than a quarter of an hour the man returned with the necessary implements.

"Martin and I went together to fetch them," he said; "I'm sorry I could not be back sooner."

Ford seized the axe, and after a few smashing blows over the lock inserted the bar and the door burst open. He stepped inside immediately, but as he did so he started back and a look of horror spread over his face. We all rushed in.

"Good God, we are too late!" he cried "She has escaped us."

"Escaped? How?" I said, pushing forward

"By death!" he answered.

He went forward and knelt on the floor of the room. In the dim light I could plainly see the body of a woman. Ford struck a match and held it close to the face. It was the body of Mme. Koluchy. Yes, there she lay. The well-known face, in all its magnificent beauty, wore now the awful repose of death. Beside her was a small hypodermic syringe, and also an open bottle containing some clear solution. From that open bottle had issued the smell which pervaded the outer and the inner laboratory.

For fully a moment we all gazed down at the dead woman in absolute silence. The sudden discovery had struck us dumb. How she had managed to obtain access to the house when it had been so closely watched was indeed a mystery. But after all it mattered nothing now. The end had come. A fit end to such a life as hers had been. We withdrew from the semi-darkness of the room into the outer laboratory. Dufrayer glanced round him.

"I wonder where the old woman can be!" he exclaimed.

"She was with us a moment ago," I answered "Is she not here now?"

"No, she has gone back into her own haunts, most likely. Had we not better call her? It is impossible that Madame could have got into the house without her assistance."

"I will go and have a look for her," said Tyler. He left the laboratory, and we heard him moving about the house, his footsteps echoing as he went. He presently came back.

"She is not in any of the kitchens," he said. "Perhaps she has gone upstairs—it does not matter much now, does it?"

"No," I answered, and then once more we were all silent, too stunned to utter many words. I never saw any one look so utterly crestfallen as Ford.

"To think that Mme. Koluchy should have done us at the very end!" he exclaimed more than once; "but it was like her; yes, it was like her."

"The message which the carrier pigeon brought meant evidently more to her than lay on the surface," I remarked. "She saw that she was hemmed in on every side, and was not the woman to be taken alive."

"Well, our search has come to an unlooked-for end," said Ford again; "but I do wonder," he added, "where Miss Beringer can be. It is very odd that we have not heard or seen anything of her."

Just then Dufrayer spoke.

"Hark!" he cried, "what is that?"

We all stood still and listened. Far away, as if from some great distance, we heard a muffled cry. Again and again it was repeated. So faint was the sound that it seemed to be away out in the street.

"What on earth can it be?" said Ford looking round him anxiously.

We moved softly round the laboratory, fearing to disturb the silent figure that lay in the awful repose of death. Again and once again we heard the cry. We stopped now and then to listen more closely. At last we reached a point where it seemed louder than anywhere else. I lay down and applied my ear to the stone flags.

"It is here!" I cried, in intense excitement, "just beneath us. Listen!"

Yes, it was now unmistakable—the sound came from beneath our feet.

"There is a cellar beneath this," I said; "some one is immured here."

We searched rapidly for any sign of an entrance, but searched in vain.

Once again the cry was repeated, but now it was as faint as that which might come from the throat of an infant.

"There is some one under here," said Dufrayer, in a tone of the greatest excitement. "We must smash the flagstone immediately."

Ford and Tyler both seized the crowbar. In a few moments they had loosened the stone, levered it up, and turned it over. As they did so, I perceived that there was a secret spring underneath, and had we looked long enough we could have removed the stone without the help of the crowbar. The moment it was turned up a breath of intensely cold air greeted us, and we saw immediately beneath our feet a dark, circular hole. A low moan came up from the darkness. I gently lowered down the crowbar; it rested on something soft.

Our excitement now was intense. Taking off my coat I lowered myself through the hole, and holding on by my hands to the edge of the hole, my feet at last touched the solid ground. The cold that surrounded me was so intense that I almost gasped for breath. In what infernal region was I finding myself? I let go and, striking a match, looked round. Good God! a woman lay in this fearful dungeon! In another moment I had raised her, and as her face caught the light I saw at a glance that it was Miss Beringer. The others quickly lifted her out, and I sprang up beside them. A pair of steel hand-cuffs were on her wrists. She was so icy cold from the awful chill of that subterranean chamber, that at first she looked like one dead. Her mouth was torn and her hands swollen. When she was brought up into the warmer air she lay to all appearance unconscious for several moments. Dufrayer quickly took a flask from his pocket, poured out some brandy, and put it to her lips. At first she could not swallow, then, to our great relief, a few drops went down her throat. She sighed audibly and opened her eyes. When she did so she stared with a dazed expression all round. In less than a moment, however, full consciousness returned, a fierce light of understanding shone in the depths of her eyes, and she sat up.

"Have you got her?" she asked, gazing wildly round.

"We have, Miss Beringer, but not alive," I answered. "Now tell us how it is you are here. Tell us what has happened, if you possibly can."

"But the old woman—Mme. Koluchy—have you got her?"

"Mme. Koluchy is dead!" I answered, thinking that she had not yet recovered her senses.

"But she is not!" she answered, in a passionate voice. "Take the old woman."

Ford turned to one of his men.

"Fetch her in," he said.

"I have had a good search for her already," said Tyler, "and could not find her in any of the lower regions."

He spoke in a whisper, and I do not think Miss Beringer heard him. She was lying back again with closed eyes. Ford's man rushed out of the room, to return in a few moments.

"I have been all over the house," he said, "and cannot find the woman high or low. She is not here—she must have gone out when Martin and I were away fetching the axe and crowbar. I remember now, we left the door open—we had no thought of anything else in our excitement."

Miss Beringer heard the words, and once again she roused herself. Now she sprang to her feet.

"I might have known it," she said. "Fools! all of you! How was it she escaped? Did not you recognize her?"

"But Mme. Koluchy is dead," I said. "Come and look for yourself, if you do not believe me. Here she lies in this very room. You scarcely know what you are saying just now, after your own awful experience; but at least Madame has not escaped. She can never harm any one again—she has gone to her long account."

Miss Beringer uttered a hollow laugh.

"I am all right," she said. "It does not take me long to come back to my senses. Oh, what fools all you men are! Madame knew what she was about when she immured me in that living grave. Do you call that Mme. Koluchy? Come and look at her again."

In the dim light of the laboratory we went and bent over the dead woman. I looked earnestly into the face, and then raised my eyes. Beyond doubt, poor Miss Beringer's senses had given way. The woman on whom I gazed was Mme. Koluchy. Feature for feature was the same.

"I see you doubt me," said Miss Beringer. "Well, listen to my story."

She stood before us and began to speak eagerly. We all clustered round her. Never before had we listened to a tale of more daring and unparalleled atrocity.

"I told you, Mr. Head," she began, "that I had work which would keep me in town. So I had. From the time you went to Hastings yesterday I began to watch this house. I had all faith in the police officers you, Mr. Ford, had placed on duty, but I also felt certain that Madame, in her unbounded resources, would find a means to return. I knew that, if such were the case, it would need all a woman's keenest wit and intuition to foil her. She knew me as well as I knew her. It is true that she feared no man in London, but I do believe she had a wholesome dread of Anna Beringer.

"Well, my watch began, and for the first hour or so nothing occurred, but as soon as it was dark I saw the old caretaker, who showed you over the house on the first occasion, come out by the area door. I immediately followed her. She went straight to a shop in the Marylebone High Street—a small grocer's. She remained there for nearly half an hour. When she came out she was carrying a bag, quite a small one, which apparently contained some provisions. I followed her again, watching her closely as I did so. Something about her walk first attracted my attention. The man on duty passed us as we went down Welbeck Street. I quickened my steps, and was in reality only two or three feet behind the woman whom I now strongly suspected to be Mme. Koluchy herself.

"Just when we reached the open gate of the area, and as I was about to lay my hand on her shoulder, she turned quick as lightning upon me, and dashed into my face a liquid which must have been a solution of the strongest ammonia. The effect was instantaneous. I fell back gasping for breath, and unable to utter a sound. She well knew what the effect of the ammonia would be, causing a sudden paralysis of the glottis, which would prevent my uttering a word for a couple of moments. Before I could recover myself, she had flung her arm around me, had dragged me down the area steps and into the house. The moment we got within she slipped a pair of hand-cuffs on my wrists and also gagged me. I was so paralyzed by the effect of the ammonia that I did not attempt to make the smallest struggle until too late. When she had gagged and bound me, she dragged me down a passage and into this laboratory where we are now standing. She then laid me on the floor and tied me down securely. When she had done this, she looked down at me and smiled a smile of devilish cruelty.

"'Yes, Miss Beringer,' she said, 'you are a smart woman, the smartest with one exception in all London. You are interested in me—I am about to gratify that interest.'

"She left me for a few moments, and presently returned dragging something heavy after her. Horror of horrors, it was a woman's dead body! I could scarcely believe the evidence of my own senses. She laid the body on the floor, and began to dress it in some of her clothes. Having done this, and having arranged it in the attitude of one who might have suddenly fallen and died, she came up to me again.

"'Two years ago,' she said, speaking slowly, and bending her face to within about a foot of mine, 'there lived a woman in Naples who was in every respect my double. She was like me in each feature, in height, proportion, even to the expression of the face. She was a peasant woman, but so strong was her resemblance to me, that twice the Neapolitan police arrested her, believing her to be me. They, of course, discovered their mistake, and she quickly recovered her liberty. The woman died, and though to all appearance she was buried, it was but a mock funeral. For I had been watching her, and I felt that in extremis she would be of the utmost use to me. I offered the woman's husband a large sum for her body. It was conveyed to my house in Naples, no matter how. The husband received his money, but in order that no tales might arise he was quickly afterwards put out of the way by one of my confederates. I kept the body at a very low temperature, and when I came to England in my own yacht, brought it with me. Since then it has remained in a frozen chamber beneath the floor of the inner laboratory, thus retaining its likeness, as under such circumstances it would perpetually.

"'The time has come when I must use my double in order to effect my own escape. The most vindictive tribunal in the world will pause at the edge of the grave. My enemies will suppose that I am dead, and I shall escape from their power, for the likeness to me is so perfect, that detection cannot be made until the autopsy. By then I shall be well out of the country, for the men who are on watch for me will have withdrawn the moment the news of my suicide is known. I mean to put a hypodermic syringe and a bottle of strong poison near the body of the woman. Thus all will be complete: This is my last trump card.

"'And now, Miss Beringer,' she added, with a strange laugh, which I hear even now echoing in my ears, 'for your part in this ghastly game. In order to insure your silence I mean to consign you to the frozen chamber from which I have just taken this woman. Gagged and bound in that place your tortures will not last long, for death will soon release you from them. But know that you can never again mingle with your fellow-men. Know also that you made a mistake when you pitted your strength against mine, for mine is the stronger. Come!'

"She raised me as if I were an infant, and lifted me into the inner room. I noticed that one of the flagstones was up—the gag prevented my speaking, the thongs which bound me prevented my struggling. Madame thrust me into the frozen chamber and sealed the stone above me. There I have remained for the last fifteen hours. What I have endured is beyond description. At last I fancied I heard footsteps overhead. I made one frantic struggle, and managed to remove the gag from my lips. The moment I did so I shouted wildly. Thank God, you heard me in time."

Miss Beringer's words fell on our ears like the strokes of a hammer. We were far too stunned to reply. Madame had been in our very grasp, under our hands, and once more she had eluded.

Chapter X

THE DOOM

THE mysterious disappearance of Mme. Koluchy was now the universal topic of conversation. Her house was deserted, her numerous satellites were not to be found. The woman herself had gone as it were from the face of the earth. Nearly every detective in London was engaged in her pursuit. Scotland Yard had never been more agog with excitement; but day after day passed, and there was not the most remote tidings of her capture. No clue to her whereabouts could be obtained. That she was alive was certain, however, and my apprehensions never slumbered. I began to see that cruel face in my dreams, and whether I went abroad or whether I stayed at home, it equally haunted me.

A few days before Christmas I had a visit from Dufrayer. He found me pacing up and down my laboratory.

"What is the matter?" he said.

"The old story," I answered.

He shook his head.

"This won't do, Norman; you must turn your attention to something else."

"That is impossible," I replied, raising haggard eyes to his face.

He came up and laid his hand on my shoulder.

"You want change, Head, and you must have it. I have come in the nick of time with an invitation which ought to suit us both. We have been asked down to Rokesby Rectory to spend Christmas with my old friend, the rector. You have often heard me talk of William Sherwood. He is one of the best fellows I know. Shall I accept the invitation for us both?"

"Where is Rokesby Rectory?" I asked.

"In Cumberland, about thirty miles from Lake Windermere, a most picturesque quarter. We shall have as much seclusion as we like at Sherwood's house, and the air is bracing. If we run down next Monday, we shall be in time for a merry Christmas. What do you say?"

I agreed to accompany Dufrayer, and the following Monday, at an early hour, we started on our journey. Nothing of any moment occurred, except that at one of the large junctions a party of gipsies got into a third-class compartment near our own. Amongst them I noticed one woman, taller than the rest, who wore a shawl so arranged over her head as to conceal her face. The unusual sight of gipsies travelling by train attracted my attention, and I remarked on it to Dufrayer. Later on I noticed, too, that they were singing, and that one voice was clear, and full, and rich. The circumstance, however, made very little impression on either of us.

At Rokesby Station the gipsies left the train, and each of them carried his or her bundle, disappearing almost immediately into a thick pine forest, which stretched away to the left of the little station.

The peculiar gait of the tall woman attracted me, and I was about to mention it to Dufrayer, when Sherwood's sudden appearance and hurried, hospitable greeting put it out of my head. Sherwood was a true specimen of a country parson; his views were broad-minded, and he was a thorough sportsman.

The vicarage was six miles from the nearest station, but the drive through the bracing air was invigorating, and I felt some of the heaviness and depression which had made my life a burden of late already leaving me.

When we reached the house we saw a slenderly-made girl standing in the porch. She held a lamp in her hand, and its bright light illuminated each feature. She had dark eyes and a pale, somewhat nervous face; she could not have been more than eighteen years of age.

248

"Here we are, Rosaly," called out her father, "and cold too after our journey. I hope you have seen to the fires."

"Yes, father; the house is warm and comfortable," was the reply.

The girl stepped on to the gravel, and held out her hand to Dufrayer, who was an old friend. Dufrayer turned and introduced me.

"Mr. Head, Rosaly," he said; "you have often heard me talk of him."

"Many times," she answered. "How do you do, Mr. Head? I am very glad indeed to welcome you here—you seem quite like an old friend; but come in both of you, do—you must be frozen."

She led the way into the house, and we found ourselves in a spacious and very lofty hall. It was lit by one or two standard lamps, and was in all respects on a larger and more massive scale than is usually to be found in a country rectory.

"Ah! you are noticing our hall," said the girl, observing the interest in my face. "It is quite one of the features of Rokesby; but the fact is, this is quite an old house, and was not turned into a rectory until the beginning of the present century. I will take you all over it to-morrow. Now, do come into father's smoking-room—I have had tea prepared there for you."

She turned to the left, threw open a heavy oak door, and introduced us into a room lined with cedar from floor to ceiling. Great logs were burning on the hearth, and tea had been prepared. Miss Sherwood attended to our comforts, and presently left us to enjoy our smoke.

"I have a thousand and one things to see to," she said. "With Christmas so near, you may imagine that I am very busy."

When she left the room, the rector looked after her with affection in his eyes.

"What a charming girl!" I could not help saying.

"I am glad you take to her, Mr. Head," was his reply; "I need not say that she is the light of my old eyes. Rosaly's mother died a fortnight after her birth, and the child has been as my one ewe lamb. But I am sorry to say she is sadly delicate, and I have had many hours of anxiety about her."

"Indeed," I replied; "it is true she looks pale, but I should have judged that she was healthy—rather of the wiry make."

"In body she is fairly healthy, but hers is a peculiarly nervous organism. She suffers intensely from all sorts of terrors, and her environment is not the best for her. She had a shock when young. I will tell you about it later on."

Soon afterwards Dufrayer and I went to our respective rooms, and when we met in the drawing-room half an hour later, Miss Sherwood, in a pretty dress, was standing by the hearth. Her manners were very simple and unaffected, and, although thoroughly girlish, were not wanting in dignity. She was evidently well accustomed to receiving her father's guests, and also to making them thoroughly at home. When we entered the dining-room we had already engaged in a brisk conversation, and her young voice and soft, dark-brown eyes added much to the attractiveness of the pleasant scene.

Towards the end of the meal I alluded once again to the old house.

"I suppose it is very old," I said; "it has certainly taken me by surprise—you must tell me its history."

I looked full at my young hostess as I spoke. To my surprise a shadow immediately flitted over her expressive face; she hesitated, then said slowly:

"Every one remarks the house, and little wonder. I believe in parts it is over three hundred years old. Of course, some of the rooms are more modern. Father thinks we were in great luck when it was turned into a rectory, but——" Here she dropped her voice, and a faint sigh escaped her lips.

I looked at her again with curiosity.

"The place was spoiled by the last rector," she went on. "He and his family committed many acts of vandalism, but father has done his best to restore the house to its ancient appearance. You shall see it to-morrow, if you are really interested."

"I take a deep interest in old houses," I answered; "and this, from the little I have seen of it, is quite to my mind. Doubtless you have many old legends in connection with it, and if you have a real ghost it will complete the charm."

I smiled as I spoke, but the next instant the smile died on my lips. A sudden flame of colour had rushed into Miss Sherwood's face, leaving it far paler than was natural. She dropped her napkin, and stooped to pick it up. As she did so, I observed that the rector was looking at her anxiously. He immediately burst into conversation, completely turning the subject into what I considered a trivial channel.

A few moments later the young girl rose and left us to our wine.

As soon as we were alone, Sherwood asked us to draw our chairs to the fire and began to speak.

"I heard what you said to Rosaly, Mr. Head," he began; "and I am sorry now that I did not warn you. There is a painful legend connected with this old house, and the ghost whom you so laughingly alluded to exists, as far as my child is concerned, to a painful degree."

"Indeed," I answered.

"I do not believe in the ghost myself," he continued; "but I do believe in the influence of a very strong, nervous terror over Rosaly. If you like, I will tell you the story."

"Nothing could please me better," I answered.

The rector opened a fresh box of cigars, handed them to us, and began.

ghost
story

"The man who was my predecessor here had a scapegrace son, who got into serious trouble with a peasant girl in this forest. He took the girl to London, and then deserted her. She drowned herself. The boy's father vowed he would never see the lad again, but the mother pleaded for him, and there was a sort of patched-up reconciliation. He came down to spend Christmas in the house, having faithfully promised to turn over a new leaf. There were festivities and high mirth.

"On Christmas night the whole family retired to bed as usual, but soon afterwards a scream was heard issuing from the room where the young man slept—the West Room it is called. By the way, it is the one you are to occupy, Dufrayer. The rector rushed into the room, and, to his horror and surprise, found the unfortunate young man dead, stabbed to the heart. There was, naturally great excitement and alarm, more particularly when it was discovered that a well-known herb-woman, the mother of the girl whom the young man had decoyed to London, had been seen haunting the place. Rumour went so far as to say that she had entered the house by means of a secret passage known only to herself. Her name was Mother Heriot, and she was regarded by the villagers as a sort of witch. This woman was arrested on suspicion; but nothing was definitely proved against her, and no trial took place. Six weeks later she was found dead in her hut, on Grey Tor, and since then the rumour is that she haunts the rectory on each Christmas night—entering the house through the secret passage which we none of us can discover. This story is rife in the house, and I suppose Rosaly heard it from her old nurse. Certain it is that, when she was about eight years old, she was found on Christmas night screaming violently, and declaring that she had seen the herb-woman, who entered her room and bent down over her. Since then her nerves have never been the same. Each Christmas as it comes round is a time of mental terror to her, although she tries hard to struggle against her fears. On her account I shall be glad when Christmas is over. I do my best to make it cheerful, but I can see that she dreads it terribly."

"What about the secret passage?" I interrupted.

252

"Ah! I have something curious to tell you about that," said the old rector, rising as he spoke. "There is not the least doubt that it exists. It is said to have been made at the time of the Monmouth Rebellion, and is supposed to be connected with the churchyard, about two hundred yards away; but although we have searched, and have even had experts down to look into the matter, we have never been able to get the slightest clue to its whereabouts. My impression is that it was bricked up long ago, and that whoever committed the murder entered the house by some other means. Be that as it may, the passage cannot be found, and we have long ceased to trouble ourselves about it."

"But have you no clue whatever to its whereabouts?" I asked.

"Nothing which I can call a clue. My belief is that we shall have to pull down the old pile before we find the passage."

"I should like to search for it," I said impulsively; "these sorts of things interest me immensely."

"I could give you a sort of key, Head, if that would be any use," said Sherwood; "it is in an old black-letter book." As he spoke he crossed the room, took a book bound in vellum, with silver clasps, from a locked bookcase, and, opening it, laid it before me.

"This book contains a history of Rokesby," he continued. "Can you read black-letter?"

I replied that I could.

He then turned a page, and pointed to some rhymed words. "More than one expert has puzzled over these lines," he continued. "Read for yourself."

I read aloud slowly:

When the Yew and Star combine.

Draw it twenty cubits line;

Wait until the saintly lips

Shall the belfry spire eclipse.

Cubits eight across the first

There shall lie the tomb accurst.

"And you have never succeeded in solving this?" I continued.

"We have often tried, but never with success. The legend runs that the passage goes into the churchyard, and has a connection with one of the old vaults, but I know nothing more. Shall we join Rosaly in the drawing-room?"

"May I copy this old rhyme first?" I asked.

My host looked at me curiously; then he nodded. I took a memorandum-book from my pocket and scribbled down the words. Mr. Sherwood then locked up the book in its accustomed place, and we left the subject of the secret passage and the ghost, to enjoy the rest of the evening in a more everyday manner.

The next morning, Christmas Eve, was damp and chill, for a thaw had set in during the night. Miss Sherwood asked Dufrayer and me to help her with the church decorations, and we spent a busy morning in the very old Norman church just at the back of the vicarage. When we left it, on our way home to lunch, I could not help looking round the churchyard with interest. Where was the tomb accurst into which the secret passage ran? As I could not talk, however, on the subject with Miss Sherwood, I resolved, at least for the present, to banish it from my mind. A sense of strong depression was still hanging over me, and Mme. Koluchy herself seemed to pervade the air. Yet, surely, no place could be farther from her accustomed haunts than this secluded rectory at the base of the Cumberland hills.

"The day is brightening," said Rosaly, turning her eyes on my face, as we were entering the house; "suppose we go for a walk after lunch? If you like, we could go up Grey Tor and pay a visit to Mother Heriot."

"Mother Heriot?" I repeated, in astonishment.

"Yes—the herb-woman—but do you know about her?"

"Your father spoke about a woman of the name last night?"

"Oh, I know," replied Miss Sherwood hastily; "but he alluded to the mother—the dreadful ghost which is said to haunt Rokesby. This is the daughter. When the mother died a long time ago, after committing a terrible murder, the daughter took her name and trade. She is a very curious person, and I should like you to see her. She is much looked up to by the neighbours although they also fear her. She is said to have a panacea against every sort of illness: she knows the property of each herb that grows in the neighbourhood, and has certainly performed marvellous cures."

"Does she deal in witchcraft and fortune-telling?" I asked.

"A little of the latter, beyond doubt," replied the girl, laughing; "she shall tell your fortune this afternoon. What fun it will be! We must hurry with lunch, for the days are so short now."

Soon after the mid-day meal we set off, taking the road for a mile or two, and then, turning sharply to the right, we began to ascend Grey Tor. Our path led through a wood of dark pine and larches, which clothed the side of the summit of the hill. The air was still very chilly, and it struck damp as we entered the pine forest. Wreaths of white mist clung to the dripping branches of the trees, the earth was soft and yielding, with fallen pine leaves and dead fern.

"Mother Heriot's hut is just beyond the wood," said Rosaly; "you will see it as soon as we emerge. Ah! there it is," she cried.

I looked upward and saw a hut made of stone and mud, which seemed to cling to the bare side of the mountain.

We walked quickly up a winding path, that grew narrower as we proceeded. Suddenly we emerged on to a little plateau on the mountain side. It was grass-covered and strewn with grey granite boulders. Here stood the rude hut. From the chimney some smoke was going straight up like a thin, blue ribbon. As we approached close we saw that the door of the hut was shut. From the eaves under the roof were hanging several small bunches of dried herbs. I stepped forward and struck upon the door with my stick. It was immediately opened by a thin, middle-aged woman, with a singularly lined and withered face. I asked her if we might come in. She gave me a keen glance from out of her beady-black eyes, then seeing Rosaly, her face brightened, she made a rapid motion with her hand, and then, to my astonishment, began to speak on her fingers.

"She can hear all right, but she is quite dumb—has been so since she was a child," said the rector's daughter to me. "She does not use the ordinary deaf-and-dumb language, but she taught me her peculiar signs long ago, and I often run up here to have a chat with her.

"Now, look here, mother," continued the girl, going up close to the dame, "I have brought two gentlemen to see you: we want you to tell us our fortunes. It is lucky to have the fortune told on Christmas Eve, is it not?"

The herb-woman nodded, then pointed inside the hut. She then spoke quickly on her fingers. Rosaly turned to us.

"We are in great luck," said the girl excitedly. "A curious thing has happened. Mother Heriot has a visitor staying with her, no less a person than the greatest fortune-teller in England, the Queen of the Gipsies; she is spending a couple of nights in the hut. Mother Heriot suggests that the Queen of the Gipsies shall tell us our fortunes. It will be quite magnificent."

"I wonder if the woman she alludes to is one of the gipsies who arrived at Rokesby Station yesterday," I said, turning to Dufrayer.

"Very possibly," he answered, just raising his brows.

Rosaly continued to speak, in great excitement

"You consent, don't you?" she said to us both.

"Certainly," said Dufrayer, with a smile.

"All right, mother," cried Miss Sherwood, turning once again to the herb-woman, "we will have our fortunes told, and your gipsy friend shall tell them. Will she come out to us here or shall we go in to her?"

Again there was a quick pantomime of fingers and hands. Rosaly began to interpret.

"Mother Heriot says that she will speak to her first. She seems to stand in considerable awe of her."

The herb-woman vanished inside the hut We continued to stand on the threshold.

I looked at Dufrayer, who gave me an answering glance of amusement. Our position was ridiculous and yet, ridiculous as it seemed, there was a curiously tense feeling at my heart, and my depression grew greater than ever. I felt myself to be standing on the brink of a great catastrophe, and could not understand my own sensations.

The herb-woman returned, and Miss Sherwood eagerly interpreted.

"How queer!" she exclaimed. "The gipsy will only see me alone. I am to meet her in the hut. Shall I go?"

"I should advise you to have nothing to do with the matter," said Dufrayer.

"Oh, but I am curious. I should like to," she answered.

"Well, we will wait for you; but don't put faith in her silly words."

The girl's face slightly paled. She entered the hut; we remained outside.

"Knowing her peculiar idiosyncrasy, I wonder if we did right to let her go in?" I said to my friend.

"Why not?" said Dufrayer.

"With such a disposition she ought not to be indulged in ridiculous superstitions," I said.

"She cannot take such nonsense seriously," was his reply. He was leaning up against the lintel of the little hut, his arms folded, his eyes looking straight before him. I had never seen his face look keener or more matter-of-fact.

A moment later Miss Sherwood re-appeared. There was a marked, and quite terrible, change in her face—it was absolutely white. She avoided our eyes, slipped a piece of silver into Mother Heriot's hand, and said quickly:

"Let us hurry home; it is turning very cold."

"Now, what is it?" said Dufrayer, as we began to descend the mountain; "you look as if you had heard bad news."

"The Queen of the Gipsies was very mysterious," said the girl.

"What sort of person was she?" I asked.

"I cannot tell you, Mr. Head; I saw very little of her. She was in a dark part of the hut and was in complete shadow. She took my hand and looked at it, and said what I am not allowed to repeat."

"I am sorry you saw her," I answered, "but surely you don't believe her? You are too much a girl of the latter end of the nineteenth century to place your faith in fortune-tellers."

"But that is just it," she answered; "I am not a girl of the nineteenth century at all, and I do most fully believe in fortune-telling and all kinds of superstitions. I wish we hadn't gone. What I have heard does affect me strangely, strangely. I wish we had not gone."

We were now descending the hill, but as we walked Miss Sherwood kept glancing behind her as if afraid of some one or something following us. Suddenly she stopped, turned round and clutched my arm.

258

"Hark! Who is that?" she whispered, pointing her hand towards a dark shadow beneath the trees. "There is some one coming after us, I am certain there is. Don't you see a figure behind that clump? Who can it be? Listen."

We waited and stood silent for a moment, gazing towards the spot which the girl had indicated. The sharp snap of a dead twig followed by the rustling noise of rapidly retreating footsteps sounded through the stillness. I felt Miss Sherwood's hand tremble on my arm.

"There certainly was some one there," said Dufrayer; "but why should not there be?"

"Why, indeed?" I echoed. "There is nothing to be frightened about, Miss Sherwood. It is doubtless one of Mother Heriot's bucolic patients."

"They never venture near her at this hour," she answered. "They believe in her, but they are also a good deal afraid. No one ever goes to see Mother Heriot after dark. Let us get quickly home."

I could see that she was much troubled, and thought it best to humour her. We hurried forward. Just as we entered the pine wood I looked back. On the summit of the little ridge which contained Mother Heriot's hut I saw dimly through the mist a tall figure. The moment my eyes rested on it it vanished. There was something in its height and gait which made my heart stand still. It resembled the tall gipsy whom I had noticed yesterday, and it also bore—God in Heaven, yes—an intangible and yet very real resemblance to Mme. Koluchy. Mme. Koluchy here! Impossible! My brain must be playing me a trick. I laughed at my own nervousness. Surely here at least we were safe from that woman's machinations.

We reached home, and I mentioned my vague suspicion to Dufrayer.

"A wild idea has occurred to me," I said.

"What?" he answered.

"It has flashed through my brain that there is just a remote possibility that the gipsy fortune-teller in Mother Heriot's hut is Madame herself."

He looked thoughtful for a moment.

"We never can tell where and how Madame may reappear," he said; "but I think in this case, Head, you may banish the suspicion from your mind. Beyond doubt, the woman has left England long ago."

The evening passed away. I noticed that Rosaly was silent and preoccupied; her nervousness was now quite apparent to every one, and her father, who could not but remark it, was especially tender to her.

Christmas Day went by quietly. In the morning we all attended service in the little church, and at night some guests arrived for the usual festivities. We passed a merry evening, but now and then I glanced with a certain apprehension at Miss Sherwood. She was in white, with holly berries in her belt and dark hair. She was certainly a very pretty girl, but the uneasiness plainly manifested in her watchful eyes and trembling lips marred her beauty. There was a want of quiet about her, too, which infected me uncomfortably. Suddenly I determined to ask for her confidence. What had the mysterious gipsy said to her? This was the night when, according to old tradition, the ghost of the herb-woman appeared. If Miss Sherwood could relieve her mind before retiring to rest, it would be all the better for her. We were standing near each other, and as she stooped to pick up a bunch of berries which had fallen from her belt, I bent towards her.

"You are troubled about something," I said.

"Oh, I am a very silly girl," she replied.

"Will you not tell me about it?" I continued. "I will respect your confidence, and give you my sympathy."

"I ought not to encourage my nervous fears," she replied. "By the way, did father tell you about the legend connected with this house?"

"He did."

"This is the night when the herb-woman appears."

"My dear child, you don't suppose that a spirit from the other world really comes back in that fashion! Dismiss it from your mind—there is nothing in it."

"So you say," she answered, "but you never saw——-" She began to tremble, and raising her hand brushed it across her eyes. "I feel a ghostly influence in the air," she said; "I know that something dreadful will happen tonight."

"You think that, because the fortune-teller frightened you yesterday."

She gave me a startled and wide-awake glance.

"What do you mean?"

"I judge from your face and manner. If you will take courage and unburden your mind, I may, doubtless, be able to dispel your fears."

"But she told me what she did under the promise of secrecy; dare I break my word?"

"Under the circumstances, yes," I answered quickly.

"Very well, I will tell you. I don't feel as if I could keep it to myself another moment. But you on your part must faithfully promise that it shall go no farther."

"I will make the promise," I said. *another confidence*

She looked me full in the face.

"Come into the conservatory," she said. She took my hand, and led me out of the long, low drawing-room into a great conservatory at the farther end. It was lit with many Chinese lanterns, which gave a dim, and yet bright, effect. We went and stood under a large lemon tree, and Miss Sherwood took one of my hands in both her own.

"I shall never forget that scene yesterday;" she said. "I could scarcely see the face of the gipsy, but her great, brilliant eyes pierced the gloom, and the feel of her hand thrilled me when it touched mine. She asked me to kneel by her, and her voice was very full, and deep, and of great power; it was not like that of an uneducated woman. She spoke very slowly, with a pause between each word.

"'I pity you, for you are close to death,' she began.

"I felt myself quite incapable of replying, and she continued:

"Not your own death, nor even that of your father, but all the same you are very close to death. Death will soon touch you, and it will be cold, and mysterious, and awful, and try as you may, you cannot guard against it, for it will come from a very unlooked-for source, and be instant and swift in its work. Now ask me no more—go!'

"'But what about the fortunes of the two gentlemen who are waiting outside?' I said.

"I have told you the fortunes of those men,' she answered; 'go!'

"She waved me away with her hand, and I went out. That is all, Mr. Head. I do not know what it means, but you can understand that to a nervous girl like me it has come as a shock."

"I can, truly," I replied; "and now you must make up your mind not to think of it any more. The gipsy saw that you were nervous, and she thought she would heighten the impression by words of awful portent, which doubtless mean nothing at all."

Rosaly tried to smile, and I think my words comforted her. She little guessed the battle I was having with my own heart. The unaccountable depression which had assailed me of late now gathered thick like a pall.

Late that evening I went to Dufrayer's room. I had promised Miss Sherwood that I would not betray her confidence, but the words of the gipsy in the herb-woman's hut kept returning to me again and again:

"I pity you, for you are close to death. You cannot guard against it, for it will come from an unlooked-for source, and be instant and swift in its work."

"What is the matter?" said Dufrayer, glancing into my face.

"I am depressed," I replied; "the ghostly legend belonging to this house is affecting me."

He smiled.

"And by the way," I added, "you are sleeping in the room where the murder was committed."

He smiled again, and gave me a glance of amused commiseration.

"Really, Head," he cried, "this sort of thing is unlike you. Surely old wives' fables ought not to give you a moment's serious thought. The fact that an unfortunate lad was murdered in this room cannot affect my nerves some twenty years afterwards. Do go to bed, my dear fellow; you need a long sleep."

He bade me good-night. I had no excuse to linger, and I left him.

Just as I had reached the door, he called after me:

"Good-night, old man; sleep well."

I turned and looked at him. He was standing by the window, his face was towards me, and he still wore that inscrutable smile which was one of his special characteristics. I left him. I little guessed ...

I retired to my room; my brain was on fire; it was impossible for me to rest. What was yesterday but a vague suspicion was now assuming the form of a certainty. Only one person could have uttered the words which Miss Sherwood had heard. Beyond doubt, Madame Koluchy had known of our proposed visit to Rokesby. Beyond doubt, she, in company with some gipsies, had joined our train, and when we arrived at Rokesby, she alighted there also. With her knowledge of the gipsies, an acquaintanceship with Mother Heriot would be easily made. To take refuge in her hut would be a likely contingency. Why had she done so? What mischief could she do to us from such a vantage point? Suddenly, like a vivid flash, the memory of the secret passage, which none of the inmates of the house could discover, returned to me. In all probability this passage was well known to Mother Heriot, for had not her mother committed the murder which had taken place in this very house, and did not the legend say that she had entered the house, and quitted it again through the secret passage?

I quickly made up my mind. I must act, and act at once. I would go straight to the hut; I would confront Madame; I would meet her alone. In open combat I had nothing to fear. Anything was better than this wearing and agonizing suspense.

I waited in my room until the steps of the old rector retiring for the night were heard, and then went swiftly downstairs. I took the key of the hall door from its hook on the wall, opened it, locked it behind me, went to the stables, secured a lantern, and then began my ascent of Grey Tor.

The night was clear and starlit, the moon had not yet risen, but the stars made sufficient light for me to see my way. After a little over an hour's hard walking, I reached the herb-woman's hut. I thundered on the door with my stick, and in a minute the dame appeared. Suddenly I remembered that she was dumb, but she could hear. I spoke to her.

"I have a word to say to the stranger who was here yesterday," I began. "Is she within? I must see her at once."

The herb-woman shook her head.

"I do not believe you," I said; "stand aside I must search the hut."

She stood aside, and I entered. There was no one else present. The hut was small, a glance showed me each corner—the herb-woman's guest had departed.

Without even apologizing for my abrupt intrusion, I quickly ran down the mountain, and as I did so, the queer rhyme which contained the key to the secret passage occurred to my memory. I had my memorandum-book with me; I opened it now, and read the words:—-

When the Yew and Star combine.

Draw it twenty cubits line;

Wait until the saintly lips

Shall the belfry spire eclipse.

Cubits eight across the first

There shall lie the tomb accurst.

Gibberish doubtless, and yet gibberish with a possible meaning. I pondered over the enigmatical words.

"There is a yew tree in the churchyard," I said to myself, "but the rest seems unfathomable."

There was a short cut home through the churchyard—I resolved to take it. I went there and walked straight to the yew tree.

"When the Yew and Star combine," I said, speaking aloud. "Surely there is only one star which remains immovable—the Pole or North Star."

I looked up at the sky—the Pole star was shining down upon me. I became excited and much interested. Moving about, I presently got the trunk of the old yew tree and the star in a line. Then I again examined my key.

"Draw it twenty cubits line."

Twenty cubits meant thirty feet. I walked on in a straight line that distance, and then perceived in the moonlight, for the moon had now risen, that standing here, and looking at the church spire, the lips of the stone carving of a saint just covered the spire itself from view. Surely the meaning of the second couplet was plain:

Wait until the saintly lips

Shall the belfry spire eclipse.

The third and last couplet ran as follows:

Cubits eight across the first

There shall lie the tomb accurst.

My heart beating hard, I quickly measured eight cubits, namely twelve feet, and then started back with a cry of horror, for I had come to a large vault, which stood open. The entrance-stone had been moved aside. Without an instant's hesitation I ran down some steps. The tomb was a large one, and was quite empty; never coffin of man had lain here, but a passage wound away to the left, a tortuous passage, down which I quickly walked. My lantern threw light on the ghastly place, and the air was sufficiently good to prevent the candle going out.

Why was the tomb open? What was happening? Fear itself seemed to walk by my side. Never before had I so felt its ghastly presence I hurried my steps, and soon perceived a dim light at the farther end. The next instant I had entered the hall of the old house. I had done so through a panel which had been slipped aside. Had any one gone in before me? If so who! Who had opened the tomb? Who had traversed the passage? Who had gone into the house by this fearful and long-closed door?

I was just about to rush upstairs, when a piercing scream fell on my ears; it came from just above me. With two or three bounds I cleared the stairs, and the next instant my eyes fell upon a huddled-up heap on the landing. I bent over it; it was Rosaly. Her features were twitching in a horrible manner, and her dilated eyes stared at me without any recognition. Her lips were murmuring, "Catch her! catch her!"

The next moment the rector appeared hurrying down the passage in his dressing-gown.

"What is wrong?" he cried; "what has happened?"

The girl clung to my arm, and now sent up scream after scream. The entire house was aroused, and the servants with scared faces came running to the spot. Rosaly's terror now found vent in fresh words.

"The herb-woman," she sobbed, "the ghost of the herb-woman. I heard a noise and ran on to the landing. I met her—she was coming from Mr. Dufrayer's room—she was making straight for yours, Mr. Head. Suddenly she saw me, uttered a cry, and flew downstairs. Oh, catch her, the ghost! the ghost!"

"Did you say the woman was coming from Dufrayer's room," I asked. A sudden maddening fear clutched at my heart. Where was Dufrayer? Surely he must have heard this uproar. I went to his room, opened the door, and dashed in. Inside all was darkness.

"Wake up," I said to him, "something dreadful has happened— did you not hear Rosaly scream? Wake up!"

There was no answer. I returned to the landing to fetch a light. The rector now accompanied me into the room We both went up to the silent figure in the bed. I bent over him and shook him by the shoulder. Still he did not stir. I bent lower, and observed on his neck, just behind the ear, a slight mark, the mark which a hypodermic syringe would make. Good God! what had happened?

"You are close to death. You cannot guard against it, try as you may, for it will come from an unlooked-for source, and be instant and swift in its work."

The words echoed mockingly in my ears. I flung down the bed-clothes, and, in an access of agony, laid my hand on the heart of the man I loved best on earth. He was dead!

I staggered back, faint and giddy, against the bed-post.

"See," I said to the old clergyman, "her work, the fiend; she has been in this house. She has entered by the secret passage. Come at once; there is not an instant to lose. As there is a God in Heaven, she shall pay the price for this crime."

Sherwood gazed at me, as if he thought me bereft of my senses. He could not believe that Dufrayer was really dead. I pointed to the small wound, and asked him to feel where the heart no longer beat.

"But who has done it?" he said. "What fiend do you allude to?"

"Mme. Koluchy; let us follow her."

I rushed from the room and downstairs. The panel in the hall had been slammed to, but my memory could not play me false, I knew its position. I found what had been so long searched for in vain, touched a spring, and opened it. Sherwood and I hurried down the winding passage. Just at the entrance to the tomb we came upon a gipsy woman's bonnet and cloak. They had been dropped there, doubtless, by Madame when she had flown after committing her deadly work. We entered the empty tomb. On the floor lay a small hypodermic syringe. I picked it up—it was broken. To its sides clung a whitish-gray substance. I guessed what it afterwards proved to be—trinitrin, or nitro-glycerine in strong solution. The effect of such a terrible poison would be instantaneous.

Sherwood and I returned to the house—the place was in an uproar of excitement. The local police were called in. I told my strange tale, and my strong suspicions, to which they listened with breathless interest.

Rosaly was very ill, going from one strong hysterical fit into another. The doctor was summoned to attend her. The fact of Dufrayer's death was carefully kept from the sick girl. Her father was so distracted about her that he could give no attention to any one else.

Meanwhile I was alone, utterly alone, with my anguish and horror. The friend of my life had fallen by the hand of Mme. Koluchy. A fire was burning in my brain, which grew hotter each instant. Never was man more pursued with a deadly thirst for vengeance. The thought that Madame was moment by moment putting a greater distance between herself and me drove me mad. Towards morning I could stand inaction no longer, and determined to walk to the station. When I got there I learned that no train left before nine o'clock. This was more than I could bear; my restlessness increased. The junction which connected with the main line was a distance of fifteen miles off. There was no carriage to be obtained. Nevertheless, I resolved to walk the distance. I had overestimated my own strength. I was already faint and giddy. The shock had told on me more than I dared to own. I had not gone half the distance before I was seized with a queer giddiness, my eyes grew dim, the earth seemed to reel away from me, I staggered forward a few steps, and then all was lost in darkness. I must have stumbled and fallen by the wayside, and my fit of unconsciousness must have been long, for when I came to myself the sun was high in the heavens. A rough-looking man, dressed as a workman, was bending over me.

"You have been real bad," he said, the moment my eyes met his. "The lady said to throw cold water on you and you'd be better."

The man's words roused me as no ordinary restorative could do. I sat up, and the next moment had tottered to my feet.

"The lady?" I said. "Did you mention a lady? What lady?"

"A tall lady," was the reply, "a stranger in these parts. She was bending over you when I come along. She had black eyes, and I thought she was giving you something to bring you round. When she saw me she said, 'You dash cold water over him, and he'll come to.'"

"But where is the lady now?" I gasped.

"There by yonder hill, just going over the brow, don't you see?"

"I do, and I know who she is. I must overtake her. Good-bye, my man, I am all right."

So I was: the sudden stimulus had renewed my faltering strength. I recognised that figure. With that grace, inimitable and perfect, which never at any moment deserted it, it was moving from my view. Yes, I knew it. Mme. Koluchy had doubtless found me by the wayside, and had meant to complete the work which she had begun last night. Had she still possessed her syringe I should now have been a dead man. Where was she going? Doubtless to catch the very train to which I was hurrying. If so, we should meet almost immediately. I hurried forward. Once again I caught sight of the figure in the far distance. I could not get up to it, and suddenly I felt that I did not want to. I should meet her in London to-night. That was my thought of thoughts.

As I approached the great junction I heard the whistle of a coming train. It was the express. It dashed into the station just as I reached it. I was barely in time. Without waiting for a ticket I stumbled almost in a fainting condition into the first carriage I could reach. The train moved on. I felt a sudden sense of satisfaction. Mme. Koluchy was also on board.

How that awful journey was passed is difficult for me to remember. Beyond the thought of thoughts that Madame and I were rushing to London by the same train, that we should beyond doubt meet soon, I had little feeling of any sort. Her hour was close at hand—my hour of vengeance was nigh.

270

At the first junction I handed two telegrams to a porter and desired him to send them off immediately. They were to Tyler and Ford.

When between eight and nine o'clock that night we reached Euston, the detectives were waiting for me.

"Mme. Koluchy is in the train," I said to them; "you can apprehend her if you are quick—there is not an instant to lose."

The men in wild excitement began to search along the platform. I followed them. Surely Madame could not have already escaped. She had not the faintest idea that I was in the train; she would take things leisurely when she reached Euston. So I had hoped, but my hopes were falsified. Nowhere could we get even a glimpse of the face for which we sought.

"Never mind," said Ford, "I also have news, and I believe that our success is near. We will go straight to her house. I learned not an hour ago that a fresh staff of servants had been secured, and the house is brightly lit up. Our detectives who surround the place are under the impression that she will be in her old quarters to-night. I have a carriage in waiting: we will start immediately."

Without a word I entered it, and we drove off. We made no plans beyond the intention in each man's breast that Madame should be taken either alive or dead.

As the carriage drew up at the house I noticed that the hall was brilliantly lighted. The moment Ford touched the bell a flunkey threw the door open, as if he were waiting for us.

"My mistress is in her laboratory," was his reply to our inquiries. "She has just returned after a journey. I think she expects you, gentlemen. Will you go to her there?—you know the way."

We rapidly crossed the hall and began to descend the stone steps. As we did so the muffled hum of machinery in rapid motion fell on our ears. Just as we reached the laboratory door Ford, who had been leading the way, stopped and turned round. His face was very pale, but he spoke firmly and quietly.

271

"There is not the least doubt," he said, in a semi-whisper, "that we are going into great danger. Madame would not receive us like this if she had not made a plan for our destruction which only she could devise. It is impossible to tell what may happen. That it will be a terrible encounter, and that it will need all our strength and presence of mind, is certain, for we are now about to enter the very sanctuary of her fiendish arts and appliances. I will go first. The moment I see her I shall cover her, and if she stirs will shoot her dead on the spot."

He turned the handle of the door, and we slipped silently into the laboratory.

It was like entering a furnace, the heat was stifling. A single incandescent burner shed a subdued light over the place, revealing the outline of the stone roof and dim recesses in the walls. At the farther end stood Madame. As we entered, she turned slowly and faced us; her face was quiet, her lips closed, her eyes alone expressed emotion.

"Hands up, or I fire!" rang out from Ford, who stepped forward and immediately covered her with his revolver.

She instantly obeyed, raising both her arms; her eyes now met mine, and the faintest of smiles played round her lips.

The next instant, as if wrenched from his grasp by some unseen power, the weapon leapt from Ford's hands, and dashed itself with terrific force against the poles of an enormous electro-magnet beside him. Every loose piece of iron started and sprang towards it with a deafening crash. Madame must have made the current by pressing a key on the floor with her foot. For a moment we stood rooted to the spot, thunder-struck by the sudden and unforeseen method by which we had been disarmed.

Mme. Koluchy still continued to gaze at us, but now her smile grew broader, and soon it rang out in a scornful laugh.

"It is my turn to dictate terms," she said, in a steady, even voice. "Advance one step towards me, and we die together. Norman

Head, this is your supposed hour of victory, but know that you will never take me either alive or dead."

As she spoke her hand moved to a small lever on the bench beside her. She drew herself up to her full, majestic height, and stood rigid as a figure carved in marble. I glanced at Ford: his lips were firmly compressed, drops of sweat gleamed upon his face, he began to breathe quickly through distended nostrils, then with a sudden spring he bounded forward, and simultaneously there leapt up, straight before our eyes, what seemed like one huge sheet of white flame. So fearfully bright and dazzling was it that it struck us like a blow, and Tyler and I fell. We were blinded by a heat that seemed to sear our very eyeballs. The next moment all was darkness.

When I came to myself a cool draught of air was blowing upon my face, and Tyler's voice sounded in my ears. I rose, staggering. Before my eyes there still seemed to dance a thousand sparks and whirling wheels of fire. The servants were running about wildly, and one of the men had brought a lamp from the hall—it lit up the wild and haggard face of my companion.

"We dare not go back," he whispered, pointing to the laboratory door, trembling and almost gibbering as he did so.

"But what has happened?" I said.

I made a rush towards the laboratory. Two of the men held me back forcibly.

"It's not safe, sir," one of them said; "the room within is a furnace. You would die if you entered."

By main force I was kept from rushing to my own destruction.

It was an hour later when we entered. Even then the heat was almost past bearing. Slowly and cautiously Tyler and I approached the spot where we had last seen Mme. Koluchy. Upon the stone flags lay the body of the detective, so terribly burnt as to be almost unrecognisable, and a few yards farther was the mouth of a big hole, from which still radiated a fierce heat.

By degrees it cooled sufficiently to allow us to examine it. It was about 8ft. deep and circular in shape. From its walls jutted innumerable jets. Their use was evident to me at once, for upon the floor beside us stood an enormous iron cylinder, such as are used for compressed gases. These had presumably been used before to create by means of the jets one vast oxyhydrogen flame to give the intensest heat known, a heat computed by scientists at the enormous temperature of 2,400 deg. Centigrade.

It was evident what had happened. As Ford sprang forward Madame must have released the iron trap and descended through a column of this fearful flame, not only causing instantaneous death, but simultaneously also an absolute annihilation.

At the bottom of the well lay a small heap of smouldering ashes. These were all the earthly remains of the brain that had conceived and the body that had executed some of the most malignant designs against mankind that the history of the world has ever shown.

THE END